Mercury Rises

Mercury Rises

A NOVEL BY ROBERT KROESE

PUBLISHED BY

Published by AmazonEncore
P.O. Box 400818
Las Vegas, NV 89140

ISBN-13: 9781612180861
ISBN-10: 1612180868

*For Mrs. Price, who told
me to "just keep writing."*

....

*With thanks to:
Joel Bezaire, for fleshing out Noah;
Michele Smith, for catching the all-too-common, errant comma;
Jocelyn Pihlaja, for zeroing in on clichés like a hawk;
Alex Hamilton, PhD, for helping me avoid violating the
laws of physics; and my wife, Julia, for helping
me avoid violating most other laws.*

PROLOGUE

To Your Holiness, the High Council of the Seraphim,

Greetings from your humble servant, Ederatz,
Cherub First Class,
Order of the Mundane Observation Corps

There comes a time in every angel's life when he is compelled to reflect on his existence and ask himself that most difficult of questions: why do I even bother?

For me, that time lasted from June 6, 1979, to August 21, 1986. This seven-year bout of existential doubt was followed by six years of relatively undisturbed self-pity, a year and a half of morose cynicism, eight months of figurative hair pulling and teeth gritting, another three months of literal hair pulling and teeth gritting, and, finally, an indeterminate period of drunken obliviousness.

It's been clear to me for some time that no one in your organization is reading these reports. I'm not sure when I first came to that realization; it may have been when no one bothered to follow up on my claim that an elite unit of nineteenth-century Turks had traveled to Ireland in 1976 through a rift in the space-time continuum in order to seed discord among the members of U2.

And yet I persist in writing. Why?

For one thing, I suppose I'm still clutching to a shred of hope that some sympathetic seraph will come across these missives and extract me from this dump of a plane. Beyond that pedestrian motivation, I seem to have fallen victim to the illusion, so common on the Mundane Plane, that committing facts to paper will somehow help me make sense of them. I long ago gave up any attempt at systematic description of events down here, but I can't quite bring myself to stop trying to herd them into some kind of semi-coherent narrative.

Speaking of which, you'll undoubtedly notice that many of the names I've used for characters are anachronistic. For example, the cherub now generally known as Mercury was obviously not called "Mercury" eighteen hundred years before the dawn of the Roman Empire. For that matter, the organization he worked for was not originally called The Apocalypse Bureau, and it is very unlikely that the biblical figure Noah ever used the words *dude* or *asshole.*

Further complicating things, I've gone and gotten myself inextricably tangled up with the plot. Despite my best efforts to remain uninvolved and objective, I've…well, to be honest I pretty much gave up trying a while back. So now I'm a character in my own story. I tried to leave myself out, but, well, it's complicated. You'll see what I mean.

I do have one advantage this time around: this time I know how the story ends. In fact, I'd better get started telling this story, or I'm going to run out of time. As a wise man once said, "We've always been headed toward the Apocalypse. It's just a question of proximity."

Years ago we learned from the Bible that the flood occurred in the year 4990 BC...Just before the flood, Noah was instructed by God that in seven days the flood would begin. Using the language that "a day is as a thousand years," it is like saying through Noah, "Mankind has seven days or seven thousand years to escape destruction." Since 2011 A.D. is precisely seven thousand years after Noah preached, God has given mankind...another infallible, absolute proof that May 21, 2011, is the date of the Rapture.

—The Rev. Harold Camping, January 1, 2010

The only thing that stops God from sending another flood is that the first one was useless.

—Nicholas Chamfort

Buena Park

Riverside Fwy

Knot's Berry Farm

Santa Ana Fwy

Buena Park Mall

Beacon **Building**

Anaheim

Orange Fwy

Anaheim Island

Euclid

Disneyland

Santa Ana

Implosion Crater

ACHOO

Cathedral of the Angels

0   1 Mi

Garden Grove

Garden Grove Fwy

ONE
Circa 2,000 B.C.

Mercury sighed as he trudged up the road to Babylon, his eyes affixed on the squat silhouette of the nearly finished ziggurat at the edge of town. He had been called away on some Heavenly errands and was anxious to see what progress had been made on the massive clay brick pyramid while he was gone.

As he expected, he found that the ziggurat was within weeks of being finished. Unfortunately, it had been within weeks of being finished for over three years now, and no perceivable progress had been made while he was gone.

He clambered up the steps of the hundred-and-fifty-foot-high structure to find several dozen idle laborers encamped at the top. The men didn't even make a show of pretending to work as Mercury reached the plateau.

"What gives, guys?" he asked, trying to maintain the nice-guy demeanor he had cultivated on the worksite. "Kinda thought you'd have started on level seven by now."

Noncommittal murmurs arose from the men.

Mercury tried again. "Anyone want to clue me in about what challenges we're facing with level seven? The first six levels seemed to go smoothly. Level seven is pretty much more of the same if I remember the plans correctly. No judgments here, just trying to get an idea of any special challenges we might have with level seven so I can make sure to give you all the resources you need. My goal is to provide an atmosphere of empowerment."

Still no one spoke up.

"Hold on, I think I've got a copy of the plans with me," said Mercury, riffling through a satchel hanging off his shoulder. "Yep, here we go. Hmmm. Yeah, nothing special for level seven. Sun-baked clay bricks on the inside, fire-glazed bricks on the outside walls, same as the other six levels. And you'll only need about half as many bricks as you did for the last level, on account of the fact that we're building a pyramid. Volume decreases geometrically as we go up, as you'll recall. I don't mean to tell you your business. We're all professionals here."

Grunts and mutters.

"OK," said Mercury. "It's cool. I'm sure you guys are tired. Why don't you take the rest of the day off and we'll meet back here first thing in the morning? I'll have Tiamat swing by in case you're more comfortable talking to her."

Suddenly the men leaped to their feet and all began talking at once. Mercury could make out nothing in the cacophony of voices.

"Whoa, hold on," he chided. "One at a time. You, Nabu. Tell me what's going on."

Mercury hated playing the Tiamat card. He took appealing to her authority as a personal failing as a manager. Besides preferring positive motivation over negative and feeling that he should be able to handle the men without appealing to an external authority, he was secretly afraid the men would someday call his bluff. He had a better chance of summoning a thunderstorm than getting Tiamat to show up.[1] Never a hands-on leader, Tiamat

---

1   He had in fact been trying to summon a thunderstorm for several weeks, but the dry air and a lingering high-pressure zone were making it difficult to say the least.

rarely even bothered these days to make the occasional unscheduled appearance to berate the laborers for their stupidity and laziness and throw a few over the edge as an example for the others. That left Mercury to rally the men on his own, a difficult enough task even when he wasn't being called off on Heavenly errands every other week.

Nabu, one of the group foremen, launched into a litany of grievances: shoddy brickmaking, lack of proper burial arrangements for workers who fell to their deaths (Tiamat had recently decreed that only one funeral would be allowed per week no matter how many men had died and no matter how hot the weather was), preferential treatment for the Amorites, and on and on. But the root problem was one Mercury knew well: an ailment he called *almost-finished-ism*.

The men had been laboring toward the completion of the ziggurat for nearly a generation, but now that it was nearly done, they feared the change its completion would bring. There would be other ziggurats, that much was certain—Tiamat's assurances that this was "most likely the last one" had always proved false in the past. But relocation was difficult on men with families, and starting over was always a bit demoralizing.

"Some of the men and I were talking," Nabu was saying. "We were thinking, why build another ziggurat when we could just make this one taller? I mean, a pair of two-hundred-foot-tall ziggurats is impressive, but wouldn't one three-hundred-foot ziggurat be better? Imagine that, a three-hundred-foot ziggurat!"

Mercury sighed. "Admittedly a three-hundred-foot ziggurat would be a sight to behold," he said. "But you understand that a ziggurat is essentially a *pyramid*, right? It's a fundamental geometric shape. The height is a function of the size of the base. You can't, you know, decide when you're ninety percent done to make it *taller*."

"Right, right," said Nabu. "But here's what we were thinking: what if we excavate, say fifty feet deep all the way around the base of the ziggurat, to a distance of a mile or two? And then we cover up the dirt at the base with more bricks? I mean, who would know we didn't just build it fifty feet higher? Pretty clever, eh?"

Mercury managed a pained smile. "Yes," he said, doing some quick estimating in his head. "Moving eight hundred thousand cubic feet of sand does *sound* like an attractive option. But here's the thing: ziggurats are meant to look impressive from a distance. You'll notice that we deliberately built it on a hill, and we even brought sand in to raise some low spots in the middle of the site before we started construction. In fact, right over there, if I'm not mistaken, is where your father died of heat stroke twenty-five years ago while carting in buckets of sand one beautiful summer day. The point is, we'd have to excavate several miles out for it to do any good. It might take a hundred years, and we'd be digging up all the work your father did—and probably your father himself, if I'm remembering what we did with the corpses that day."

Nabu was quiet for a moment. Mercury could tell he was still trying to think of a way to make his excavation idea work, so he pressed the attack.

"Also, there's the flooding problem. Remember last year when your brother-in-law died in that flash flood because he couldn't get out of the limestone quarry in time? Basically you're talking about making all of Babylon into one big limestone quarry. Whenever it rained, we would all have to flee to the surrounding hills where we had dumped all the sand from the excavation. And there we'd sit, looking down on our pitiful ziggurat sticking out of the mud. No, Nabu, I'm afraid it's no good. We just need to finish this thing and move on. So what do you say, guys? We start bright and early tomorrow morning on level seven?"

The men grumbled assent. Mercury thanked them for their hard work and trudged back down the steps. "I'm not cut out for this job," he muttered to himself. "Bloody ziggurats. Where's the point?"

TWO

Some four thousand years later a demon called Eddie Pratt sat alone in a pub in Cork, Ireland, nursing a pint and massaging his left hand. He had been writing (and drinking) almost nonstop for the past six weeks, and he was very close to completing his opus. Stacks of papers littered the booth that had become his office, by virtue of the fact that Eddie seemed to have an inexhaustible thirst for Guinness (and a wallet that miraculously always had a few more pounds in it)—and the fact that no one wanted to clean it.

"Another pint, Eddie?" asked the bartender, a dour-faced old man who went by the name Cob.

Eddie, his eyes still fixed blearily on his work, held up the empty glass in answer. Cob took it and returned a moment later with a refill of stout.

"Och, what's all that?" he asked.

"Same as always," Eddie grunted. "Report."

"Aye," said Cob. "But what are all those ticks? Tick, tick, tick. Every line more ticks."

"Those are quote marks," replied Eddie, tiredly. "It's dialogue."

"Och, I know," said Cob. "Too much dialogue. People hate all those ticks. You need more action."

"You're a writer now?" Eddie asked, peering up skeptically at Cob.

"Ah, no. But I know what I like. Reading all those ticks would drive me to drink."

"You don't read the ticks. They're punctuation. And you're a bartender, Cob. That's not much of a drive."

"Tick, tick, tick," repeated Cob.

"This isn't easy, you know," grumbled Eddie.

"Och, I'm sure not."

"Are you familiar with Plato?"

"Aye."

"You realize that the work of Plato is one of the cornerstones of Western civilization, and that everything he ever wrote was dialogue?"

"Everything who wrote?"

"Plato. You said you were familiar with him."

"Och, I thought you said, 'Play-Doh.'"

"No, you imbecile. *Plato.* The disciple of Socrates. Plato believed that all of the things we experience are really just impressions of some greater, ultimate reality that underlies the Universe."

"Impressions?" said Cob doubtfully. "I think you may be thinkin' o' Silly Putty. Remember, you could pick up pictures from the funny pages. Darned if I could read 'em though, 'cause they were all backwards. Kind of a dirty trick, making the words backwards, don't you think?"

Eddie gritted his teeth and went back to work.

"Tick, tick, tick," said Cob again. "Too much talking."

"You got that right at least," said Eddie.

"Sod off," grunted Cob, and returned to the bar.

A moment later, the door to the pub opened and an attractive woman with stern, vaguely Asian features walked in. By her clothes and demeanor, Eddie judged she was American. When she opened her mouth to reveal perfectly straight, gleaming white teeth and a propensity for over pronouncing the letter *r*, his suspicion was confirmed. She walked straight up to him and said, "Eddie Pratt?"

Eddie grimaced. There were only a handful of reasons for an attractive American woman to be seeking him out in a pub in Cork, and none of them were good.

"Mind if I have a seat?" she asked.

Eddie shrugged, as if to say, "If you can *find* a seat, you can have it."

Carefully relocating several stacks of papers, the woman sat down across from him. "Mr. Pratt," she said, "my name is Wanda Kwan. I'm not sure exactly how to broach this subject, so I'll just say it: I know who you are."

Eddie winced. Could it be? Had he somehow been found out? If someone had figured out that he was an angel exiled on Earth—which was bad enough in itself—they might suspect he had something to do with the recent horrific events in Southern California. He was in no physical danger, of course; Eddie, like all angels, had at his disposal the miraculous power of the interplanar energy channels, which would keep him out of any prison designed to hold mortals. What he feared wasn't imprisonment or torment by humans; it was the loss of face among angels.

The worst thing that can happen to an angel on the Mundane Plane—particularly an agent of the Mundane Observation Corps, an organization whose activities are supposed to remain completely invisible to humans—is to be outed as angel. Beyond embarrassing, it's akin to the feeling that overcomes a substitute teacher who has been outsmarted by a class of third graders. Despite his current exile, Eddie still hoped to someday leave this plane, and if he ever wanted to show his face in Heaven again, he would have to find a way out of this bind.

"So," Eddie replied, trying to appear nonchalant. "What do you want, exactly?"

Wanda smiled. "Good, yes, let's get right down to it. What I want is you. Your gift, that is."

Eddie nodded slowly. "My gift," he repeated.

"Yes," said Wanda. "We—the company I work for, that is— we're aware of your abilities, and we need your help to take care of a certain thorny problem. The job will pay very well, but before I say any more, I need you to assure me that you can be discreet."

What the hell? thought Eddie. What is this, rent-a-cherub? Where do people get these crazy ideas?

"Hmm," said Eddie. "Here's the thing. I'm not really interested in money. That is, it's useful on occasion, but I have ways of making a few pounds here and there. Let's just say my wallet always has enough money in it for what I need."

"That sounds like a very sensible way of looking at things," said Wanda. "But it does make me wonder, if you weren't doing it for the money, what was in it for you in your deal with Katie Midford?"

Eddie frowned. How did this woman know about that? How could anyone know he had agreed to nudge Harry Giddings toward the Apocalypse in exchange for extraction from the Mundane Plane? And why the hell would she bring that up, considering that Katie Midford never lived up to her side of the deal?

He said, "The deal with Katie Midford didn't work out so well for me. Our arrangement was supposed to be my ticket out of this place, and as you can see…" He trailed off, gesturing at his surroundings.

Wanda replied, "If you need a visa, I'm sure we can help with that as well. My company is connected with some very important people."

A *visa*? thought Eddie. What the blazes was she talking about? "In fact," she went on, "I believe we can get you a temporary work visa right away. We'll put you up in the finest hotel in Los Angeles. A suite, of course, so you'll have a dedicated place to write."

Eddie stared at her dumbly, trying to make sense of what she was saying. "To write?" asked Eddie. "Yes, I'll need a place to write. What, ah, am I going to be writing, exactly?"

Wanda appeared puzzled. She motioned toward the stacks of papers. "Why, *this*, of course."

"This?" he replied. "Why would you be interested in the adventures of a rogue angel named Mercury on the brink of the Apocalypse?"

"Oh, I'm sorry," said Wanda, "I assumed this was, you know"—her voice dropped to a whisper—"*the last book*."

"The last book," repeated Eddie, uncomprehendingly.

"You know," said Wanda, "the final book in the Charlie Nyx saga."

"Ah…" replied Eddie, not knowing what else to say.

Wanda went on, "Before she…disappeared, Katie told us that she was nearly done with the final book in the series. We all knew, of course, that…well, Katie was a smart gal and all, but it was pretty obvious she didn't have the follow-through to write a three-hundred-page book, let alone seven of them. We knew she was fronting for someone, but she was a rather secretive person, as I'm sure you know, so we could never figure out who the real author was. We eventually decided that if the real author of the Charlie Nyx books wanted to remain outside of the limelight, and if he or she had come to some mutually beneficial arrangement with Katie Midford, well…who were we to upset the applecart, as they say? But when Katie disappeared after that whole tragedy in Anaheim, our connection to the real author disappeared with her. Fortunately we have some investigative resources at our disposal, and we were able to ascertain that an employee of Katie's paid you several visits in this very pub shortly before her disappearance. When our sources reported that you spent all of your time in this pub, writing, well, we knew we had our man."

Eddie stifled a laugh at his earlier fears. This woman wasn't an agent of some insidious entity looking to employ a disgraced angel to do their dirty work for them; she was a representative of Midford's publishing company, who thought she had located Midford's elusive ghostwriter.

"Hold on," said Eddie. "You're trying to finish the series even though Katie Midford is presumed to be dead and the setting of the book is a three-hundred-yard-wide crater in the middle of Los Angeles?"

"Yes, well," said Wanda, "I'll admit it's a bit distasteful when you phrase it like *that*. But the book is already completed, right? And what better way to honor the memory of Katie Midford than to release the final book in the series as she had intended, along with the accompanying movies and merchandising."

Eddie frowned. Something still didn't make sense.

"If you have the finished book, what do you need *me* for?" he asked.

"Ah," said Wanda. "As I say, we're going on Midford's assurances that the book was nearly done shortly before the...Anaheim incident. We've never actually seen the book, but we assumed from her comments that the writer...that is, that you were nearly finished at that point."

"So," said Eddie, "the official story is that Katie Midford handed you the completed manuscript only days before her tragic death, and that you are fulfilling her final wishes by publishing it?"

"Oh my," said Wanda excitedly. "You do have a way of spinning a story. Yes, that's exactly it. We want to be true to Midford's dying wishes. I must remember that."

Eddie's brow furrowed. "And you're doing that by tracking down her ghostwriter in an attempt to get him to finish the series she was pretending to have written?"

"Exactly," said Wanda. "Of course, as I said, we assumed from Katie's assurances that the book really was nearly done. But if you're working on…" she looked somewhat distastefully down at his scribblings, "…something *else*, then I suppose we'll just have to accept the fact that Katie Midford's dream will go unfulfilled, along with our fourth-quarter revenue projections. Oh, Mr. Pratt, it breaks my heart to think of the poor children who will never get to see the seventh Charlie Nyx movie, and the poor shareholders who will, through no fault of their own, lose a valuable piece of intellectual property. Breaks…my…*heart.*"

"Shareholders," murmured Eddie, the word echoing meaninglessly in his head. His brain had screeched to a halt in front of an earlier word in the sentence, and it now stood (in a figurative sense) stock still, with its eyes wide and its jaw open, staring at the word in awe. Lovely Wanda Kwan, the vaguely Asian-American publishing company representative, had uttered, through her lip gloss and perfect teeth, the one word that every writer secretly yearns to hear. That word is *movie.*

"Ms. Kwan," he began.

"Call me Wanda, please."

"Wanda, there is something I need to confess to you."

"Yes?"

"This manuscript, this book I'm working on...it's not really about an angel named Mercury."

"No?"

"No. It's about a young boy with a dream and a magical staff. A boy named Charlie Nyx."

"But you said—"

"I know what I said, Wanda. I was lying. You see, I was nearly done with the seventh book when I heard about Anaheim and Tia...Katie..."

"You call her Tia Katie?"

"Er, yes," said Eddie. "It's Spanish for *aunt*. She was like an aunt to me, you know. You know, a, um, Spanish aunt."

"She was like a Spanish aunt to so many people," said Wanda.

"Yes," Eddie went on, "and I didn't think there was any way the book would ever get published with Anaheim in ruins and Tia Katie dead, so I...changed it. I renamed a few characters and made them angels instead of, you know, what do you call them...?"

"Troglodytes?"

"Right, instead of troglodytes, because I was hoping to get it published with a different title...but underneath those superficial changes, it's still Book Seven of the Charlie Nyx series."

"Oh!" Wanda exclaimed. "This is so wonderful! Think of how happy the children and their parents, the shareholders, will be, when we announce that Katie Midford's dying wish, the publication of *Charlie Nyx and the Undead of Anaheim*, will proceed!"

Eddie felt a gnawing in his gut. *The Undead of Anaheim*? Good lord, was there any way that this project could be in poorer taste? "Right," said Eddie, trying to maintain his enthusiasm. "We're married to that title, are we?"

Wanda laughed. "It's only printed on the back covers of thirty million copies of *Charlie Nyx and the Tunnels of Doom*," she said. "So sure, we can change it." She chuckled and shook her head.

"So not really then?" asked Eddie.

"No, not really," Wanda replied cheerily. "You'll have to work with that title. I'm sure you can come up with a tasteful way of handling it."

Eddie began, "I'm a writer, not a—"

"I know, not a miracle worker. Don't worry, we've got a whole staff of writers who can help you work out these little problems."

"Oh, miracles I can do," said Eddie, "but *this*…"

She pretended not to hear him. "And once Book Seven is done, we'll have to talk about other projects. A lot of people are saying angels are the next big thing. I'd love to hear your ideas for a movie about a rogue angel at the…how did you phrase it?"

"The adventures of a rogue angel on the brink of the Apocalypse," said Eddie numbly. Wow, could it be possible? His report, ignored by the angelic powers in Heaven, made into a Hollywood movie?

"Oh, I do love the sound of that," gushed Wanda. "First things first, though. What's the earliest you can make it to Los Angeles?"

Eddie smiled. "If I leave right now, I can be there in four hours."

Wanda laughed. "You writers and your crazy imaginations," she said.

THREE

As the writing career of Eddie Pratt seemed poised to take off, that of Christine Temetri was about to crash and burn in the wake of a series of events that turned out, once again, not to have been the Apocalypse.

Her employer, the Christian news magazine known as the *Banner*, soldiered on despite having been deprived of its *raison d'être*, its headquarters, and its leader, Harry Giddings. Nearly a third of the *Banner*'s staff had been killed in the earthquake that had leveled its building, and Harry had been violently sucked out of Mundane existence at the peak of his career by one very bad apple.

Troy Van Dellen, the *Banner*'s irrepressibly chipper news editor, had rallied the staff at an abandoned strip mall in Yorba Linda two days after the Anaheim Event, as it was being called, and had even managed to put out a special edition of the magazine covering the near-Apocalyptic events that had occurred in Southern California of late (besides the earthquakes and the puzzling obliteration of Anaheim Stadium, a mysterious wildfire had blazed for days in the San Bernardino Forest). Now, six weeks later, it was becoming clear that without some firm direction from the *Banner*'s corporate parent, the magazine would fold in short order. Deadlines were being missed, stories were going uncovered, and the staff members who weren't dead or missing were shell-shocked and demoralized.

Thus it was almost a relief when Troy informed Christine of an emergency meeting in the *Banner*'s makeshift offices at nine o'clock on a Saturday morning. It was undoubtedly bad news, but at least their days in limbo would be mercifully brought to an end.

Christine trudged into the cavernous, fluorescent-lit building that had once served as an electronics outlet store. The folding chairs, Formica tables, and haphazardly placed phones and laptop computers reminded her of her meeting with General David Isaakson in a concrete block house on the Israeli-Syrian border—a meeting that had ended abruptly when the house collapsed, killing Isaakson and nearly killing her. And yet, somehow this hollowed-out shell of a store, with its stark lighting and faded sale posters that advertised long-expired special offers on electronic components that nobody needed five years ago and certainly didn't need now, managed to be even more depressing than the building that had tried to kill her. The most cheery item in the whole place was a poster depicting a starving African child, at the bottom of which were the words YOU CAN HELP. Christine sighed and sank into a chair, gripping her caramel macchiato with both hands.

Christine was tired. She hadn't slept well since she and Mercury had averted the Apocalypse. Partly she was having trouble readjusting to Mundane reality after having seen the strings holding it all up, but mostly she was finding it difficult to sleep on Troy Van Dellen's couch because his house smelled oppressively of lavender and his cat kept trying to sleep on her face.

She hadn't returned to her condo in Glendale since it had been invaded by demons. Her stated reason was that the earthquake had damaged the walls—which was true—but in reality she couldn't shake the image of the hulking, demonic Don materializing uninvited in her breakfast nook. Presumably the linoleum had been torn out by Uzziel's lackeys, but she wasn't feeling up to confirming the fact herself.

As she sat nursing her coffee, two men Christine didn't recognize were engaged in hushed conversation with an uncharacteristically somber Troy Van Dellen in a distant corner of the room. While they talked, the rest of the *Banner*'s extant staff trickled in and, after a few forced pleasantries, seated themselves in anticipation of some kind of announcement from the higher-ups. They didn't need to wait long. One of the men, an older, balding gentleman in an expensive gray suit, left the huddle and strode toward the tables. A few paces behind him followed the other stranger, a stocky, pink-faced fellow sporting a blond crew cut. The older man stopped a few paces in front of the assembled staff members, cleared his throat, and spoke for precisely fifty-three seconds.

He said, in a staccato style that reminded Christine of movies from the 1940s, "Good morning. My name is Gardner Vasili. I'm an attorney representing the estate of Harry Giddings. I am, in accordance with Mr. Giddings's will, ordering the immediate dissolution of the entire *Banner* organization. All of the *Banner*'s remaining assets have been sold at a private auction to a company known as the Finch Group. The Finch Group is, as you may know, the publisher of several magazines, including the country's fastest-growing news publication, the *Beacon*. As the *Beacon* is rapidly adding staff, I encourage each of you to consider applying for a position at their headquarters here in Los Angeles. I have in my hand," he said, waving a stack of envelopes, "an envelope for each of you. Inside are your last paycheck and a business card with the phone number of the *Beacon*'s head recruiter. When you call, please tell them that you were an employee of the *Banner* and that you were personally referred by Gardner Vasili. Your dedicated service to the *Banner* will be taken into account. My associate, Dave, will lock up." He handed the stack of envelopes to the blond fellow, evidently named Dave, and walked out.

The room was silent for a few seconds. Then the staff erupted into a flurry of questions, pleas, accusations, and epithets, all directed at the hapless Dave, who had clearly been selected for this job due to his lack of knowledge of virtually everything other than how to hand out envelopes and lock doors behind him.

Christine took her envelope and grabbed Troy's as well. She handed it to him, and he smiled wryly.

"Guess I'll see you at the *Beacon*," said Troy, with a wink.

"Oh, absolutely," said Christine. They each opened their envelopes, pulled out the business cards, and tore them to pieces in unison.

"See you tonight?" asked Troy.

Christine nodded grimly. "One more night," she said.

"No worries," replied Troy. "I think Morrissey is starting to like you." Troy had named his cat Morrissey. Christine was afraid to ask whether it was because the cat physically resembled Morris from the old 9 Lives cat food commercial or because he temperamentally resembled the lead singer of the Smiths.

Christine had to admit that although she still didn't really get along with Troy, he had been exceedingly gracious about letting her crash at his house. And she and Troy shared another bond: their unmitigated hatred for the glorified birdcage liner known as the *Beacon*.

The *Beacon* was, in many ways, the mirror image of the *Banner*. Whereas the *Banner* had been established by a religious fundamentalist looking to herald the Biblical Apocalypse, the *Beacon* had been founded by a strident atheist who was hoping to usher in a glorious era in human history based on Science and Reason. The *Beacon* was, in fact, founded as a direct response to the *Banner* by Harry Giddings's chief rival (some would say nemesis), Horace Finch. Finch was a secular Jew who had assembled a network of television and radio stations throughout Eastern Europe after the collapse of the Soviet Union. His secular media empire gradually expanded toward the west as Harry's Christian empire moved east, and the two men had once met for drinks and a fist-fight in Tours, France.

Neither magazine had ever made a profit, both having been founded for ideological rather than pecuniary reasons. Toward the end, in fact, the rivalry had mutated into a contest of which magazine could bleed more red ink and still survive. Every day the *Banner* lost its thousands and the *Beacon* lost its tens of thousands. And now that Harry was dead and the *Banner* was on the verge of collapse, Finch had evidently decided to take the high road by looting its rival for its assets and staff. The *Beacon* didn't need any more reporters or editors; Christine could only assume that Finch's true motivation was to obliterate any memory of the *Banner* and prevent it from ever rising from the ashes.

As ambivalent as Christine had been about the *Banner's* strategy of combining proselytizing and news reporting, she found the *Beacon's* methodology even more distasteful. At least Harry was up-front about his motivations (excluding the bit about proclaiming the Apocalypse); there was never any attempt to conceal the faith-driven agenda of the *Banner*. The *Beacon*, however, was another story.

The *Beacon* was run by the sort of cynical atheists who stuck four-legged fish symbols labeled "DARWIN" on their cars in response to the Jesus fish that marked the hatchbacks of their Christian counterparts. Admittedly, the Jesus fish trend had always seemed a little silly to Christine. The fish had been used as a secret identifier by the early Church in the days of persecution by the Romans; sticking it on your car in the twenty-first century reeked of the sort of smug camaraderie that afflicted aging fraternity brothers and those old women who wore red hats when they met for brunch at Denny's. But the Darwin fish—that was something else entirely. Once it stopped being an amusing, ironic commentary (after about the eight hundredth time she had seen one), it began to strike her as somewhat petty and mean-spirited. Beyond that, it had the unintentional effect of elevating Darwin to the position of secular messiah, which seemed to Christine to be a telling marker of the subconscious motivations of the amphibi-anists, the automotive decal version of a Freudian slip.[2]

In other words, the *Beacon*'s staff patted themselves on the back for advancing the cause of Reason and Science, but in reality their motivation was more negative than positive; more anti-religion than pro-science. This wasn't entirely their fault; it's much easier to rally people behind the idea of a miraculous savior than the idea that the purpose of the Universe, if there is one, can only be pieced together through a painstakingly dull process intelligible only to the sort of people who took honors calculus in high school. And since magazine editors tended to be yearbook committee people, the *Beacon*'s involvement in the scientific process was essentially reduced to the role of yelling, "GO SCIENCE! BEAT RELIGION!"

2   The Christians had then struck back with a decal of a larger fish, labeled "TRUTH," eating the Darwin fish, which distilled Christianity to its core principle: the ultimate devouring of Science by the giant, horrific Jesus-fish.

That sort of deluded secularism was the last thing Christine needed after three years of dealing with deluded religiosity, and in any case she was more convinced than ever, thanks to her involvement in the events of the almost-Apocalypse, that she was not cut out to be a reporter. Unlike the *Banner's* other employees, she had the additional burden of knowing exactly what had happened in Anaheim and not being able to tell a soul.

What had happened was that her boss and sometimes friend, Harry Giddings, had been duped into proclaiming the onset of the Apocalypse by a Machiavellian schemer who turned out to be not only a demoness but a bad sport and a plagiarist. As a result of his duping, Anaheim Stadium and everyone in it had imploded, sucked through a pinpoint portal into an adjacent plane. That was a tough truth to face, and an even tougher one to keep quiet about. And as skeptical as anyone at the *Banner* might have been about that story, she knew that the smug twits at the *Beacon* would be even less receptive. Not that she planned on telling anyone, but somehow the idea of working among diehard skeptics filled her with dread. It would be like Troy Van Dellen moving to the rural Midwest: he still showed no signs of coming out of the closet, but even a closeted homosexual had to feel more comfortable in a place like Los Angeles than a place like Iowa.

"What are we going to do?" she asked Troy.

Troy shook his head, trying manfully to maintain his characteristic smirk-smile. "Maybe I'll finally finish that novel," he said. Troy had been working for the past five years on a novel that was, as he described it, a cross between *In Cold Blood* and *My Fair Lady*—a cross that Christine wasn't sure anyone could bear.

"What about you?" Troy asked. "I hear the *Times* is looking for copy editors. Not glamorous, but you'd get your foot in the door."

"Ugh," said Christine. "Maybe I'll go back to substitute teaching for a while. I need a change. Something drastic." Her eye fell on the poster of the African child. "YOU CAN HELP," reminded the poster. Below the words was the logo of Eternal Harvest, an interdenominational organization founded by Harry to alleviate poverty, famine, and disease in Africa. The logo was comprised of the letters EH followed by a sheaf of grain and a soaring dove, a combination of icons that had always looked to Christine like a question mark, so that the logo seemed to be saying, "EH?"

Despite its ambiguous logo, Eternal Harvest was a worthwhile organization, probably Harry's greatest legacy, despite his belief that his primary mission on Earth was to usher in the Apocalypse. Eternal Harvest had provided hands-on assistance to remote tribes in various areas of eastern Africa, digging cisterns to provide them with clean drinking water, building chicken coops to supply them with eggs, and inoculating them against diseases, among other worthy endeavors. Christine had on occasion thought to herself that Harry's efforts to promote the Christian faith would be better served if he were to shut down the *Banner* and send the whole staff to Africa to work for Eternal Harvest.

She had not, of course, been inclined to move to Africa *herself*, as she had a career as a journalist to pursue and linoleum to pay for. Things had changed, though. She jotted down the phone number of Eternal Harvest on the back of the envelope and walked out of the cavernous building for the last time.

FOUR
Circa 2,000 B.C.

After doing his best to rally the workers at the top of the ziggurat, Mercury reluctantly returned to Tiamat's palace to report on the situation. He sat across from her in the drawing room—so named because it was where she drew up the plans for the ziggurats.

"I'm not going to lie to you," Mercury said. "We've got problems on the ziggurat. I'm starting to think we should tell these guys we're doing eight levels next time. When they begin to lose steam after level seven, we'd be like, 'Hey, guess what? We're done!'"

Tiamat was busily examining sheaves of parchment laid out on a marble slab before her. "It doesn't matter," she said finally. "We're building in the wrong place. *Again.*"

"Are you kidding?" cried Mercury. "This is the perfect spot for a ziggurat. High elevation, close to shopping, a stone's throw from the Euphrates…The only way someone could have picked a better spot for a ziggurat is if they, you know, actually knew what the hell a ziggurat was for."

Tiamat looked up from the papers and regarded him piteously. "Poor Mercury," she said. "Your problem is that you're too smart to be a cherub. You'd make a pretty good seraph, but alas, it was not to be."

"I'd make a lousy seraph," Mercury replied. "Too much pressure. Besides, I'd probably get stuck with some two-bit civilization like those idiots pushing stones around Britain. I don't know who's running that civilization, but whoever it is evidently has no idea we're in the middle of a global pyramid race here."

Tiamat laughed. "You should be so lucky as to get your own civilization," she said. "Do you know what the competition is like to get into the Seraphic Civilization Shepherding Program? I could hardly believe it when they told me I got the Babylonians. I mean, I was hoping for Egypt; we all wanted Egypt, but Babylon is pretty damn good."

Mercury nodded in assent. "It was lucky that Babylon opened up after Marduk got caught using alchemy to prop up the economy. If he had melted down those solid gold pigs before trying to sell them to the Egyptians, the muckety-mucks at the SCSP might never have caught him."

"Marduk!" Tiamat spat. "What a horse's ass. Have you heard what he's up to these days?"

"I'm sure I have no idea."

Tiamat peered at him suspiciously. "Mercury."

"What?"

"You know something."

"No, I swear," Mercury insisted. "I don't know where he is."

"Uh-huh. Tell me what you *do* know."

Mercury threw up his hands dismissively. "Oh, you know how the guys talk at the jobsite. They've got this whole mythology they've built up about you and Marduk. Crazy stuff. Just talk, you know."

"What are they saying, Mercury? Tell me. Now."

"Well, they've got this nutty idea that you're, you know, evil."

"Evil!" she howled. "Evil! No one accuses me of being evil! Tell me who it was and I'll throw him off the ziggurat! Never mind, I'll throw them *all* off the ziggurat! It's not like the lazy, incompetent, slandering fools are doing any work anyway. But first, I'll boil their children in oil while they watch! Call me evil, will they? I'll show them!"

"Yes, and as you've noted," Mercury went on, "Marduk hasn't been around much lately, so you get all the blame for, you know, throwing people off the ziggurat and whatnot…"

"Lies!" Tiamat hissed. "Scandalous lies! Tell me who it was and I'll throw them off the ziggurat!"

"Meanwhile," Mercury continued, "they've built up this exaggerated image of Marduk as some sort of conquering hero who's going to come back and save them."

"Save them!" Tiamat cried. "From what? Gainful employment? The chance to be part of history? The excitement of knowing that at any moment you could be thrown to your death from a ziggurat?"

"I told you it was crazy," Mercury said.

"So," Tiamat asked, "what do they say the great Marduk is doing these days, while his worshipers await his triumphant return?"

"Well, supposedly he's preparing for battle with you," Mercury said. "Of course, as you know, he's been away for longer than anyone expected, so the stories of his preparations are getting pretty involved.

"Involved?"

"Yeah, they asked me to write it down for them because they were starting to lose track of it all." He felt around in his satchel until he found a scrap of well-worn parchment. "Ah, here it is. OK, first Marduk has to make a bow, which takes a while, then he has to make the arrows for it, then he has to get his mace…Don't ask me how he's going to use a mace and a bow at the same time; maybe he's got like six arms in this scenario or something. Let's see, he throws lightning before him, fills his body with flame…wow, that's a good one, huh? Filling his body with flame. Nice. Makes a net to encircle you, gathers the four winds, creates seven *new* winds, such as the whirlwind, tornado, um, I don't seem to have the others written down, but they were all pretty similar. Dust devil, funnel cloud, that sort of thing. Oh, and they just added this one, the rain-flood. That's as far as they've gotten. Crazy stuff, like I said."

"Insolent fools," Tiamat muttered.

"It's just talk," assured Mercury. "I wouldn't take it too seriously. Anyway, now that I've told you all this stuff, you're probably going to want to finally level with me about what we're doing here in Babylon."

"We're building a great civilization," chided Tiamat.

"Right, sure," said Mercury, nodding. "But I can't help think how much greater it could be if we didn't spend thirty percent of our GDP on ziggurats. I mean, I get the national pride angle, but seriously, we've got like eighteen of these things now. What's the point?"

"The point," Tiamat growled through gritted teeth, "is to keep building them until we get it right!"

Her statement was punctuated by a distant rumble of thunder.

"What the hell?" Mercury exclaimed. "I've been trying to get it to thunder for weeks, and now, out of the blue…"

"You've been trying to get it to thunder?"

"A little side project I've been working on," Mercury admitted. "I always thought it would be neat to be able to make a grave pronouncement and have it punctuated with thunder. You know, something like, 'You shall pay dearly for eating the last chicken dumpling!'"

Thunder rumbled obediently in the distance.

"Oh, I do like that!" Tiamat exclaimed. "Let me try again." She cleared her throat and growled, "I shall cast you and your descendents to twelve generations to your deaths off the top of the highest ziggurat!"

A light drizzle began to fall. Tiamat frowned.

"I think maybe you used too many prepositional phrases," ventured Mercury. "Keep it simple, like 'Stop teasing your sister or I'll turn this oxcart around!'"

Thunder boomed again, closer this time.

"Forget it," grumbled Tiamat. "I don't need cheap parlor tricks to make my point."

"Or *do* you?" Mercury asked, an ominous tone in his voice. There was another rumbling in the distance.

"Stop that!" Tiamat barked.

"Stop what?" asked Mercury spookily. "I'm *not doing anything*." There was a flash of lightning followed by a loud clap of thunder.

"Damn you, I said stop it! If you persist, I shall boil you in oil until you cry to the heavens for mercy!"

The rain intensified slightly.

"Huh," said Mercury. "I honestly thought you nailed it with that one."

They watched out the window as the rain continued to fall harder and harder.

"Quarry's gonna flood again," said Mercury.

Tiamat nodded.

A few minutes later, he spoke again. "Probably the kilns as well."

Tiamat nodded again. Shouts arose throughout the city as streets turned into rivers. The sound of fists banging against wood could be heard below them.

"Did you remember to lock the palace doors?" Tiamat asked.

"Yep."

A moat began to form around the palace.

"Second-floor windows?" Tiamat asked.

"Yep."

Mud-brick houses deteriorated in the torrent. The city's wretched denizens slogged desperately against the current to get to higher ground. As the water rose higher and higher, it became clear that only one place would be safe.

"Look at them, scurrying up the ziggurat like ants!" Tiamat laughed. "Pathetic!"

"Yeah, about that..." said Mercury.

"What?"

"If this rain keeps up, the palace will be underwater in a couple of days. We might want to look into reserving some space on the ziggurat."

"It would take quite a flood to submerge this palace," Tiamat said. "Every living thing that moves on the Earth would perish. I doubt it will come to that."

"And if it does, and the top of the ziggurat is full?"

Tiamat smiled wickedly. "Why, then we'll..."

"I know, I know," said Mercury wearily. "Throw some people off the ziggurat."

FIVE

Los Angeles was a revelation to Eddie Pratt. He had been in Ireland for so long that he had begun to think of the Mundane Plane as an endless landscape of moss, cobblestones, and fog. Southern California was warm and dry, and the oppressive fog of Cork had been supplanted by a pleasant brownish haze that hung in the distance like a cozy blanket hugging the city. As an angel Eddie was immune to lung cancer, emphysema, and stray bullets, but not, it turned out, to depression and ennui. Driving down Rodeo Drive in a rented BMW convertible, he scolded himself for not daring to abandon his post earlier. No wonder they called this the City of the Angels.

After checking into his suite at the Wilshire, Eddie had procured the BMW on his newly acquired expense account and spent the next several hours driving around the city, admiring—and, he hoped, being admired by—the beautiful people. At two p.m., he strode into the executive conference room on the fifteenth floor of the Beacon Building wearing aviator sunglasses and a forest green velour jumpsuit that he thought made him look stylish while retaining comfort. He was half right.

Wanda Kwan introduced him as "the man behind the success of Charlie Nyx," and he smiled and shook the hands of the representatives of the various aspects of the Charlie Nyx franchise. There was a representative from the movie studio, someone who handled the Charlie Nyx action figures and other merchandising, a woman from the *Beacon* who was doing a feature on the Charlie Nyx phenomenon, a small, roundish man whom Wanda introduced as the marketing director for the Charlie's Grill chain of restaurants, and several others.

"Horace Finch sends his regrets," Wanda said. "He's out of the country right now, but he asked me to personally thank you for coming to Los Angeles, Eddie. I'll be his acting representative during this meeting, and if there is anything you would like to communicate to Mr. Finch, I'll be happy to relay it for you."

Eddie nodded understandingly.

"So," said Wanda to Eddie, "I think the big question on everyone's mind is, how's the book coming?"

Eddie affected a smile, trying to appear confident. In fact, although he couldn't explain why, this syndicate of Charlie Nyx-related interests was making him profoundly uneasy. It was ridiculous that he, a six-thousand-year-old angel, could be made to feel uneasy by this gaggle of money-grubbing bureaucrats, but here he was, fidgeting nervously under the table. He took a deep breath.

"Well," he said, "The book is fantastic. I mean, I really think it's the best one yet."

Nods and appreciative murmurs went around the table.

"Here's the thing, though," Eddie went on. "Given the recent, ah, *events* in Anaheim, there are certain elements of the story that need to be, well, *massaged*, so as to not appear insensitive to those aggrieved by this terrible tragedy."

The syndicate nodded and murmured in respectful agreement. No one wanted to be insensitive to those aggrieved by a tragedy, especially if being insensitive in any way tarnished the Charlie Nyx brand or the Finch Corporation's public image, thereby adversely affecting the beloved shareholders.

Thank God, thought Eddie. If they think I have to rewrite a significant part of the book, it might give me enough time to locate a copy of the actual manuscript.

"We completely understand," said Wanda. "In fact, I believe Tim has an idea in that regard." She motioned to the dwarfish man that had been introduced as Tim Scalzo, the marketing director of Charlie's Grill.

"Yes," Tim piped up. "As you know, sales at most Charlie's Grill stores have been down for the past several weeks. In addition to the weak economy, which has affected all of our respective interests, Charlie's Grill has had to face a number of unique challenges lately. First, there's the bad press that has resulted from the class action lawsuit regarding Charlie's Triple Bacon Sausage Burger. Despite the fact that all four meats used in the burger were of the finest quality, six highly publicized deaths have turned this into an expensive and embarrassing public relations nightmare for us. Then there are the religious extremists who are boycotting Charlie's Grill because they didn't see the humor in our 'Be the Antichrist' promotion. I mean, come on, people, don't take things so seriously. It's not like Karl Grissom was the actual Antichrist!"

The syndicate laughed. Eddie shifted nervously in his chair.

Tim went on, "And frankly it's a bit unfair that they're refusing to call off the boycott even though Karl was shot in the head and was then absconded with, never to be seen again. I mean, how badly wrong does a marketing campaign have to go before we're forgiven?"

Murmurs of sympathetic understanding arose from the syndicate.

"And on top of all that," Tim continued, "our research indicates that seventeen percent of our frequent patrons have stopped eating at Charlie's Grill because they're afraid they might get shot at. Because of *one* shooting at *one* restaurant. I mean, how do you combat that kind of thinking? It's completely irrational. You're probably twice as likely to be struck by lightning as you are to be shot in the parking lot of Charlie's Grill."

"And six times as likely to die from eating the food," offered Eddie helpfully.

Tim glared at Eddie. "The cause of death for three of those cases hasn't yet been proven." He continued, "The point is that Charlie's Grill could use some good publicity, especially now, as we embark on a new phase in the expansion of the Charlie's Grill concept. As you know, before this run of bad luck, we began construction on the new Charlie Nyx Travel Plaza and Family Fun Place in Laguna Hills, just south of L.A. The Laguna Hills location was to be our flagship, the shining gem in the crown of the Charlie's Grill chain. Of course, there are always naysayers, and especially with the bad press we've gotten lately, many commentators are insisting that we've overextended ourselves. It goes without saying, then, that our grand opening this winter has to be a smashing success. What I'm suggesting is that we use the power of Charlie Nyx to revitalize the Charlie's Grill brand."

Eddie stared dumbly at Tim. "You...want to hold some kind of Charlie Nyx–related event at this travel plaza thing?"

"No, no," said Tim. "I mean, yes, of course. But more importantly, we want to incorporate the Charlie Nyx Travel Plaza and Family Fun Place into the book somehow. Maybe Charlie stops there on the way to the tunnels of the lizard king to take a shower or play some video games or something."

"I love it," gushed Wanda. "The *Tunnels of Doom* movie is already scheduled to premiere at the adjacent Charlie's Cinemas, so we'll do a huge grand opening slash movie premiere slash book-release party. It's a perfect storm of corporate synergy. The shareholders are going to *pee* themselves. Of course, that does mean an aggressive publishing timeline for the book. We'll need a draft by next Friday. That won't be a problem, will it, Eddie?"

"Wha…er," Eddie started. "So I have find…er, rewrite the book to take out any references to Anaheim and add a chapter where the main character swings by a *truck stop?* In a *week?*"

"A truck stop!" exclaimed Tim. "This is a Travel Plaza and Family Fun Place, Eddie. Complete with one-hour napping rooms, luxury showers, and a Family Massage Center. We just need Charlie to take twenty minutes out of his busy adventuring schedule to drop by there. He can't spend all his time whacking goblins with his magical staff, after all. You know how fifteen-year-olds are."

A stern-looking man at the end of the table cleared his throat.

"Oh, I'm sorry, Dan," Wanda said. "You had some legal concerns you wanted to mention."

"Yes," said Dan. "As you know, the entire Anaheim Stadium site is an ongoing crime scene, which means that under no circumstances is the book to make any reference to it. I trust that won't be a problem, Mr. Pratt."

"Well, I can't just…" Eddie began.

An editor for Finch Books, a bookish woman named Linda, spoke up. "Although, of course, it's very important that we maintain continuity with the rest of the series."

Eddie protested, "But how can I maintain continuity if I can't mention the setting of…"

"Yes, yes," the man in charge of action figures and merchandising said. "Continuity is very important. Also, the outfits."

"Outfits?" Eddie asked, confused.

"In the series thus far, Charlie's sweetheart Madeline changes outfits an average of three and a third times per book. We'd like to up that to five for this one. Sales of Sweetheart Madeline dolls are down forty percent this year, but we think we can make most of that up by offering several new accessory sets."

"And explosions," added the movie studio representative. "Receipts from the last Charlie Nyx movie were down fifteen percent, and our research indicates this is partly due to the relatively low number of explosions in that installment. We need at least six explosions to keep the interest of our core audience."

"*Tasteful* explosions," Wanda clarified. "The main thing, of course, is that the book reflect the true wishes of the late Katie Midford. What her wishes would have been if she had written them, I mean. And that we get the finished manuscript by next week."

"I'm sorry," Eddie began. "I just don't see how I can…"

"And once that's out of the way," Wanda went on, "we can talk about your angel book."

"Ooh, you've got a book about angels?" asked the studio rep. "How many explosions does it have?"

For a moment, Eddie stared at them in disbelief. Then, with the slightest hint of hope in his voice, he asked, "Do implosions count?"

SIX

The day after the *Banner* was shut down, Christine made a pilgrimage to the Anaheim Crater, the capacious hole in the ground where Anaheim Stadium had once stood. She hadn't been back since the stadium was destroyed.

Traffic, always bad in Los Angeles, had gotten exponentially worse since the Anaheim Event forced the closure of several main roads. Christine got lost and ended up cutting through an alley only to be trapped in a seemingly endless sea of immobile vehicles. All around her, horns honked and drivers hurled curses. Some of them had gotten out of their cars and were screaming and gesturing wildly at someone or something ahead of her.

"This whole city has gone insane," Christine muttered, gripping the steering wheel. She and Mercury might have averted the Apocalypse, but you certainly couldn't tell from the atmosphere in L.A. recently. Even before Anaheim, people had been on edge because of the earthquakes, but now things were really getting bad. It reminded her of those wretched movies about the teenagers who were supposed to die in an accident but somehow cheated Death only to be painstakingly hunted down one by one by Death over the next two gruesome, pointless hours. The Apocalypse, not to be cheated of its moment in the sun, seemed to be asserting itself in the collective psyche of Los Angeles: where earthquakes and implosions had left off, mass hysteria was taking over.

After five minutes of sitting immobile behind a great white plumbing van bearing the markings of "Kip's Plumbing," Christine turned off the engine of her Scion. Another three minutes and she threw the door open and got out of the car.

"What the hell is going on?" she demanded of no one in particular. Looking around the van, she could make out some sort of disturbance about ten cars up. She locked the Scion and marched forward, determined to find out what was going on. What she found was a crowd of maybe fifty people standing in a rough circle. Squeezing through to the front of the crowd, she saw the source of all the trouble: an unkempt, elderly man had parked his pickup in the middle of an intersection. In front of the pickup was a metal barrel, in which a fire was burning. The man was hollering something incomprehensible at the crowd, and they were hollering something incomprehensible right back at him. In his hand was a hardcover Charlie Nyx book.

"Oh, jeez," muttered Christine. This old kook had arranged an impromptu book burning in the middle of a busy intersection. And he was about to get himself lynched, judging by the mood of his audience. She doubted many of them were die-hard Charlie Nyx fans, but quite a few of them seemed to be fans of "Get out of the road, asshole!"

A beefy, balding man wearing blue coveralls had stepped forward and was berating the old man furiously, jabbing his finger into the man's ribs. Embroidered on his chest was the name "Kip." Great globs of saliva were fleeing Kip's lips in droves, landing on the old man or anywhere else they could find refuge. What the old man lacked in size, he made up for in intensity, shrieking like a wounded seagull about "blasphemous books" and "signs of the End Times."

While this altercation was going on, a young man in a business suit rushed forward and gave the barrel a kick, knocking it over and spilling a mass of flaming books into the street. Several onlookers dove out of the way of the conflagration, creating havoc in the crowd. Meanwhile, a new fracas had broken out closer to Christine, with an angry contingent castigating the man who had kicked over the barrel. Kip had brought his fist back in an effort to cow the old man, and two other men had stepped up to restrain him. In the distance, Christine heard sirens and saw the flashing lights of emergency vehicles, but they seemed to be making little progress toward the source of the trouble. Chaos was spreading through the scene like germs at a preschool.

Christine had had enough. Clearly she wasn't going to be able to do anything to quell the chaos, and bedlam could go on just as well without her. Leaving her car in the de facto parking lot, she trudged off toward the place where Anaheim Stadium once stood. She figured it was about a mile away; at the rate things were going, she'd have plenty of time to get back to her car. And if not, what was the worst that could happen?

She realized that she didn't really want to think very hard about the worst that could happen. However, if the worst did happen, it would be just as well for her to be a mile away at the time.

Walking briskly, it took her less than twenty minutes to get to the scene of the Anaheim Event. She couldn't get very close; construction fencing ringed the entire area a good hundred feet from the crater's edge. She walked up to the chain-link fence, finding a place among the other gawkers and picture takers. Her view was mostly obscured by the dozens of vehicles, tents, and other temporary structures that skirted the crater.

She could only assume that the figures scurrying about inside the perimeter fence were trying to figure out what exactly had happened there. She imagined they probably weren't having much luck.

Her eyes alighted on a small, thoughtful-looking black man wearing civilian clothes who was crouched on the shallow slope just inside the jagged swath of asphalt that marked the crater's edge. Sand filtered between the fingers of his left hand, and he stared vacantly into space as if waiting for inspiration to strike. Who was he? Christine wondered. Not a cop, certainly, and not military. He didn't look like a government bigwig or bureaucrat either. A researcher or investigator of some kind, maybe? Maybe, she thought with a tinge of pity, he was the one that all the bureaucrats and bigwigs were expecting to explain this mess.

Part of her wanted to call out to the man, to tell him she knew exactly what had caused the crater. But what would she say? That Anaheim Stadium had been imploded by a supernatural device that could fit in the palm of one's hand? If she were lucky, she'd be dismissed as delusional, and if she were unlucky, she'd be charged with interfering with a federal investigation—or worse. And her situation wouldn't be improved by spilling her guts about who had used the anti-bomb, and why.

She had tried her best to put all those details out of her mind during the six weeks since the Anaheim Event, and now that she forced herself to think about it, she realized she was having a hard time keeping it all straight. She wasn't sure she'd be able to offer a cogent narrative of the events leading up to the Event even if she wanted to. The politics of Heaven and Hell were just too damned complicated.

First, there was that conniving bastard Gamaliel, who was working for that conniving bitch Katie Midford, who was really the demoness Tiamat, who wanted to—how did she put it?—subjugate humanity with an iron fist.

Then there was that imbecile Izbazel, who was a minion of Lucifer aka Satan, who wanted to destroy the world.

Then there were Uzziel and Michael and all the other the agents of Heaven, who couldn't seem to agree on much of anything; and Harry Giddings, who thought he was working for Heaven but wasn't; and Karl Grissom, the accidental Antichrist.

And then, of course, there was Mercury. Mercury was infuriating, exasperating, callous, and self-absorbed, and she was having a hard time coming to grips with the fact that she would most likely never see him again. She didn't exactly miss him; she felt more or less the way she had felt that day she came home from school to find that her father had sold the bright orange Oldsmobile Toronado that he had driven as long as she could remember. The car was horrifically loud, belched huge clouds of blue smoke for a good ten minutes every time it was started, and always inexplicably smelled like overripe peaches, but Christine had cried herself to sleep that night because she couldn't imagine life without it.

The man she had been staring at glanced her direction, and for a moment she thought he was looking directly at her. She half expected him to walk over and launch into a series of questions about what exactly she knew about the Anaheim Event, but he simply muttered something under his breath, stood up, and then walked away.

Of course he wouldn't question her. There was no reason to suspect she had had anything to do with the destruction of the stadium. In fact, she reminded herself, she *hadn't* had anything to do with it.

Yet, for some reason, she felt a twinge of guilt whenever she thought about what had happened here. That guilt was the main reason she hadn't visited the implosion site until now. She wasn't sure her brain would be able to process the reality of the aftermath; until now it had seemed like something out of a half-remembered nightmare, and a part of her expected to break down completely at the sight of the destruction. But standing here overlooking the crater, she felt like an extra in a Hollywood film. The vast gray crater dotted with tents and portable offices bore no resemblance to the image of Anaheim Stadium packed with True Believers that was etched into her mind. Surveying the scene now, she simply felt numb—and somehow that was worse than the tsunami of guilt she had expected.

Fraternizing with Mercury has warped my soul, she thought. Seeing this hole in the ground instead of a stadium filled with tens of thousands of people should make me feel *something*. After all, I was the reason Karl was onstage in the first place. If I hadn't saved him and delivered him to Harry wrapped up with a nice bow, he wouldn't have been here, and Izbazel wouldn't have detonated the anti-bomb. It's *my fault*.

But she couldn't make the words mean anything. Damn it, she thought. Maybe I just need to get out of here. Away from this place, this city. Somewhere I can do something meaningful.

She fingered the scrap of paper on which she had written the number of Eternal Harvest. Africa? she thought. That was a bit extreme, wasn't it?

On the other hand, her career as a journalist seemed to be over, and she still dreaded returning to her condo. Why *not* move to Africa, far away from the aftermath of the Anaheim Event, the cynical machinations of the *Beacon*, and her infernal linoleum? A remote village in eastern Africa sounded positively welcoming compared to this unholy place. She couldn't possibly feel more useless and unfulfilled there than here, and who knows? She might even be able to do some good—real good, helping people in a meaningful, concrete way for once, rather than spreading a combination of false hope and cynicism through her Apocalyptic columns.

Gunfire erupted in the direction from which she had come, followed by screams. Police cars and National Guard vehicles raced past her toward the scene. Pandemonium was taking hold of Los Angeles.

Christine pulled her cell phone from her pocket and began to dial.

SEVEN

In high school Jacob Slater had been diagnosed with Asperger's syndrome, a vaguely defined condition which, in the final analysis, meant that people gave him the heebie jeebies.

He didn't like crowds, and he liked smaller groups of people even less. One-on-one contact with a person he didn't already know was roughly as painful for him as a third-degree sunburn. To compensate him for this deficiency, the Almighty had given him a keen intellect and a preternatural ability to make sense of disparate data and recognize patterns, abilities he had put to good use as a forensic blast expert for the FBI.

Technically he was a "forensic explosive investigator," but his interest was not in the explosives, but rather the explosions. He had always loved explosions, even as a child. When he was ten he had once poisoned a neighborhood stray cat by feeding it liverwurst laced with gunpowder, and his protests that the poisoning had been an accident didn't save him from several trips to the school psychologist. Technically he was telling the truth: he hadn't meant to poison the cat; he had meant to blow it up. This admission didn't help his case either. Ironically three days later the cat was apprehended by an animal control officer who took it to the city pound, where it died by lethal injection after a miserable, frightening, weeklong incarceration in a small cage surrounded by dozens of other doomed animals. Young Jacob concluded, not unreasonably, that his parents and teachers weren't really concerned about keeping the cat alive; what they wanted was for the cat to die quietly and alone rather than in an exciting and very public explosion.

Jacob never tried to blow up another animal after that, partly because it was clearly too much trouble and partly because as annoying as stray cats and raccoons could be, at least they weren't hypocrites. He did, however, blow up plenty of inanimate objects, from model airplanes to mailboxes, both because he liked to see things explode and because he liked the challenge of trying to reassemble the pieces. He would occasionally videotape his projects but was disappointed to learn that the typical camcorder recorded only thirty frames per second—not enough to dissect an explosion in much detail.

The FBI didn't call Jacob Slater when they wanted to keep a bomb from going off; they called him two minutes after a bomb had gone off. His job was essentially to tell the story of what had happened during the fraction of a second before everything went to hell. He did his job exceedingly well, and he had been waiting his entire adult life for the call he had received six weeks ago.

At least, he thought it was the call he had been waiting for. A massive explosion at Anaheim Stadium, they had said. But once he got there he found...nothing. That wasn't hyperbole; he had literally found *nothing*. Where there once had been a stadium filled with people, there was now only a gigantic bowl-shaped hole in the ground. They were calling it the Anaheim *Event* rather than the Anaheim *Blast* for a reason, that reason being that everyone who had seen the devastation in Anaheim who knew anything about explosions knew that it hadn't been caused by any known type of explosive device.

Jacob Slater was, above all else, a scientist, and science works by systematically isolating and eliminating unknowns. Unfortunately, the crater in Anaheim was one big, gaping unknown, and there were very few definite knowns to be had.

The fact was that no one knew what had happened in Anaheim, just as no one really knew what was wrong with Jacob Slater. The doctors who had analyzed him two decades earlier hadn't actually found anything definitively wrong with him. Yes, they had offered an authoritative-sounding diagnosis, but it wasn't as if they had discovered anything concrete like an imbalance of bodily humors or a band of angry dwarves living in his small intestine. All they had done was to confirm that, yes, there was something a little off about young Jacob, and lump him into a category with a few million other kids who were a little off—a category called "Asperger's." When all else fails, science comes up with a label, like "gravity" or "inertia" or "Asperger's" and calls it a day. And that, in a nutshell, is how the Anaheim Event was born. It was a name that explained nothing and meant nothing, but it stuck the phenomenon into a category around which life could go on more or less as usual.

Jacob was, in fact, one of seven explosive experts from various agencies who had been called on to help explain the Event. Experts in other disciplines had been recruited as well, of course—some three dozen men and women bearing laminated badges identifying them as hailing from some arm of the government or other wandered about the crater at any given time, jotting down God-only-knew-what in government-issued notepads and talking to God-only-knew-whom on government-issued mobile phones. Jacob couldn't fathom who all these people were, and he didn't make much of an effort to find out; he communicated only with his direct superiors and the other blast guys, not only because of his aforementioned discomfort with strangers, but also because that seemed to be what his superiors wanted. Interagency cooperation was all well and good, but it was understood to be the sport of the aristocracy; rank-and-file workers like Jacob were expected to keep to their own kind.

Jacob's own notepad was empty, because despite having been on-site for six weeks, he still didn't know where to begin. None of his training seemed to apply; it was as if they had called him to investigate the site of a UFO landing or diagnose a case of lycanthropy. The only inference he could draw from the scene was so bizarre, so far outside anything he had ever experienced, that he dared not even write it down for fear of where it would take him. So he had spent six weeks walking in circles trying to devise a reasonable explanation when it was clear that whatever happened here was anything but reasonable.

Jacob sat in a crouch at the edge of the Anaheim crater, letting sand fall between his fingers and wondering what he was going to tell his superiors. A hundred or so feet away, behind a barrier of hurriedly constructed fencing, a handful of tourists stood gawking and taking pictures. The authorities would have preferred to keep the public farther away from the crater, but the blast site (as those in charge insisted on calling it) was so huge and so close to the center of bustling downtown Anaheim that isolating it had been effectively impossible. Still, they made a good public show of keeping the area secret as a matter of national security, with twenty-foot-high chain-link fencing topped with barbed wire marking a perimeter some hundred feet outside the rim of the crater, and National Guardsmen patrolling the streets a quarter mile out. The sight of armed men in camouflage gear driving around town in Humvees made for a surreal juxtaposition with the amusement park atmosphere of Anaheim, prompting one cynical joker to spray paint a nearby building with the moniker FASCISM-LAND. The perpetrator was arrested and held for three days without access to an attorney as an "enemy combatant" before being handed over to the local police, a regrettable episode that not surprisingly failed to quiet protests that the military had overstepped its authority.

"Hey, um, Slater," called a voice. "You are, um, going to be late." It was Kevin Samson, another member of the blast team. That's what they were calling it: the "blast team." Jacob found the name ironic not only because he was pretty sure that what had caused this crater was in no way any kind of blast, but also because the members of the team were some of the dullest people he had ever met. What was it about explosive guys that made them so impossibly boring? Did a life centered on explosions cause a man's personality to somehow implode? Not that Jacob minded; he actually preferred dull people, because they made few social demands and tended to make him look interesting by comparison. "Team" was also a stretch, as once the bus from the blast site deposited them back at their hotels, each team member went his separate way, not seeing the others again until the bus picked them up the next morning. This "blast team" was as big a blast and as much of a team as the 1962 Mets.

"I'm coming," muttered Jacob. He turned and trudged along the edge of the crater toward a parking lot crammed with the double-wide trailers that acted as the Anaheim Command Headquarters, On-site Operations, which had the unfortunate acronym ACHOO. He made his way through the maze of trailers to the one marked Central Briefing. Below the official sign identifying the building was a hand-painted piece of laminated cardboard that read GOOFIE. All of the trailers had been given cartoon character names that later had to be modified due to threat of a lawsuit. As a result, GOOFIE now sat nestled between MICKEE, DONULD and MINNEE. The U.S. military feared no fighting force on earth, but even it was no match for the army of attorneys that served the Mouse.

Jacob walked up the ramp that led to GOOFIE and went inside, taking a seat at a table at the front of the room, along with the other members of the blast team. They sat with their backs against the wall, facing an assortment of military and civilian higher-ups that had gathered to hear them speak. This was to be the third briefing delivered to the Heads of the Joint Anaheim Command (unofficially known as HeadJAC) by the blast team. The previous two briefings consisted mainly of the blast team members pleading for more time to assess the situation, and there had been a lot of pressure leading up to this latest briefing to deliver some kind of preliminary report on what had happened. The blast team had, as a result, written up a sketchy eight-page report that was long on descriptive information and very short on causality. The report had been distributed to the HeadJAC members the previous day, but the real trial by fire was going to be the Q&A period following the briefing.

After the briefing had been called to order, Kevin Samson began to read the report word for word, pausing often for generous drinks of water. Kevin had been chosen as the de facto spokesperson of the blast group because of his painfully deliberate, halting way of talking. Only thirty minutes had been allotted for the briefing; it was conceivable that he could use up the entire time reading the report and the Q&A period would have to be postponed.

"Preliminary report on the kinesthetic dynamics of the Anaheim Event," Kevin began. "Um." He picked up a water bottle from the table in front of him, unscrewed the lid, put the opening to his lips, took several small swallows, screwed the lid back on, and set the bottle back down on the table. He continued, "Before drawing any conclusions from the, um, physical evidence present at the scene of the Anaheim Event, hereinafter referred to simply as 'the Event,' it is necessary to…undertake a, um, thorough cataloguing of the…data at hand." Kevin cleared his throat and continued, "To wit." He cleared his throat again, said, "Excuse me," and picked up the water bottle again. He unscrewed the lid, took several more sips, screwed the lid back on, and set it down once more. He began again, "To wit. Um."

A gruff voice from the back of the room broke the silence. It was the deputy assistant director of the FBI, Dirk Lubbers. "Look," he said. "Do you know what kind of bomb this was or not?"

Kevin paled. He riffled through the eight-page report as if looking for a section entitled "What Kind of Bomb It Was." He didn't find anything of the sort. "Um," said Kevin. "Before drawing any conclusions, um…"

"For Christ's sake," Lubbers growled. "There are seven of you, and you've had six weeks to examine the scene. Surely you can tell us *something*." Murmurs of assent bubbled up from the assembled members of HeadJAC.

Brighton Quincy, another member of the blast team, spoke up. "We have a theory," he said, which was news to Jacob and the rest of the team.

"Go on," said Lubbers.

"We believe that a device producing an extremely high-temperature, symmetrical blast could conceivably have vaporized the stadium, converting much of the matter within range to plasma. The super-heated plasma would have shot upwards, creating a massive vacuum at the scene that would have sucked everything into it from immediate vicinity. This would explain the inverted blast pattern we found, as well as the lack of any glazing or other typical signs of an explosion, such as…"

He was cut short by the sound of harsh, barking laughter. It was Lubbers. "You're telling me that what caused…*this,*" he said, gesturing toward the giant crater visible outside, "was a bomb that was so effective it *destroyed the evidence of its own explosion?*"

Kevin leaped to the rescue. "I think that what Mr. Quincy is saying is that *theoretically,* um."

Quincy tried again. "It isn't inconceivable that a very high-energy blast, not nuclear because we'd have detected some fallout, but some sort of controlled plasma reaction…"

"Jesus Christ," spat Lubbers. "I scraped through physics in high school with a C minus and even I know that's bullshit. You guys don't have a damn clue what caused this. A hundred and forty thousand dead, and you don't have a goddamned clue."

Jacob found himself on his feet, clearing his throat. Suddenly all eyes were on him. Good God, he thought, what am I doing?

"It wasn't a bomb," he said.

"'Scuse me?" said Lubbers.

"I, uh, suspect that it, uh, was not actually a bomb," said Jacob. Great, he thought. I'm turning into, um, Kevin.

"Not a bomb," chuckled Lubbers. "OK, I'll bite. What was it then? A UFO? Bigfoot? The world's largest Dyson vacuum?"

The room erupted in laughter.

Jacob took a deep breath. He stared at his feet because he dared not confront the jeering faces in the room, but spoke clearly, willing each word out of his mouth. "Something like that," he said. "Clearly this…*event*…was not caused by any kind of ordinary explosive device. In fact, other than the, uh, sheer devastation, there's no evidence of an explosion at all."

"No evidence of an explosion," said another voice. "You mean other than the quarter-mile diameter crater in the middle of Anaheim."

Nervous laughter filled the room.

Still Jacob did not look up. He went on, "Yes, uh, as I said, no evidence other than the crater. That is, we're assuming it was an explosion because, well, that's the only phenomenon we've ever experienced that is capable of creating a scene remotely like this. But if you look at the scene as its own thing, that is, not as something under the heading of 'blast crater,' you would come to the conclusion that it was caused by something else entirely. Something, uh, not an explosion."

"Something, uh, not an explosion," repeated Lubbers mockingly. "Can you be just a little bit more specific?"

"I believe I can," said Jacob. He took a deep breath and looked Deputy Assistant Director Lubbers straight in the eye. "I believe what caused this," he said, "was an *implosion*. Rather than exploding outward, the device—call it an anti-bomb—sucked Anaheim Stadium into it. It imploded the whole area. "

"Imploded?" said Quincy, doubtfully. "That's impossible. And even if there were such a device, which we know there isn't, where did everything go? Where did a hundred and forty thousand people and five thousand tons of earth and concrete disappear to?"

"Well," replied Jacob nervously. "It's impossible to say. Outer space, maybe."

"Are you shitting me, Slater?" growled Lubbers. "Anaheim Stadium was sucked into outer fucking space?"

"Not necessarily," answered Jacob hurriedly. "That's one possibility. But to remove that much matter that quickly would require some kind of rift in space-time itself, some kind of wormhole or portal. The other end of the portal might open somewhere in deep space, but it could just as well open into another dimension. Once you've established the possibility of a rift in space-time, there's really no limit to…" Jacob broke off, having come to the uncomfortable realization that everyone in the room, including his "teammates" in the blast group, thought he was crazy. It didn't matter what he said at this point; no one was going to hear him. He might just as well be talking about leprechauns and the Easter Bunny as wormholes and other dimensions.

Lubbers narrowed his eyes at Jacob. "You're telling me," he said, "that it is your professional opinion that Anaheim Stadium was *sucked through a portal to another dimension?*"

Jacob had to admit that when he phrased it like that, it did sound a little silly. "Sir," he said haltingly, "I have no professional opinion on the matter. I, uh, my expertise and experience fail me. What I'm offering you is an attempt at an assessment uncolored by prejudice. I'm shooting in the dark, sir. We all are."

"Well, Mr. Slater," said Lubbers, "you'd better hope to God that your alternate dimension exists, because that sort of fairy tale *Star Trek* bullshit sure as hell isn't going to fly in this one."

With that, he walked out of the trailer. The briefing was over.

EIGHT
circa 2,000 B.C.

"Well, this is ridiculous," observed Tiamat irritably. "We're going on, what, three weeks of rain now?"

Mercury nodded. "It'll be twenty-one days on Thursday."

"And no word from Nabu," she said. "We're running out of food."

Nabu had left four days earlier on a raft with three other men on an expedition to the mountains to the east in an attempt to scrounge up some food.

"OK, that's it," Tiamat said. "You need to go find out what's going on."

"Me?" asked Mercury. "What am *I* going to do? I don't know anybody in Weather."

"This is more than weather," said Tiamat. "This is a cataclysm. The Department of Weather might be involved, but they can't do something like this without approval from higher up. We need to go to the top and ask them what the hell they're trying to pull."

"And by 'we,'" said Mercury, "I assume you mean me."

"Well, *I* can't go, can I?" said Tiamat. "I've got a civilization to run." She motioned at the hundreds of bedraggled lumps of humanity huddling together under makeshift shelters. She and

Mercury sat in comfort in a luxurious tent on the northwest corner of the ziggurat guarded by a dozen cherub henchmen.

"Wouldn't you rather take a little vacation at the Courts of the Most High?" Mercury asked. "The weather there is beautiful this time of year. I'm sure I can manage the civilization for a few days."

"No, no, it wouldn't do for me to leave my people," Tiamat said, watching an elderly woman struggling to cross a torrent of water that had formed where the rain poured off Tiamat's tent. "Move it, you old battle-ax! You're blocking the view! Also, there are some pending legal matters that make a visit to the Courts inconvenient for me at the present."

"Another outstanding warrant?" Mercury asked wearily.

"Don't judge me, Mercury," Tiamat snapped. "You don't know what it's like, trying to build a great civilization while abiding by all these ridiculous regulations. Did you know they've outlawed human sacrifice? How are the people supposed to express their devotion if they can't occasionally sacrifice one of their children to me?"

Mercury frowned. "Didn't you just have a child burned on an altar last week?"

"That was a mercy killing," Tiamat said. "He had a harelip."

"Many harelips live long and productive lives," Mercury replied.

"I know," said Tiamat, "but nobody could understand a word he said. It was very frustrating."

"I see," said Mercury.

"The point is," Tiamat went on, "I've got to sort out a few things down here before I can show my face in Heaven again. Those idiots at the Seraphic Civilization Shepherding Program keep trying to micromanage the situation down here, but they'll change their tune once Babylon is the greatest civilization on the

Mundane Plane. All of my minor transgressions will be forgiven then. But until that happens…"

"You need me to be your go-between," said Mercury. "I got it."

The next day, Mercury made his way to the Megiddo Portal, which was some four hundred miles to the west. Traveling by air most of the way, it took him a little over two hours.

The Megiddo Portal was located on a small rock outcropping that was virtually impossible to reach by foot. For an angel, however, it presented no challenge. Mercury alighted on the intricate pattern carved into the rock and blinked out of Mundane existence, reappearing a split second later in the arrivals area of the planeport.

He walked to the portal bearing the markings of the Courts of the Most High and soon found himself walking the gold brick paths of Heaven's most prominent plane.

Mercury strode the path to the great pyramid-shaped building that housed the Apocalypse Bureau. Once inside, he made his way to Uzziel's office and knocked. A curt "Come in!" greeted him, and he opened the door.

Uzziel was on the phone. "No, I won't hold!" he shouted. "I'm a deputy assistant director of the Apocalypse Bureau, and I demand to…Damn it all, they've put me on hold again. Sit down, Mercury. Let me guess, you're here to complain about the flooding? You and every other cherub assigned to the Mundane Plane."

Mercury shook his head innocently. "Flooding? No, I was just stopping by to see how things are holding up here at the home front. What's this about flooding?"

"Half the damn Mundane Plane is underwater," Uzziel said. "My phone is ringing off the hook with angels asking me if we're running some kind of drill. You really haven't noticed any flooding?"

"Oh, there's been a little rain," Mercury said dismissively. "It doesn't bother me. I find it soothing."

"No, I *don't* want to be transferred to the Apocalypse Bureau!" Uzziel shouted. "I *am* the Apocalypse Bureau. My name is Uzziel. I'm trying to find out if you...Damn it all to Hell!"

"On hold again?" Mercury asked.

Uzziel sighed. "I'm actually glad you're here," he said. "Maybe you can figure out what the hell is going on with this flooding."

A nasal voice spoke from Uzziel's intercom. "Sir, you have a call on line two. Should I have them call back?"

"No, I'll take it," said Uzziel. "These idiots have me on hold anyway. Who is it?"

The voice spoke again. "She said her name was Susie. From the Punk Lips Bureau."

"The *what*?" Uzziel demanded.

"That's what she said. She said she was transferring Susie from the Punk Lips Bureau with a question about budding."

"Whatever," Uzziel said wearily. "Just transfer her." He punched the button for line two on his phone.

"Apocalypse Bureau, Deputy Assistant Director Uzziel speaking," Uzziel said into the phone. "Uh-huh. Yep. OK, I got it." He hung up and smiled humorlessly at Mercury. "I just hung up on myself."

"I admire your patience," Mercury said. "I'd have hung up on you hours ago."

"Seriously, Mercury, this is a disaster. I guess the worst of the flooding hasn't hit your area yet, but trust me, it's like the end of the world down there. Which, of course, it can't be, because I'm in charge of the Apocalypse and I don't know a damn thing about whatever is going on."

"Really?" Mercury asked. "So you didn't approve this rain?"

"No," replied Uzziel firmly.

"Not even in Europe?"

"No," said Uzziel, shaking his head. "I didn't approve the rain in Europe."

"What about in Asia?"

"No," said Uzziel. "I didn't OK the rain in Asia either."

"Hmm," said Mercury. "But Africa, though. Surely—"

"I most certainly did not bless the rains down in Africa!" growled Uzziel.

"OK," said Mercury. "Let me see what I can find out."

"Thanks, Merc," said Uzziel. "I'll owe you one."

Mercury left Uzziel's office. Now what? Not only did Uzziel not know anything, evidently Mercury wasn't the first angel to arrive from the Mundane Plane to complain in vain about the rain.

It occurred to him, however, that if a large number of angels had fled the Mundane Plane through the planeport, someone who spent a lot of time at the planeport might have overheard something useful. Mercury sighed. There was only one thing to do: head back to the planeport and find Perp.

Perp wasn't difficult to find, as he was the only cherub Mercury knew who had assumed the appearance of a young human child with vestigial birdlike wings.[3]

"Hey, Perp," called Mercury as he spotted Perp's winged figure buzzing down the concourse of the planeport. "Still doing the baby-with-bird-wings thing, eh?"

---

3   All angels can fly, of course, but as flight is simply a matter of using interplanar energy to warp gravity, wings are hardly necessary. In the Pre–Comic Book (PCB) era, it was not uncommon for angels to sport wings on the Mundane Plane to establish their Heavenly credentials and to offer a visible explanation to the plane's primitive inhabitants of their ability to defy gravity. Mercury himself briefly experimented with wings on his shoes and on his hat, the former making walking difficult and the latter inevitably prompting the question, "OK, but how does the hat stay on?"

"Hmph," replied Perp as he changed directions to approach Mercury. "Just wait until the Renaissance. Then we'll see who's at the height of fashion."

"The Ren-what?" Mercury asked.

"Forget it," Perp said. "In this job, I hear stuff about Mundane history that you wouldn't believe."

"Actually," said Mercury, "that's what I wanted to talk to you about. Have you heard about the flooding?"

"Have I heard about the flooding!" Perp exclaimed. "It's all anybody's talking about. I must have escorted five hundred angels through here in the past two weeks, every one of them soaking wet and whining nonstop about the incessant rain on Earth. Lousy fair-weather cherubim, taking an assignment on the Mundane Plane because they thought it was going to be all puppies and rainbows. And now they all want transfers. Well you can't have a rainbow without rain!"

"Maybe they're just in it for the puppies," suggested Mercury.

"Hmph," replied Perp. "Herbs such as rosemary and eucalyptus can help repel fleas."

"I guess I deserved that," said Mercury. "So have you heard anything about why it's raining so much? I just talked to Uzziel, and the Apocalypse Bureau is clueless."

"*Everybody's* clueless," Perp whispered. "And you know what that means."

Mercury didn't.

"It means," whispered Perp, "that this cataclysm wasn't cleared through channels. The entire bureaucracy is out of the loop. In other words, it came down from *on high.*"

"'On high?'" Mercury asked. "You mean the archangels?"

"Shhh!" Perp hissed. "Higher. The order came from *them.*"

There was only one *them* that Perp could mean: the legendary beings known as the Eternals, who were to the angels what angels were to humans. Mercury wasn't even certain they really existed, but the official story was that the Eternals provided guidance to the High Council of Seraphim, which was comprised of the archangels and a few senior members of the Seraphic Senate. Mercury had always suspected that the High Council perpetuated the belief in the Eternals to cover the fact that they were making things up as they went along.

"Come on, Perp," Mercury said. "You don't really buy all that crap about the Eter—"

"Shhh!" Perp hissed again. "Doubt if you like, but I know when the entire Heavenly bureaucracy is out of the loop on something. Now if you don't mind, I've got work to do. We've got a V.I.A. coming through this afternoon."

"Ooh, who is it?" Mercury prodded. "A senator? Somebody from the Council?"

Perp responded only with a look of disdain.

"An archangel?" whispered Mercury. "Gabriel? Michael?"

An expression of alarm swept across Perp's face.

"Wow, Michael? God's own general?"

"Quiet!" Perp hissed. "This is top-secret stuff. Only planeport security and a few key employees of Transport and Communications have been told. So keep your mouth shut!"

"I want to meet him," said Mercury.

"What? No! You can't meet Michael! He's passing through the planeport on official business. He doesn't have time to stop and sign autographs."

"I don't want an autograph. I want to ask him what he knows about this rain."

"I told you," said Perp irritably. "Nobody knows anything."

"Then it won't hurt to ask."

"Absolutely not," said Perp, folding his pudgy arms in front of his chest.

"Fine," said Mercury. "Then I'm going to walk over to that information desk and ask that they page the Archangel Michael. *Archangel Michael, please pick up the white courtesy phone.*"

"You can't do that!" Perp snapped. "That's a violation of security protocols."

"How could I violate security protocols for something I have no way of knowing about? I mean, unless *you* told me. Wow, I bet you could get in trouble for something like that."

"But I didn't tell you anything!" Perp protested.

Mercury shrugged. "Well, you've got *me* convinced, but I'm a sympathetic audience."

"OK, OK," grumbled Perp. "You can be part of the official escort. But asking him about the flood is out of the question. Under no circumstances are you to initiate a conversation with Michael."

"What if he starts a conversation with me?" Mercury asked.

"Why in hell would he do that?" Perp growled.

Mercury shrugged. "I have a friendly sort of face. People like talking to me."

"Whatever," said Perp. "Just don't start anything, and don't antagonize him. No talking about religion or politics."

"Works for me," said Mercury. "I'll stick to completely non-controversial topics. Like the weather, for instance."

NINE

After the meeting at the Beacon Building, Eddie spent two days holed up in his hotel room reading books one through six of the Charlie Nyx series and then watching the five movies that had been released on Blue-Ray, looking for clues as to the author's identity. He was surprised to find that the books weren't actually bad. The writing style was a bit tired; clearly the author had talent, but Eddie got the impression that he or she wasn't trying very hard. Underneath the unremarkable prose, however, lay a story with mythical potency. It reminded Eddie of some of the ancient epic poems, but updated and translated to tween-speak. The movies, on the other hand, were absolute dreck, combining an overly literal reading of the books with a ten-year-old's obsession with shit blowing up. By the end of the last movie, Eddie was actually sick to his stomach—although that might also have had something to do with the two cartons of Whoppers and three gallons of Mountain Dew he had ingested during his Charlie Nyx marathon.

Having learned almost nothing about the author of the books, Eddie drove the BMW across town to the posh neighborhood that had once been home to Katie Midford. The drive helped relieve the nausea induced by the intake of excessive sugar and computer-generated graphics, but he was still experiencing a funk that even the warm weather and comforting smog blanket of Los Angeles couldn't dispel. It was dawning on him that even if he found the manuscript, it would undoubtedly be unusable in its current form, as it had been written before the Anaheim Event. Eddie knew enough about human nature to realize that releasing a young adult fantasy adventure that made frequent references to a place where a hundred and forty thousand people had very recently died would be considered in very bad taste, no matter what Wanda Kwan and her beloved shareholders thought. Not only that, but it was probably only a matter of time before someone discovered that there really *was* a secret network of tunnels under Anaheim Stadium, a fact that would raise a lot of uncomfortable questions that would undoubtedly be directed at Eddie himself. Maybe the authorities had found the tunnels already and simply hadn't revealed the fact publicly. But if they had, he reflected, he most likely would have been approached in Cork by FBI agents rather than the lovely Wanda Kwan. So they hadn't found them yet. And maybe, with a little luck, they never would.

So, if he could avoid being arrested on the suspicion that he was the most dangerous terrorist in U.S. history, and if he could somehow locate the manuscript that had eluded the Finch Group's professional investigators, and if he could remove the horrifically offensive bits of the manuscript that were undoubtedly critical to the arc of the entire Charlie Nyx series without ruining the book, and if that book were then made into a blockbuster movie, and if he could then parlay the success of that movie into another movie deal, Eddie Pratt would be an actual honest-to-goodness Hollywood screenwriter—and wasn't that worth the risk? Of course it was. Eddie Pratt, the misplaced cherub of Cork, was going to be the biggest thing that ever came out of the M.O.C.

Eddie drove up Katie Midford's driveway and waved his hand at the gate sensor. The sensor, mistaking an electrical irregularity caused by the manipulation of a minute amount of interplanar energy for a valid entry code, obediently opened the iron gate for the BMW. Eddie zoomed up to the house and squealed to a stop. Then, performing a similar trick on the front door locks and the house's security sensors, he entered the mansion.

The house was large but sparsely furnished; he moved rapidly from room to room, looking everywhere he thought somebody might possibly have hidden a manuscript. Eventually he came to a heavy wood door at the end of a hallway that had evidently been locked from the other side. Once again taking hold of a slim vein of interplanar energy pulsing through the air, he created a slight kinetic push that nudged aside the latch of the door. Opening the door, he strode in and was immediately greeted with five very loud pops that startled him tremendously, temporarily distracting him from the five bullet holes that had been torn in his chest.

Before Eddie could even appraise his condition, Katie Midford's tile floor leaped up from behind him and cracked him on the back of his head. He lay there, dazed and bleeding, nearly insensible with pain, while a well-built blond woman in a stylish black leather jacket and sunglasses approached him coolly. In her right hand was a smoking Glock 17 pistol.

"You gonna get up?" the woman asked.

This struck Eddie as rather rude. If there was any condition that gave a man *carte blanche* to lie down and take it easy for a bit, it was being shot five times in the chest with a nine-millimeter automatic pistol. But then Eddie wasn't a man. Still, he was in an awful lot of pain, and a great deal of blood that by all rights should still have been inside him was now re-coloring Katie Midford's grout lines. He lay on the tile and groaned.

"Reason I ask is," said the woman, who was still pointing the pistol in Eddie's direction, "I need to know if I should reload or get a shovel."

Eddie managed a chuckle. "Shoot me again and you'll regret it," he said.

The woman squeezed the trigger again. Nothing happened. She checked the gun's magazine, releasing a handful of bullets into her palm. She peered at them curiously for a moment before popping one in her mouth. "Nice," she said. "Chocolate bullets. Haven't seen that one before. Gonna be a bitch to clean the Glock though." Melted chocolate dripped from the gun's barrel.

She replaced the gun in a shoulder holster and held out her hand to Eddie. "Name's Cody," she said. "Cody Lang." She seemed profoundly unsurprised by Eddie's supernatural abilities.

With Cody's help, Eddie struggled to his feet. "I'm Eddie Pratt," he said.

"Sorry about shooting you, Eddie Pratt. My line of work can be dangerous. And you *are* trespassing, you know. Come on, let's sit in the parlor. I'll make you a drink."

"Your line of business," Eddie echoed weakly. "And what would that be, exactly?" He stumbled along after Cody and collapsed in an easy chair in the parlor. Cody made them a couple of gin and tonics from the bar and sat down across from him. She handed Eddie one of the drinks. Eddie took it, wincing with pain as muscles in his not-quite-healed-chest tightened.

"Actress slash private investigator," Cody said.

"Um, what?" Eddie replied.

"That's my line of business. Lines of business."

Eddie was puzzled. "That's sort of an odd combination, isn't it?"

"In this town," Cody said, "there's a surprising amount of overlap." She reached into her jacket, and for a split second Eddie prepared to pull the chocolate bullet trick again. But her hand came out bearing only a small white card. She handed it to Eddie. It read:

Cody Lang,
Actress and Private Investigator

Specializing in:
- Infidelity
- Bail Bonds
- Polygraphs
- Body Double
- Thigh Model
- Crying on Command

"Crying on command?" asked Eddie.

"Would you like to see?" asked Cody.

"Oh, uh, that's OK," said Eddie, who was secretly wishing he had asked about something higher on the list.

"Fine," said Cody. "I don't...really like doing it anyway. It tends to stir up some things that I don't...It's hard to talk about." She removed her sunglasses and wiped her eyes with the back of her hand. They were moist and red.

"Hey, that's impressive," said Eddie.

"Thanks," said Cody, suddenly sanguine again. "That's gotten me cast as the grieving wife at least a dozen times. It's also handy in infidelity cases, you know, when I have to break the news about some cheating bastard. People love it when you pretend to care." She took a swallow of her drink and said, "So you're one of *them*. A demon."

This last caught Eddie off guard, but there didn't seem to be much point in pretending after his miraculous recovery from five gunshot wounds to the chest, not to mention the chocolate bullet thing. "Yes," said Eddie. "I'm one of them. But I'm not a servant of Ti…Katie Midford, if that's what you're thinking."

"Yeah," replied Cody. "I kinda figured that from the fact that you broke into her house. So what's your deal?"

Eddie told her about Wanda Kwan and his need to find the real Charlie Nyx ghostwriter. Cody laughed. "A screenwriter, eh? That's aiming a bit low, isn't it?"

"What about you?" said Eddie, a bit defensively. "What are you doing here?"

"I work for Katie. Or I did, anyway. Lately I've been trying to figure out what happened to her. She owes me twenty grand."

"Twenty grand? For what?"

"Heh, that's the funny part," said Cody. "You and I have something in common. She hired me to find out who the real writer of the Charlie Nyx books is."

TEN

Christine had been in the remote Kenyan village of Baji for three hours before becoming violently ill. She lay moaning in a cot in the back room of the rundown concrete building that served as the local headquarters of Eternal Harvest. On the wall across the room was the same poster she had seen in the former electronics store in Yorba Linda. It continued to assure her, despite much evidence to the contrary, that "YOU CAN HELP." It then went on, less certainly, "EH?"

So far she was proving to be a severe drain on the personnel and resources of the already strapped Eternal Harvest organization. Leaning over the edge of the cot, she vomited into a bucket, which was then spirited away and presumably emptied in some unhygienic fashion before being returned to her. She was under constant watch by two local women who doubtlessly had better things to do. Far from helping to make this godforsaken place more livable, she had actually managed, in the few hours she had been here, to detract significantly from the local quality of life. She could only hope that whatever malignant entity had seized her insides would kill her quickly, putting her out of her misery and letting the locals get on with their already miserable lives.

The EH facility was currently staffed by a total of six people, three men and three women, most of whom seemed to be volunteers. One woman had some medical training; the others filled a variety of roles from construction foreperson to nutritionist. Any overt proselytizing that occurred was secondary to the hands-on work EH was doing in the community. At least that was the impression Christine got from the materials she had read on the plane to Nairobi and the three hours she had spent touring the town before being overcome by nausea.

The next day she felt somewhat better, and was volunteered to assist Maya Keenan, the director of the group, in an errand: they were to drive to an agricultural test facility to pick up a shipment of surplus seed that Maya intended to use to help the locals produce more of their own food.

Barely recovered from her illness, Christine was experiencing a new round of vertigo precipitated by a jarring ride in an ancient Land Rover down a remote track in Kenya.

"Can we pull over?" she moaned. "I'm going to be sick."

"Again?" asked Maya Keenan, who was driving. "How can you possibly have anything left to throw up?"

Maya, a tall, wiry ex-Manhattanite, was a no-nonsense do-gooder who applied to charity work the sort of drive that most people reserved for some combination of career, family, and dental hygiene. In short, she didn't appreciate impediments to efficiency such as unscheduled vomiting.

"I think my pancreas is coming up," moaned Christine.

"Stick your head out the window. We need to be back before nightfall. Can't stop now."

In fact they were barely moving as it was. What they were driving on wasn't so much a road as it was a vague idea of a road; a roughly linear stretch of ground littered with barely navigable rocks. Their destination was a mere twenty miles away as the crow flew, but they had been on the road for nearly an hour and they were only halfway there.

Christine couldn't recall a time when she had been more miserable. She was nauseous, tired, uncomfortable, and dirty, and part of her couldn't help wishing that the world had ended six weeks earlier. Maybe she and Mercury shouldn't have interfered with the plans of Heaven. Maybe the world was *meant* to end. Sure, the archangel Michelle had assured her that the Apocalypse was indefinitely on hold, but maybe there were powers at work that trumped even the best intentions of the most influential angels. Maybe Michelle was as powerless to stop the Apocalypse as she was.

But if the Apocalypse was still proceeding, wasn't there a whole lot of other bad stuff that was supposed to go down before the final act? Rivers turning to blood and a third of the moon falling out of the sky, stuff like that.

It occurred to her that she was thinking like Harry Giddings, a realization that actually made her feel worse. No matter how bad things were, she wasn't about to adopt Harry as a role model.

Was there even such a thing as destiny? There must be, she mused. If not, then aren't we all just bouncing around aimlessly like ping-pong balls? But if everything is predetermined, then what's the point of doing anything at all? Maybe Mercury was right: we're all just splashing around in the inexorable stream of fate. Of course, Mercury had ended up splashing a little too hard, and had nearly been pulled under by the weight of the Heavenly bureaucracy. Now he was God-knows-where, presumably still on the run from the powers-that-be.

Christine sighed. These sorts of thoughts weren't helpful. She needed to focus on the here and now, not on abstract philosophical notions. And certainly not on the late Harry Giddings or the vanished angel Mercury. She needed to focus on whatever good she could do here in Africa, for whatever time she had left.

At last they reached the remote agricultural testing facility, which consisted of a small aluminum building attached to a greenhouse about half the size of a football field. The entire facility was ringed by a twenty-foot chain-link fence topped with barbed wire. Inconspicuous signs identified the structure as "TRI-FED TESTING FACILITY 26." Maya pulled the Land Rover up to the gate and honked.

"What do they do here?" Christine asked.

"They test bioengineered crops," Maya said. "It has to be remote to prevent contamination with the local varieties."

"Remote?" Christine said. "We passed *remote* about ten miles back. This is…like…godforsaken."

A pudgy, red-faced man with an enormous head emerged from the building and unlocked the gate, swinging it open to let them enter. Thin wisps of pale yellow hair arced out from his gigantic cranium in a futile effort to block some minute fraction of the radiation pummeling his scalp. Christine tried to make out the name on the man's embroidered nametag, but the second half of the name was obscured by a sizeable scorch mark. What she could decipher looked like *Crisp*—an unlikely, albeit appropriate name.

"Drive around back," the man said. "I've got a pallet ready for you." He lumbered toward the rear of the building, his arms and legs splayed widely in an apparent attempt to prevent any one part of his body from contacting any other part. As they followed slowly in the Land Rover, Christine found herself transfixed by the sweat marks on the man's shirt. There was one big puddle on his upper back, another slightly smaller one on his lower back, and one under each armpit. The dark spots seemed to be growing before her eyes, and she found herself rooting for them to join together as one the one big, happy, sweat stain she knew they were destined to be.

The man, whose name was Crispin Guthbertson, was unaware of the sacred sweat communion about to occur on his back, but he was used to being the source of entertainment for those around him. It had been that way ever since he had arrived at Testing Facility 26. To say that Crispin was ill suited to live in the wilderness of Kenya was like saying that mayonnaise is an inadequate remedy for smallpox. Crispin was so physiologically and temperamentally unsuited to living in an equatorial climate that his own subconscious mind, in an attempt to knock some sense into him, caused him several times a day to nearly trip over an invisible line on the ground which some primordial part of his brain recognized as the dividing line between the two hemispheres of the globe.

Crispin had been designed, through six thousand years of careful inbreeding, to be perfectly adapted to live in the frigid low latitudes of Scandinavia. His body wasted no effort developing melatonin and other pigments to protect his pale, porcine flesh from a distant and ineffectual sun, preferring instead to manufacture copious rolls of fat that it systematically placed around the organs that it considered to be Crispin's most valuable components: his intestines, first of all, followed closely in priority by his stomach, liver, and kidneys. His heart and lungs were given a perfunctory wrapping of blubber, while his brain, in a forgivable oversight, was left out of the calculations completely.

What Crispin's head lacked in fatty deposits, however, it made up for with calcium. Crispin's ancestors lived on an island that had been cut off from the Scandinavian mainland, and the combination of an oversupply of seafood and an undersupply of leisure activities resulted in the primordial Guthbertsons spending a surprising proportion of their time attempting to bash one another over the head with sticks, rocks, and whatever other weapons they could devise with whatever undamaged brain matter that was left in their heads. As a result, an inordinately thick skull had become a significant survival advantage among his people: those with the thickest skulls tended to survive the bashings, allowing them to produce more offspring than their thinner-skulled rivals. These thick-skulled children were, not coincidentally, more than happy to carry on the skull-bashing traditions of their forebears, and thus both massive skulls and massive skull-bashing were passed down for dozens of generations, until it was every mother's dream that her son would grow up to have a skull so massive that he was unanimously elected to be the tribe's chief. The last chief of the tribe, in fact, had a skull that was so heavy that toward the end of his reign he required the assistance of several advisors simply to nod his own head—a fact which raised questions about undue influence of his cabinet and might ultimately have led to the end of his dynasty if his entire government hadn't been wiped out by a neighboring tribe that had developed an unquestioned military advantage by pioneering the use of rowboats and sharpened sticks.

Crispin's ancestors were absorbed into the neighboring tribe, who were equally large and pale, but possessed, on average, slightly smaller skulls and slightly larger brains. The massive-skulled people nearly died out completely, but occasionally, even thousands of years after the whole skull-bashing business started, a combination of recessive genes would result in the birth of a man like Crispin Guthbertson, whose albino features and frequent neck aches would have made him feel right at home with his prehistoric forebears.

These days, however, skull bashing was generally frowned upon and paid poorly, leaving Crispin with few career options in the field to which he was most suited. He majored in chemistry and then attended pharmaceutical college, but due to genetic programming that limited his capability to resolve conflicts without resorting to skull smashing, he was not particularly suited for customer service and ended up working as a lab technician for a small Danish biotech company. This company was then bought by a larger company, based in Germany, which then merged with two other companies to become Tri-Fed, one of the world's leading biotech firms. Tri-Fed closed its Northern European locations and relocated Crispin to a remote agricultural research facility in Kenya, thereby flouting 250 generations of breeding designed to make Crispin Guthbertson the ideal survival candidate for a near-sunless arctic village.

Crispin's official title was "site administrator," but he was essentially a glorified supply clerk for the facility. The Kenya facility, officially known as Tri-Fed Testing Facility 26, was sort of the redheaded stepchild of the Tri-Fed family; only half a dozen scientists worked at the facility at any given time, and most of them had been reassigned there because of some sort of personnel issue, generally a sexual harassment lawsuit. Most Tri-Fed locations were several hundred times the size of the Kenya facility, but an edict from senior management required that all research facilities use the same staffing guidelines, and according to those guidelines the number of "productive personnel" in Testing Facility 26 justified 0.125 security guards, 0.108 cooks, 0.281 clerical workers, and 0.333 other support personnel, totaling 0.847 nonscientific employees. Crispin Guthbertson was assigned to fill all of these positions and given a fifteen percent pay cut on top of it, to make things fair.

Mercifully Crispin was generally ignored by the group of sexual deviants making up the research staff. He spent most of his days reading mystery novels and doing paperwork in an aluminum trailer, which, thanks to the modern marvel of air-conditioning, often got as cool as ninety-three degrees Fahrenheit. One day he made the mistake of eating his lunch outside; he had fallen asleep in the shade but woke up drenched in sweat, the sun beating down on his blistered skin. Crispin was an amazingly sound sleeper; even the sunburn might not have woken up if it weren't for the fact that his glasses (which were nearly as thick as his skull) had slipped down his nose and focused the sunlight perfectly on his embroidered name tag, burning completely through his shirt, obliterating the *in* at the end of his name, and lighting his left nipple on fire. The burns had taken weeks to heal, and the incident had earned him the predictable nickname "Crispy" among the staff.

Crispin's least favorite part of his job, though, was burning seeds. As an agricultural research site, the facility produced a high volume of seeds from genetically modified crops. Most of this seed would never get legal approval to be sold in Africa or anywhere else in the world, and Tri-Fed's protocols required that it be incinerated. That meant that Crispin had to leave his air-conditioned trailer to go to a non-insulated metal building that was always at least a hundred and twenty degrees Fahrenheit, fire up the incinerator, and then toss many large bags of seed into the fire. It got so hot in the incinerator building that on heavy seed-burning days, he actually feared for his life.

Then those guys from Tri-Fed corporate showed up in a helicopter and delivered a shiny metal briefcase to the scientists. Crispin had no idea what was in that briefcase, but after that, there was even more seed burning to be done. Crispin had had enough.

One day he was sitting at his desk when a seed-burning order came through, and he happened to look up and see a poster for a Canadian relief organization[4] working nearby, and he had an idea—an idea that would mean no more trips to the incinerator, not to mention a few bucks in his pocket: he would sell the excess seed to the relief workers. He had called them up and talked to a woman named Maya, who was cautiously receptive to the idea. The first time, Maya had arrived with two men, but the next few times—having evidently been convinced that Crispin posed no threat—she had come alone. This was the first time he had seen this other woman. Kind of cute, he thought, although there was something not quite right about her face.

Maya followed the dirt driveway around the metal building to the greenhouse. A pallet of burlap bags marked TRI-FED lay on the ground. Maya and Christine exited the truck.

"How much?" asked Maya.

"Two hundred," replied Crispin.

"Two hundred? That's double what it cost last time!"

"This is really good stuff. Hey, if you don't want it, I can burn it. Got the incinerator all ready."

"I'll give you a hundred and twenty."

"A hundred and fifty. No less. I've got student loans to pay off, and this job doesn't pay shit."

"Fine," said Maya. "A hundred and fifty." She counted out a hundred and fifty dollars and handed it to the man.

"Nice doing business with you," he said, smiling, and turned to waddle back to the building.

"You're not going to help us load it?" Maya asked.

"Not for a hundred and fifty bucks. Have fun."

---

4   Eternal Harvest was not, in fact, Canadian. Crispin had made this erroneous assumption based on the fact that at the bottom of all their posters appeared the word *EH?*

"Asshole," Maya muttered. "OK, help me load these bags into the truck. We gotta get going."

"What was that all about?" Christine asked. "I thought they were giving you surplus seed."

"More or less," Maya replied. "Not so much surplus as not-yet-commercially approved. They can't legally sell it, so they give it to us."

"Except that you just bought it."

"I have to give Crispin some spending money or he won't give it to us."

"Oh, so you're not *buying* it," Christine said. "You're just exchanging money for something you want."

Maya sighed. "We're not buying it from Tri-Fed. They're giving it to us. But sometimes to get somebody to give you something, you have to grease the wheels a bit. It's how things work down here."

"Why can't they sell it? What's wrong with it?"

"Nothing's wrong with it. They just haven't gotten approval to sell it yet. It takes forever for the new seed patents to get approved, and every country has its own rules. They end up having to incinerate thousands of pounds of perfectly good seed. Crispin gives me a call when he's about to burn it."

"And this doesn't strike you as suspicious?"

"Christine, you've seen where we work. People are starving to death every day. I'm not going to let 'suspicious' stand in the way of me helping these people produce their own food. Now shut up and help me load these bags."

Christine did what she could to help, but was still feeling weak from her illness and nearly passed out loading the third bag. She went and sat in the truck while Maya finished up.

Maya was predictably irritated by Christine's inability to help, and on the way back she drove faster, seemingly in an effort to punish Christine. It worked: some ten miles from the Tri-Fed facility, the Land Rover's right front tire hit a cavernous pothole, ejecting several of the seed bags and nearly overturning the vehicle.

"I'll get it," Christine said, getting out of the Land Rover. She steadied herself against the truck, took a deep breath, and then set about reloading the ejected bags. When she had finished, she returned to the truck.

"Oh, shit," she said.

"What?" demanded Maya.

"I think we've got a flat tire."

Maya walked around the truck and inspected the tire. It had lost most of its pressure already, and was hissing more air as they watched.

"You have a spare?" Christine asked.

"That was the spare," Maya replied.

"What?" Christine asked. "We drove twenty miles into the godforsaken Kenyan wilderness without a spare tire?"

"If I didn't pick up the seed today, Crispin was going to burn it. Usually there's no hurry, but he called me yesterday and told me that if I didn't pick it up today, he was going to have to burn it all. Tri-Fed bigwigs coming out to inspect the place or something. I had no choice."

Christine bit her tongue.

Maya used the walkie-talkie to call Brian, the resident EH mechanic, but he was away in Nairobi for the day, picking up supplies.

"Looks like we may have to hunker down for the night," said Maya, bending down to inspect the tire.

"Hunker down?" Christine asked, dismayed. "Is that safe?"

Maya replied, "It's unlikely any of the raiders will come this far out…"

"Raiders?" Christine exclaimed. "There are raiders?"

"Look, we'll be fine," Maya said. "Just don't panic."

"Uh huh," replied Christine. "So, these raiders. Are they tall, mostly naked black guys with spears?"

"Spears?" Maya asked. "Why do you…?"

She looked up to see a group of half a dozen tall, lean men wearing loincloths and bearing spears, standing in front of the Land Rover. The men didn't look happy to see them.

ELEVEN

Not long after the disastrous briefing at which he had floated the idea of a rift in space-time sucking Anaheim Stadium into another dimension, Jacob Slater was pulled off the Anaheim Event and instructed to return immediately to Washington, D.C. He had packed his duffel bag and was currently waiting for the army transport helicopter that would take him to the Los Angeles airport. The helicopter wasn't just for him, of course; HeadJAC had arranged regular flights to and from LAX for the convenience of Deputy Assistant Director Lubbers and the other VIPs at ACHOO.

While he waited, he continued to pace the implosion area (as he insisted on thinking of it), eyeing the dozens of men and women going about various mysterious tasks at the site. He could only assume these were other investigators or scientists of some sort (geologists? structural engineers? immunologists?) developing their own narrative of what had happened at the site. Jacob couldn't help but think of the story of the blind men assessing the elephant: one man, feeling the elephant's tail, described the elephant as being like a rope; another, feeling the elephant's trunk, likened it to a snake; a third, feeling the elephant's leg, said that the elephant was more like a tree trunk.

I'm like the blind man at the elephant's tail, thought Jacob. Except that studying the tail wasn't enough for me. I had to keep pushing, and now I'm elbow deep in elephant shit.

His fellow blind elephant observers milled about the site, oblivious to what the other teams were doing. Each team would write up a report, and that information would work its way up the chain of command until it had reached someone with the appropriate security clearance to compare it to six other reports he couldn't make heads or tails of—probably D.A.D. Lubbers. Lubbers would report to the director of the FBI, who would report to the president of the United States, who would order a bombing raid on some backwater dictatorship that had nothing to do with the Anaheim Event but really wished they had.

Israel's war with Syria still dragged on, and some hawks in Congress were already hinting that Syria "couldn't be allowed to use an Anaheim-type device on Israel." This was such an absurd assertion that it was virtually impossible to argue against. In addition to the fact that no one had any idea what type of device (if any) had been used at Anaheim and that there was no reason to suspect the Syrians of being involved, it was unclear how anyone could stop them from using such a device if they *did* have one. Furthermore, if they did have another device, why hadn't they used it already to wipe out Tel Aviv? And for that matter, why had they used the first one in Anaheim, a city that most scholars agree is not one of the major points of contention in the ongoing Arab-Israeli conflict? Still, the hawks urged preemptive action due to the "scale of the threat," an argument that boiled down to the notion that it was better to be wrong than dead. Jacob feared that unless the various factions at the site of the implosion managed to come up with some compelling alternate explanation, escalation of the conflict in the Middle East was inevitable.

As Jacob regarded the surreal landscape, he took special interest in three large green canvas tents that had been erected roughly in line with each other, about a hundred feet apart. They were round like circus tents and maybe fifty feet in diameter. He had seen men moving in and out of these tents carrying all sorts of equipment, most of it apparently excavation related. They were digging something up inside of those tents, he knew, but so far he hadn't been able to find out what. National Guardsmen maintained a perimeter thirty feet around each tent, and his protests that he needed to take soil samples from the area inside one of the tents were met with curt rejection.

"What's under the big top?" he muttered to no one in particular. In the distance he heard the *whup-whup-whup* of an approaching helicopter. Slinging his bag over his shoulder, he trudged toward the helipad on the other side of ACHOO.

The helicopter waited on the ground for twenty minutes, but when it finally took off the only passengers were Jacob and a junior congressman from Delaware who, failing to have elicited any interest from the media in his presence at Ground Zero, decided to cut his trip short and head home. As the chopper lifted away from the crater, Jacob pulled his phone from his jacket pocket and snapped a picture of the site—a memento of the high point of his career.

He got to LAX a mere half hour before his flight was to depart, but the airline had overbooked the flight and was offering a free ticket to anywhere in the U.S. to anyone who would wait three hours for the next flight. Jacob, who badly needed a vacation and was in no hurry to return to Washington, D.C., jumped at the offer. As a result, he spent the next two hours dozing in the waiting area of the departure gate.

While he slept, he dreamed of a snake about to bite its own tail. As the snake's fangs sank into its flesh, he awoke with a start, falling out of the chair and frightening a nearby family. Wiping drool from his cheek with the back of his hand, he stood up and went for a walk down the concourse.

Something was bothering him about the implosion site, but he couldn't put his finger on what it was. Still not fully awake, he unthinkingly pulled out his phone to call his now ex-girlfriend, Karen, which is what until three weeks ago he had always done when he was feeling uneasy. She had broken up with him because, as she put it, "You're always bringing me down with all this heavy shit." He reflected ruefully that if he had ceased his practice of calling her when he was uneasy a week earlier, he might still have a girlfriend, albeit one who no longer served what was, in his mind, the primary purpose of a girlfriend.

Jacob had no friends, per se. He had mastered the basics of social interaction but found it nearly impossible to make any sort of deeper connection. The closest he had come to making a friend was in graduate school, over ten years earlier. Jacob had graduated from the University of Michigan with dual degrees in chemistry and physics, and before deciding to work for the FBI, he had intended to go into theoretical physics. He was accepted into the graduate program at MIT, where he met an eccentric young professor named Alistair Breem. Allie, as they had called him, became Jacob's advisor and mentor, and the very first thing he advised Jacob to do was to get out of theoretical physics. After two years of study, during which he realized that the only quark he was interested in was a bartender on *Star Trek*, Jacob obliged him. He had felt a special bond with Allie, but they lost touch when Jacob dropped out of the program, and he heard that Allie had been killed in a car wreck not longer after.

As a result, Jacob now stood in front of a newsstand at LAX with his phone in his hand but no one to call. His eyes alighted on one of those children's activity books filled with mazes and connect-the-dots puzzles. On a whim, he brought up the photo of the implosion site he had taken from the chopper. The picture was small and grainy; the three tents were merely dark green dots in a field of gray. "Connect the dots," he mumbled to himself.

An idea struck him. At the newsstand he bought a map of Los Angeles with a detailed blowup of Anaheim and a souvenir ruler. He then walked across the concourse to a coffee shop where he sat at a table and laid the map out in front of him. Examining the picture on his phone, he carefully made three dots on the map with a ballpoint pen and then, with the ruler, found a fourth point that was equidistant from the other three. He marked this point as well.

Next, to the puzzlement of several onlookers, he removed his shoelace and tied one end around the pen. Holding the pen as close to vertical as he could, he place the tip of it on the dot marking the location of the middle tent and with the fingers of his left hand pulled the shoelace taught across the map, pinning it to the fourth point with his index finger. Keeping his index finger still, he traced an arc that traveled east past the Costa Mesa Freeway, down to the Santa Ana, across to Garden Grove and up to Fullerton before returning to the implosion site.

Sitting back, he regarded his work. A circle some four miles in diameter now enclosed much of the southeastern Los Angeles metropolitan area. The epicenter of the circle, where he had put the fourth dot, fell at the intersection of two streets with portentous names: Euclid and Beacon. Jacob pulled his phone from his pocket and brought up a map of the area, zooming in on the intersection. A chill shot down his spine: at the corner of Euclid and Beacon sat the pyramidal structure known as the Beacon Building. What did this circle represent? he wondered. And why was the Beacon Building at its center?

He wished he knew what they were digging up in those tents. It seemed to him that there were two possibilities: either HeadJAC had found something that had to do with the cause of the implosion, or the implosion itself had unearthed something, something possibly unrelated to the implosion. He tended to think it was the latter, because the tents were located off-center of the crater. If they had found the remnants of some sort of implosion device, one would have expected to find it near the crater's center. So, Jacob thought, I will assume for now that the implosion uncovered something that had been hidden under the stadium. But what? Some sort of prehistoric structure, maybe? The ruins of some ancient civilization?

But if it were some sort of archaeological find, why the secrecy? And why were they using earthmovers and backhoes? Any kind of archaeological find would seem to require a little more finesse. No, HeadJAC had found evidence of something deep underground, something that they needed to move a lot of dirt to get to. But what? A vein of some precious metal? Gold, maybe? Uranium? The discovery of a vein of uranium under Los Angeles would warrant a fair amount of secrecy. But that didn't explain the circle with the Beacon Building at its center. Or was that merely a coincidence?

Jacob's ruminations were cut short when he realized he was being eyed circumspectly by a security guard across the concourse. It took him a moment to realize why, but it eventually occurred to him that sitting in an airport with a shoelace tied to a pen, making strange markings on a map, and muttering to oneself might conceivably fit under the heading of "suspicious behavior."

He smiled sheepishly, slipped the map into his duffel bag, and re-threaded his shoelace. He got to his feet and made his way to the rental car counter.

TWELVE
Circa 2,000 B.C.

Although angels are capable of existing in a purely spiritual form, most find that being unincorporated is, generally speaking, rather impractical. Other than a few obvious benefits (like having a good excuse for not being able to help a friend move), there isn't much advantage to going *sans corporealis*. Every angel in Heaven has a job to do, and with a few exceptions (contemplating the Infinite, waiting in line at the DMV, etc.) most of these jobs require having some sort of physical form.

Angels do have some control over what form they take, but their choices do tend to reflect their inherent characteristics and also tend to gel over time. The closest human analog is probably posture: you can choose to walk differently than you ordinarily do, but unless you're extraordinarily talented, you probably can't keep it up for very long.[5] And if you walked with a slouch when you were sixteen, you'll probably find it difficult to straighten up when you're sixty.

Due to the malleability of their physical forms, angels have no definitive physical identifiers such as fingerprints or a DNA

---

5   Some angels have, through a combination of natural ability and practice, achieved the ability to assume various forms at will, but even these angels tend to specialize within a narrow range. Angels that can switch between genders at will, for example, are rare. This narrative uses male pronouns to refer to angels in general, because although technically angels have no gender, most of those who have chosen to take human form tend to favor one gender over another. For roughly eighty percent of angels, this form is male, probably because the complexities of the female human psyche are beyond the understanding of most angels.

signature. An angel's one unique identifying feature is his name. An angel, whether seraph or cherub, comes into being with a name already encoded into his being. In a sense, an angel *is* his name, in the same way that a human being can be said to be described *en toto* by his or her DNA sequence.

Because of the relative ease with which angels assume different forms, the Heavenly Authorities very early on realized that they would need a foolproof method for identifying angels regardless of their appearance. What they came up with was an artifact known as an identity disc.[6] Observe:

A tall figure wearing a hooded leather cloak strode silently through the corridors of the planeport, flanked on all sides by four massive cherubim garbed in black except for a white star insignia marking them as members of the Angelic Special Protection Force. A small group of servants, also wearing hooded cloaks, brought up the rear. Perp, flanked by two planeport security guards with flaming swords, led the way. The guard on the right wore a sash marking him as the head of the group. Mercury, accompanied by two more guards, trailed behind. Mercury had taken the place of another escort cherub from Transport & Communications who was more than willing to take a long lunch rather than trail behind some bigwig seraph.

Occasionally Perp would issue a shrill "Make way!" but for the most part those occupying the planeport's corridors got out of the way well in advance. The entourage seemed to project an air of reverent silence. Only the occasional announcement over the planeport's PA system and a few hushed murmurs guessing at the identity of the tall angel could be heard.

---

6   Angelic identity discs are not to be confused with the "identity discs" used by programs in the movie *TRON*. The identity discs in *TRON* served as a combination of personal identification, recreational aid, and weapon, sort of like taping your Social Security card to a razor-edged Day-Glo Frisbee.

Mercury didn't care who the tall angel was. He knew who it *wasn't*, and that's all that mattered. Who it *wasn't* was the Archangel Michael, commander in chief of the Heavenly Army. The figure walked with a swagger, the sort of affectation that gave away a pretender to power, someone who was overly enthusiastic about his status as the lead dog of the pack. No, whoever that hooded character was, he wasn't Michael, that was certain.

Mercury was more interested in a smaller figure who lagged behind the entourage as if consciously forcing herself to remain out of sight. She—Mercury couldn't see her face, but was convinced by her size and her walk that it was a she—moved anxiously back and forth across the concourse, like a jockey waiting for an opening. Curious behavior for a servant, Mercury reflected.

The entourage entered a narrow corridor leading to a restricted area of the planeport that allowed access to mysterious planes that were only open to very high-ranking seraphim. He noticed the guards to his left and right move their hands closer to the hilts of their swords, smoldering in scabbards hanging from their sides. Had they sensed something? Mercury wondered. If somebody was going to attempt an attack, he realized, this would be the place to do it: the narrow corridor would even the odds between a small attacking force and the sizeable planeport security forces. All the attacker would have to do would be to seal off the opening of the corridor that led back to the main part of the planeport. The entourage would be completely isolated.

As these thoughts went through his mind, he noticed that the two planeport guards up front had abruptly stopped and turned to face the black-garbed henchmen flanking the hooded angel. They unsheathed their swords.

At that moment, the two guards flanking Mercury ran forward, drawing their swords as well. All four guards fell upon the four henchmen, decapitating two of them before they could react. The remaining two henchmen drew their swords simultaneously, and one of them managed to stab a guard before they, too, were cut down. Just then, the tall figure drew his sword, taking a step back to get all four attackers in front of him.

The servants fled past Mercury down the corridor, except for the slight figure Mercury had observed earlier. She drew a fiery blade as well and advanced toward the melee.

"Oh, no you don't," whispered Mercury, grabbing the back of her cloak. She whirled to face him. Beneath the hood, a stern young female face was visible.

"Get your hands off me," she growled, in a tone that made Mercury want to run and hide. He released her cloak.

"Ma'am," Mercury said, with a slight bow. "No disrespect, but you're going to lose this battle. You need to get the hell out of here."

The girl turned back toward the fray. The tall man was swinging his sword wildly, valiantly beating back the four attackers. The aggressors seemed to be trying to encircle the hooded man and disarm him in an attempt to subdue him without serious injury. Meanwhile, Perp buzzed frantically back and forth across the hall, shouting, "Security! Security!"

"Please," whispered Mercury urgently to the girl. "If you're who I think you are, you need to get out of here before these guys realize they've been had."

As he spoke, the blade of one of the attackers sliced through the hooded man's arm at the elbow, cutting his forearm clean off. He fell to his knees, clutching the stump. The head guard leaped on top of him, pinning him to the floor and pushing the hood back to reveal a head of thick, curly blond hair. "Quickly! The disc!" he barked.

Another guard handed him a silvery disc about the size of a half-dollar, which he pressed against the blond angel's forehead.

Suddenly Mercury stepped in front of the girl. "Hey, guys!" he yelled. "Wanna see a magic trick?"

"Decapitate the idiot," said the head guard.

"You should be more specific," Mercury said. "How am I supposed to know which one you're talking about?"

Two guards moved toward Mercury, brandishing their swords.

"Blast!" yelled the head guard, studying the silver disc. "It's not him! The identity disc says it's Malchediel."

"Michael's personal bodyguard," said another guard. "A clever ruse. But our intelligence is good, I'm sure of it. So where is he?"

"Or *she*," said the head guard, peering down the hallway past Mercury. "Stop her!"

A guard moved to run past Mercury after the girl, but Mercury stuck his foot out, tripping the guard and sending him sprawling down the hallway. As another tried to run past him on the other side, Mercury gave him a shove between shoulder blades, and he, too, lost his footing and fell facedown on the floor.

"Ten-yard penalty for clipping," Mercury said. "Unsportsmanlike, I know, but you guys have me outnumbered."

The third guard took a step toward Mercury, drawing his sword back over his shoulder as he did so.

"I hope you've got better offense than your teammates," Mercury said, "because they weren't much of a challenge."

"In the name of Lucifer," growled the head guard, "seize her!"

The guards scrambled to their feet and ran down the hall. The head guard smiled, drew back his blade, and sliced Mercury's head off. The last thing Mercury saw before losing consciousness was the guards converging on the girl.

THIRTEEN

"The good news," said Maya, "is that these aren't raiders."

"And the bad news?" asked Christine.

"They're Tawani tribesmen," Maya replied. "They aren't known for being particularly friendly to outsiders."

Maya greeted the men deferentially, speaking a few stilted words in the Tawani language and gesturing toward the flat tire and to Christine, who tried to appear harmless.

There was a brief, halting exchange between Maya and the men.

"They want us to go with them," Maya said to Christine.

"Go with them? Where?"

"To their camp. They think we've come to get someone they call *Matu-ku-oto*."

"Matu-ku-oto? Who is that?"

"Dunno," said Maya. "A visitor to their camp. A white man, apparently. They seem rather anxious to get rid of him."

"A white man named Matu-ku-oto?" asked Christine.

"I don't think that's his actual name," replied Maya. "They have a hard time pronouncing European names. Matu-ku-oto is just what they call him. A nickname, basically. I think our best bet is just to go with it."

"What does it mean?"

"Matu-ku-oto? Well, my Tawani isn't very good, but I believe it means 'silver-haired stranger.'"

Christine's heart skipped a beat. Could it be true? Had Mercury been hiding out among a primitive tribe in remote Africa? It certainly was a good hiding spot; this area had apparently been overlooked by Heaven for some time now. And the Tawani tribesmen's eagerness to get rid of Matu-ku-oto weighed in favor of the notion as well. Mercury was a bit much to take in doses of a more than a few minutes at a time. It was absurdly unlikely that Christine would have happened upon his hiding place, but she had learned to take such occurrences in stride. Evidently the Universe wanted her to find Mercury once again.

She and Maya were escorted by the men down a narrow trail through the brush. While they traveled, Maya told her what she knew about the Tawani.

The Tawani were a seminomadic people who lived for roughly half of the year in each of two locations, one of which was within twenty miles of Maji. The tribe would graze its cattle on a nearby plateau until the grass became sparse and then return to the bushlands some twenty miles farther north across a series of rocky hills. The Tawani were only going to be in the area for a few more days, and were hoping to ditch Matu-ku-oto as soon as possible.

After a good half hour, they reached the Tawani camp. Several Tawani women, as dark as rubbed walnut and naked to their waists, worked outside over large earthen pots. The returning men were intercepted by three other men, whom Christine would have guessed to be tribal leaders, except that they didn't look any older than the other men. They all looked to be in their mid twenties.

One of them mentioned the word *matu-ku-oto*, at which point several of the others sighed and looked wearily at each other, the way Christine's parents used to look at each other when asked about her cousin Olivia who kept trying to convert the family to Seventh Day Adventism and sell them Amway products. The men gestured toward a hut near the center of the village. Maya smiled and thanked them, and she and Christine walked to the hut.

As they approached, a figure emerged from the hut, leaning forward to fit through the hut's small doorway. For a moment, all they could see was the top of a man's head, covered with thick, silvery-gray curls. Christine's breath caught in her throat. She had never expected to see Mercury again.

Once outside, the man stood up straight, to his full height of maybe five feet, eight inches. Below the silver curls was a round, olive-colored face with a hooked nose and two small brown eyes. He wore a Hawaiian shirt, khaki shorts, and sandals.

"Hi!" shouted the man in a small, high-pitched voice. "I'm Horace Finch. To what do I owe the pleasure?"

Christine felt like she was going to be sick again. "Horace... Finch? The owner of the *Beacon*?"

"Indeed," said Finch. "Hey, aren't you that reporter from the *Banner*? The one who used to do the Apocalypse stuff?"

Christine nodded dumbly. She felt dizzy.

"Wow," said Finch. "I've read all your columns. Really phenomenal stuff. Hysterical, really. You know who you should do an article about, though? *Me*."

Christine fainted.

FOURTEEN

Having procured a more detailed map of the Anaheim area and a $2.97 protractor, Jacob sat at a donut shop across from the Beacon Building and proceeded to make a more precise version of his shoelace drawing. What he found was both vindicating and troubling: the center of his imaginary circle was, as near as he could determine, the exact tip of the Beacon pyramid. There was some margin of error due to the fact that the tents concealed the exact location of the excavation, but assuming that they were more-or-less centered on the objects of HeadJAC's interest, the center of the circle was within a few yards of the Beacon's tip.

Jacob finished his coffee and bear claw and walked across the street to the Beacon. He entered the building and strode across the massive marble foyer to the bank of elevators at the center of the pyramid. According to some cursory Internet research he had done, the Beacon Pyramid had fifteen floors, and sure enough, the elevator's top button was labeled "15." Jacob noticed, however, that the number 13 was missing from the elevator's control panel. If his research was correct and the building really did have fifteen floors, then that meant that the top floor should be 16, not 15. That presumably meant that there was an additional floor that was not indicated on the elevator's controls. He took the elevator to the nominal fifteenth floor, which seemed to be taken up by the offices of various corporate bigwigs and midsize-wigs. There was no indication of another floor above him, but the fifteenth floor was clearly large enough to permit at least one more floor on top of it. There had to be something up there, after all, even if it was just air-conditioning units. Or, Jacob thought wryly, a secret temple used by some mysterious sect to communicate with the gods.

What is happening to me? Jacob wondered. This morning I was a respected FBI forensic specialist. Now here I am, looking for the damned Holy Grail in Anaheim. You can draw a circle to incorporate any three equidistant points that aren't absolutely parallel, he thought. Simply drawing the circle doesn't make it an objectively real thing any more than drawing a tunnel on a sheer rock face allows the Road Runner to run through it. And the center point of that circle would have to fall somewhere; why *not* the Beacon building? Maybe his calculations were off and the actual center was the donut shop he had just left. Maybe, in fact, he had just accidentally eaten the Mystical Bear Claw holding the Secrets of the Universe.

If so, he thought, the Secrets of the Universe were damned tasty, and he was going to have a few more before flying back to Washington. Checking his watch, he saw that he had just enough time to grab another bear claw and make it back to the airport to catch his flight. This little side trip would be his secret; no one in D.C. needed to know that he had made a temporary detour into a Dan Brown novel.

The donut shop was fresh out of bear claws, so he had to settle for a custard-filled éclair. By the time he had made up his mind on this world-shattering matter, he was on the verge of being late for his flight, and he hurried to his little rented Chevy subcompact with the sticky pastry clutched in his right hand and peeled out of the parking lot.

The quickest route to the airport would take him north, but a manure spreader had jackknifed on the Santa Ana, forcing him to head south in order to take the Garden Grove Freeway west back to LAX, along with tens of thousands of other drivers. As the Chevy crept along the highway, he was dimly aware that the car's radio was playing the maudlin strains of "Stairway to Heaven." Jacob wasn't much into rock music, but he left it on because he enjoyed the challenge of trying to figure out what Robert Plant was saying in the third verse. He was pretty sure it was "If there's a bustle in your hedgerow, don't be a lawn man. It's just a sprinkling for the banking." He had a vague idea that the song was about gardening.

He had gotten only a mile from the Beacon building when he saw something that made him forget his efforts at deciphering the string of nonsense syllables emanating from the car's speakers. An electronic billboard on the side of the road was displaying the message:

JACOB WAS A QUIET MAN,
STAYING AMONG THE TENTS.

GENESIS 25:27

Having given up the hope of getting to the airport on time, Jacob pulled onto the shoulder in front of the sign. Was this a coincidence, too? Or was somebody playing a joke on him? *Jacob* was a common name, of course, and the Biblical Jacob was a key figure in mythology of the ancient Hebrews, but still, it was odd, wasn't it? Why *that* verse? If you were going to pick a Bible verse to put on a sign, wouldn't you use something about salvation or Jesus or homosexuality or something?

The radio crooned, "...and she's buuuuuyyying a staaaaair-way to heaven..." Jacob looked down to turn off the radio, and when he looked up, the sign had changed. Now it read:

HE HAD A DREAM IN WHICH HE SAW A STAIRWAY RESTING ON THE EARTH, WITH ITS TOP REACHING TO HEAVEN, AND THE ANGELS OF GOD WERE ASCENDING AND DESCENDING ON IT.

GENESIS 28:12

Jacob found himself getting angry. Somebody was screwing with him, and he didn't like it. If God, or whoever, had something to say to him, then why didn't they just come out and say it? Enough of this passive-aggressive pussyfooting around. As a scientist, he was accustomed to seeking out facts and prying meaning from them; this business of being led around by the nose by vague clues was getting old.

The sign changed again. Now it read:

WHEN JACOB AWOKE FROM HIS SLEEP, HE THOUGHT, "SURELY THE LORD IS IN THIS PLACE, AND I WAS NOT AWARE OF IT." HE WAS AFRAID AND SAID, "HOW AWE-SOME IS THIS PLACE! THIS IS NONE OTHER THAN THE HOUSE OF GOD; THIS IS THE GATE OF HEAVEN."

GENESIS 28: 16–17

"OK!" Jacob shouted at the sign. "I get it! You're trying to get my attention! Now just TELL ME WHAT YOU WANT!"

The sign changed again. Now it read:

IT DOESN'T WORK LIKE THAT.

Jacob threw the Chevy into gear and punched the accelerator. He was going to find that damned church and unplug their sign. Or blow it up, if he needed to. "We'll see what God has to say about *that*," he muttered. "Of course, You won't be able to talk without your damned sign, will You?"

He exited the freeway and made his way toward the church. It wasn't difficult to find: it was a huge, cathedral-like structure, paneled on all sides with glass. He had to admit that gaudy as it was, it was impressive. Parking on the side of the street, he strode up to the base of the sign. It was bigger than it looked from the highway: a good twelve feet across, it rested on two thick steel poles arising from a concrete base. Encircling the base was a thick evergreen hedge about four feet tall. Jacob approached it, looking for a way through.

Something moved within the hedge, and Jacob took a step back, startled.

"*Trust me*," said a deep voice from the hedge. Jacob's breath caught in his throat.

There was a loud POP! followed by a wisp of smoke arising from the hedge. The sign went dark.

"I told you," said another voice. "The green wire is the ground."

"Whoops," said the deep voice.

"At least it doesn't say 'IT DOESN'T WORK LIKE THAT' anymore."

"Hey, that was *your* idea," said the deep voice.

"No, you asked me what I wanted on the sign, and I said, 'It doesn't work like that.'"

"Ohhhh. I thought that's what you wanted on the sign. Doesn't work like what?"

"I meant, I shouldn't have to tell you what I want on the sign. The whole point of this sign was that it's programmable. I'm supposed to just be able to pick a verse on my computer and have it show up on the sign."

"Wasn't it doing that? I thought we were trying to get it to stop showing Bible verses."

"No! I mean, it was showing verses, but just random crap from Genesis. I can't get it to display the verse I have selected on the computer."

"Oh. Sounds like a software problem."

"That's what I was trying to tell you! I told you there was nothing wrong with the sign. Of course, there is *now*."

"Oh, I can fix that. Here, I'll just put the ground back."

Nothing happened.

"Great, now the sign is broken."

"Nah, it's probably just a circuit breaker. I'll go check." A heavyset, balding man in a dirty T-shirt and jeans stood up behind the hedge, and shortly after him a wiry, sandy-haired man in a navy polo and khakis.

"Oh, hey," said the wiry man. "Nice of you to join us."

"Um, hi," said Jacob.

"I'm Pastor Bob," said the wiry man. "I'm the one who called. The girl on the phone said you'd be here at noon. Anyway, Shane's been messing with the sign and he seems to have blown a breaker. So that's the first thing you'll need to deal with."

Jacob found himself nodding.

"I can do it," said Shane.

"You've done enough, Shane," said Pastor Bob. "Why don't you take a break. Give…what did you say your name was?"

"Jacob," said Jacob.

"Give Jacob your keys. Might as well get our money's worth. It costs us a hundred bucks every time they send someone out."

Shane grumbled something and unsnapped a ring of keys. He handed them to Jacob. "Through the lobby, downstairs, second door on your left."

Jacob took the keys and stood for a moment, staring blankly at them.

"Do you…need me to write that down?" Pastor Bob asked, a bit condescendingly.

"Um, no," replied Jacob. "I got it." He trudged off toward the church. He was a bit at a loss regarding what to do next, since the Almighty seemed to have called his bluff by preemptively short-circuiting His own sign. Additionally, his anger at God had been supplanted by anger at Pastor Bob. Maybe he was being overly sensitive, but this wasn't the first time he had been mistaken for a serviceman. Or gardener. Or busboy. He wanted to growl, "I'm not here to fix your damn sign. I'm a scientist! I work for the government!"

But it wasn't in Jacob's nature to yell. He was a soft-spoken, introverted man who abhorred confrontation. Also, the pronouncement that he was a government scientist would undoubtedly provoke any number of uncomfortable questions, chief among which would be, "Why is a government scientist standing in front of a church sign?"

He was tempted to toss the keys in the bushes and leave, but it occurred to him that he would have to walk past Pastor Bob and Shane to get back to his car. Maybe he could surreptitiously drop the keys in the bushes and then make a wide loop to sneak back around to his car, but he suspected that such a laborious effort to avoid confrontation would drain the gesture of most of its emotional impact. Trying to explain at this point that he wasn't the man they had been waiting for would be extremely awkward. No, all he could do at this point was to head to the electrical panel and flip the tripped breaker. He could probably help them figure out why they couldn't get the right verse to show up on the sign, too. How complicated could church sign software be? Pastor Bob was probably just pushing the wrong buttons.

He was aware of the irony—that he had somehow been drafted into repairing a sign that he had moments earlier sworn to destroy. He justified this about-face by rationalizing that the sign's messages hadn't been directed at him after all: they were just verses randomly selected by a software glitch—or perhaps just human error. He was under a lot of stress, given the debacle at ACHOO and his resulting reassignment; obviously he wasn't thinking clearly. So: he would flip the breaker, help Pastor Bob figure out his software, and then drive to LAX and hop the next flight to Washington, D.C.—at which point he could begin repairing the damage he'd done to his career.

Following Shane's instructions, he found the church's electrical room. The church evidently had a ridiculous number of incandescent lights; it had twelve separate electrical panels lining the wall of a room in the church's basement. Wait, no, he thought. There was a thirteenth panel set apart from the others. The others were labeled one through twelve, but this one had no label. Additionally, a schematic of the church's electrical system had been posted on the wall, with every section labeled with a number corresponding to one of the boxes. There was no thirteenth section.

Jacob opened the cover of the thirteenth panel. A bank of some twenty breakers greeted him. Why would someone install twenty breakers for a nonexistent section of the church?

An idea struck him. He pulled the Anaheim map from his pocket and located the church. The circle he had drawn cut right through the small gray square denoting the church's property. Doing some quick calculations, he determined that if the tip of the Beacon really was the center of the circle, then the nearest point on the circle to his present location would lie about thirty yards to the southeast of the electrical room. Forgetting the reason he was there, Jacob left the room and traversed the storage room to the south. He ended up staring at a steel door marked "PERMITTED USE ONLY."

The door was locked, and the key ring proved to be no help. Jacob clutched and pulled at the doorknob to no avail.

He felt like he should be angry, but he wasn't sure whom to be angry at or what to be angry about. It wasn't like anyone had forced him to go exploring beneath a church in Glendale. He was here of his own free will. Having experienced a series of random phenomena, he had decided that there had to be some sort of unifying explanation—that *someone* was trying to communicate *something* to him. An impenetrable obstacle like a locked door weighed against that hypothesis, but it wasn't the fault of the hypothesis that it was inadequate. The hypothesis hadn't asked to be brought into being, and it would be perfectly happy to be allowed to run free with others of its kind in the Land of Inadequate Hypotheses.

What Jacob needed, he realized, was a new hypothesis—one that didn't involve a supernatural entity attempting to communicate with him through vague signs and symbols. Why would a being with such power choose to communicate in such an imprecise, haphazard manner anyway? Surely God, if He existed, could just pick up a phone if He had something to say. This method of communication, if that's what it was, had to be the most inefficient way of delivering a message since the time of Pheidippides.[7]

---

7   Pheidippides was the Greek soldier who was sent from the battlefield of Marathon to Athens in 490 BC to announce that the Persians had been defeated. It is said that he ran the entire distance

No, thought Jacob, if the Almighty was trying to send him a message, He was going to have to do better than this. Unless, of course, the message was "Fuck you, Jacob."

Suddenly he became aware of cool air blowing on his face.

Holding out his hand, he felt a jet of air escaping around the door. The air was a good ten degrees cooler than the storage room.

Strange, he thought. Some kind of ventilation system? Maybe a cold room, like they use for banks of web servers?

Pressing his ear against the door, he heard a sort of rattling-humming sound. It rapidly grew louder until it sounded like whatever-it-was was right on the other side of the door. There was a clanging noise, and a sound like a metal grate being shoved aside. And then voices, just behind the door.

The door handle turned.

As the door opened, Jacob spun out of the way and flattened himself against the wall to the left of the hinges. The door swung wide open, concealing the figures that entered the room. One of them spoke.

"Well, that's done with," he said.

"Yeah. Kind of a shame after all the work that went into it," said the other.

"It's just a tool," said the first man. "Soon the Order will have the new one up and running, and then..."

(26.2 miles) without stopping, burst into the assembly exclaiming, "We have won!" and then died. A complete transcript of this incident follows:

Pheidippides: We have won!

Assembly: Wow, that's great. So do you guys need reinforcements or anything?

Pheidippides: No. [gasps for breath] Didn't you hear what I said? [gasps for breath] We won already.

Assembly: Oh, OK. So, um, what's the big hurry? Do you need something from us?

Pheidippides: No. [gasps for breath] Just really [gasps for breath] excited. [gasps for breath] About the victory.

Assembly: Got it. Well, good show and all that. Anyway, we're a little busy discussing taxation and whatnot, so if you don't mind waiting in the lobby for a bit...

Pheidippides: Oh. [gasps for breath] Sure. I'm pretty much [gasps for breath] done anyway. [gasps for breath] Do you think I could [gasps for breath] have a drink of... [collapses]

Assembly: What a remarkable man! I move that we start a series of footraces in honor of this brave soldier. Did anyone get his name?

The men had reached the stairs, and the remainder of their words was drowned out by the sound of their footsteps.

Jacob might have gotten a look at the men, but he had made a split-second decision to turn back toward the door and reach around to keep it from latching shut again. When he was sure they were gone, he pulled the door open.

Behind it was a metal gate, the kind used on old-fashioned elevators. While maintaining his hold on the door, he hooked his foot around a cardboard box that rested against the wall near the door and dragged it to prop the door open. He then slid open the gate and walked inside the small room that lay on the other side.

The gate was spring-loaded, and it snapped shut as soon as he let go of it. The room was completely featureless except for a dim light bulb in the ceiling and a small metal panel on one wall. In the center of the panel was a single red button. Clearly he was in some sort of elevator.

He stood for a moment, staring at the button. The sensible thing to do would be to get the hell out of here and hightail back to D.C. He had no rational reason to believe that pushing the red button would provide him with any meaningful answers. In fact, he wasn't even sure what question he was trying to find the answer *to*. You're a scientist, he told himself. This isn't how science works. First you identify the question. Then you form a hypothesis. Then you test the hypothesis. You don't go running around Los Angeles looking for Signs from Above. Still, intuition played an important role in scientific discovery, didn't it? After all, how did Einstein come up with the principle of relativity? He didn't methodically piece it together from bits of data; he just took a wild guess and then spent the next twenty years proving it. The idea came first, and the data followed. Einstein didn't let a lack of data stop him;

he just dove in, confident that things would somehow work out. Jacob took a deep breath and pushed the button.

The elevator dropped so fast that he felt like he was in freefall. It fell for three or four seconds at least, and then slowed so rapidly that his knees buckled. By the time it stopped, he estimated that he was a good hundred feet underground.

The elevator opened into a large room filled with ancient-looking technical equipment of some kind. Rows of vacuum tubes protruded above control panels filled with banks of switches and levers, and copper pipes and wiring hung from the ceiling. In the far wall was a large pane of dirty glass that appeared to look onto an adjacent room. To the left of the window was a door ominously labeled:

DANGER! DO NOT ENTER WHEN CCD IS ACTIVE!

Jacob had no way of being certain, but he strongly suspected that CCD hadn't been active since some time before the Eisenhower administration. He tried the door and found it unlocked.

It opened not onto a room, but rather a narrow hallway that was mostly taken up by a three-foot-diameter metal pipe that rested on steel supports every ten feet or so. There was just enough room on either side of the pipe for a person to walk. The hallway was dimly lit by incandescent panels in the ceiling, and appeared to extend indefinitely in both directions. It reminded Jacob of one of the gigantic particle colliders, like the Hadron Collider in Europe, which he had once toured with his mentor Alistair Breem, as a graduate student in physics.

As he peered to his left down the hallway, he noticed that it curved slightly to the right. In the opposite direction, it curved left. He pulled out his now-tattered map and compared it to his surroundings. There was no doubt about it: the circle he had drawn corresponded perfectly with the curved hallway. But if the circle really did indicate the extent of the hallway, then the hallway was some *fifteen miles* in circumference, nearly as big as the largest particle accelerator in the world! Was this, then, some sort of particle accelerator, an "atom smasher," as they used to be called? The very notion was insane. Why would you build a particle accelerator under some of the most expensive real estate in the world? And *how*? Even in the 1940s or whenever this place was built, it would have been virtually impossible to undertake a project like this just outside of Los Angeles without somebody noticing.

He was too far into this—literally and figuratively—to leave without getting some answers. He began walking down the hallway to his right.

The tunnel went on and on, with very little variation in the scenery. After about two miles, he came upon another door, but it was locked. He kept walking. After another mile, he found that the tunnel was blocked by debris. Apparently there had been a cave-in. The location corresponded to the outskirts of the crater where Anaheim Stadium had once stood. Evidently the implosion had caused part of the tunnel to collapse. That explained the digging: HeadJAC had found shafts leading to the tunnel, but the tunnel itself was filled with dirt and rock. HeadJAC was clearly unaware, then, that there was at least one place where the tunnel was still accessible, which presumably meant that HeadJAC didn't know much more about the particle accelerator than he did. They probably didn't even realize that the tunnel was a circle; they had just found shafts leading deep underground and had started digging. He knelt on the ground and pressed his ear to the rubble, straining to hear the sound of the machines digging out the shaft, but he heard nothing.

As he looked back the way he had come, his eyes alighted on something near the bottom of the pipe that didn't seem to fit the surroundings: a small LED display that displayed three numbers, 6:56.

As he watched, the display changed to 6:55. Then 6:54. A sickening sensation washed over him as he realized he was watching a countdown. Countdowns, in Jacob Slater's world, were rarely good things.

He got down on his knees and examined the device. It was a simple LED timer connected to a trigger device, embedded in a fist-sized glob of what looked like Silly Putty. C-4, thought Jacob. Plastic explosive. Enough to collapse another hundred feet or so of the tunnel, depending on its structural support.

He delicately disconnected the trigger device and then hurriedly made his way back down the tunnel. After about fifty feet, he spied another timer. He left this one in place and jogged another fifty feet, finding still another timer.

Jacob cursed at himself. The whole place was rigged to blow. How could he have missed it? And how could he have been so stupid to come down here in the first place?

If the timers were to be believed, he now had five minutes and forty seconds to either disarm all of the charges or get out of the tunnel. Disarming only a few might spare a section of the tunnel, but that would only delay his doom: he would be trapped a hundred feet underground, where he would slowly die of thirst or, if he was lucky, asphyxiation. *Unless...*

Jacob took off on a sprint. After a minute, his heart was pounding and his lungs were burning. In college, he could run a five-minute mile, but that was nearly twenty years ago. He checked his watch: less than four minutes left. Gasping for breath, his side aching and his chest feeling like it was on fire, he pressed on. After the longest three minutes of his life, he collapsed a few yards from the locked door he had found earlier.

Drenched with sweat and barely able to see straight, he crawled to a C-4 charge that had been placed under the pipe a few feet from the door. He peeled the glob from the pipe and disconnected the timer. It read 0:44.

Wiping the sweat from his eyes, hands shaking, he pulled the timer from the device and managed to reset it to fifteen seconds. Twisting the glob of C-4 in his fingers, he removed most of it and then reconnected the timer. He stuck the small glob just under the door handle. Then he got to his feet and stumbled a few yards down the tunnel before his legs gave out and he crumpled to the ground. Every muscle in his body screamed in agony. He didn't even have time to cover his ears before the charge exploded. The blast echoed deafeningly through the tunnel.

Groaning in pain, barely able to control his shaking limbs, Jacob crawled back to the door. Fortunately, his estimate had been generous: the door had been blown clear from its hinges. Behind the door was a short hallway that ended at a steel grate: an elevator.

Jacob pulled himself to his feet and staggered down the hallway. Mere seconds remained before the rest of the charges would blow. He felt like he was in one of those dreams he used to have as a child, where he was running as fast as he could from something, but his legs wouldn't do what he wanted them to do. He eventually managed to make his way down the hall. He pulled open the grate, stepped inside the elevator, and pressed the red button on the wall.

There was a blinding flash and everything went dark.

FIFTEEN

Christine regained consciousness inside a mud hut in the Tawani encampment. She was weak but the dizziness had passed. Outside she heard Maya conversing with Horace Finch. Finch had donated the spare tire from his own truck, which fortuitously had the same size wheels as the Land Rover. Maya was leaving, but Finch was assuring her that "Christine is better off staying here for the night." He told her he'd take good care of her and she thanked him and said good-bye. Christine struggled to get up, but the dizziness returned and she had to lie down again. She heard the Land Rover drive away. She was stranded with a strange man in a primitive village miles from anything that even remotely resembled civilization.

Finch entered a moment later and informed her that Maya would be returning for her tomorrow afternoon. "You have excellent timing," he said excitedly. Tomorrow morning the tribe is embarking on their yearly pilgrimage to the peak of Mbutuokoti."

"Mbutu…" Christine mumbled, slowly sitting up.

"Mbutuokoti. You probably saw it on your drive over. It's the highest mountain in the area, which frankly isn't saying much, as this area is flatter than my first wife. At its peak Mbutuokoti stands about five hundred feet above the surrounding plain. The

Tawani believe that Mbutuokoti is where Earth meets Heaven. They believe that at the peak of Mbutuokoti, their shamans are able to tap into mysterious streams of spiritual energy that allow them to communicate directly with the gods."

"Interesting," said Christine.

"Oh yes," said Finch. "Of course, it's all bullshit, but try telling them that. I've been here for a month and I still haven't been able to get through to them."

Christine was puzzled. "Why are you here, if you think it's bullshit?"

"Oh, I didn't say it wasn't interesting bullshit. Worthy of recording anyway, before, you know, this culture is erased."

"Erased? Who's going to erase their culture?"

"Please, Christine. These people are doomed. More and more of their territory is taken by developers every year. There are only about four hundred Tawani left. And in any case, they're a primitive, superstitious, polytheistic culture. They haven't advanced a whit in five thousand years. Hell, they had never seen a wheel until a few years back when the first white people showed up in Jeeps. Can you imagine? They're a nomadic culture. They move their whole civilization back and forth a couple of times a year, and it's never occurred to them to put any of their shit on wheels. Every six months they look at their heaps of crap and ask, 'How the hell are we going to move all this stuff three hundred miles?' And the best answer they can come up with is, 'Well, we could *drag* it.' Ridiculous. It's a dead-end culture."

It was a little ridiculous, Christine thought. Still, wasn't there something to be said for preserving the indigenous culture? She was used to a sort of thinly veiled cultural imperialism from fundamentalists like Harry Giddings, but she hadn't expected it from an atheist like Horace Finch. Weren't they supposed to be tolerant of cultural differences?

"And don't start with the need to be tolerant of cultural differences," Finch went on. "I'm not saying their culture is in any way inferior to ours. What I'm saying is that, right or wrong, our culture is going to crush theirs. Facts is facts. The best we can do is to educate them about the crushing in advance, to make it as painless a process as possible."

Christine was starting to understand the looks the Tawani men had flashed each other when Maya had asked about the silver-haired visitor. Finch had set himself up as the benevolent ambassador of an empire that was nevertheless going to destroy them. It was a wonder they tolerated him at all.

Finch went on, "If these people spent as much time trying to develop a written language as they did making up deities, they wouldn't be in this jam. They've got rain gods, cloud gods, sun gods...I've documented three hundred different deities so far, and I'm not even close to covering them all. At this point there are probably more Tawani deities than there are Tawanis."

In fact, the Tawani only had seven gods and goddesses in their pantheon; the remainder they had made up just to screw with Horace Finch. Finch had made it his mission to debunk their mythology, one deity at a time, and the Tawani had cleverly responded by manufacturing an unlimited number of deities. At first it had been an enjoyable diversion, but as Finch showed no sign of tiring of his debunking, it had become something of a chore. More worrying, they were on the verge of running out of natural phenomena that could be used as an excuse for supernatural intervention. Lately they had devised gods of acid indigestion, night sweats, and chafing, respectively. A recent secret meeting of the tribal elders had focused on whether the tribe should start reusing deities and hope that Finch didn't notice, or pretend to convert to pantheism.

In truth, they had started inventing deities in an attempt to determine whether Finch could tell the difference between a real god and a fake one, a test that he decisively failed in their eyes. If the silver-haired stranger couldn't even determine which gods had been around since the beginning of time and which ones had been created in the last five minutes, what kind of spiritual wisdom could he possibly have to offer? Once they had determined he was merely a charlatan who was pretending to understand the spirit world, they decided there would be no harm in having a little fun at his expense. But now, a month into Finch's stay, the joke was getting a little old.

The Tawani had also concluded that anyone who wanted so badly to believe that the gods did not exist must have done something very evil in their sight. Perhaps, they thought, Finch had murdered his own brother or given his seed to an ox. In an effort to get him to admit to the latter, in fact, they had created a god who was half ox and half man, an ominous figure called Tuwambo that they claimed crept into the huts of evildoers and gave them terrifying nightmares.[8] In fact, *tuwambo* was the Tawani word for jock itch, which explained the confused looks Finch got from the local children when he facetiously urged them to "be good or Tuwambo will get you."

If the primitive Tawani were confused by the motivations of Finch, Christine was even more so. Horace Finch was a multi-billionaire. Surely he had more important things to do than disabuse an African tribe of their superstitions. Finch seemed amused by the question.

---

8   Tuwambo, they claimed, occasionally worked in concert with Mawtaba, god of night sweats, and Buwandanta, god of that thing where you are half awake and can feel yourself lying in bed but you can't move.

"What could be more important than furthering the advancement of science and reason?" he asked. "And tribes like the Tawani represent a unique opportunity: most of the world's people have progressed gradually from polytheism to monotheism on their way to a completely secular, scientific worldview. But by getting to the Tawani early, maybe we can get them to make a quantum leap over that intermediate step. Maybe if I can get them to dismiss superstition entirely, they can create an entirely new culture without any of the vestigial trappings of religion that still plague Western civilization. If that happens, then rather than Western civilization wiping out the Tawani culture, the new and improved Tawani culture will transform Western civilization as we know it!"

Great, thought Christine. The only other Westerner for miles around, and he's...what did Mercury call it? *Batshit crazy.*

"So you're a missionary, then," Christine said. "Except that instead of spreading Christianity, you're spreading atheism."

"Something like that," agreed Finch. "But I'm more up-front about my motivations. I don't pretend to be interested in distributing food and medicine in order to smuggle in my beliefs."

"Yeah," Christine replied dryly. "I know how people hate that make-believe food and medicine Eternal Harvest is distributing."

Finch nodded, apparently not picking up on her sarcasm. "Exactly," he said. "Also, I happened to be in the area."

Christine was skeptical. "You happened to be in the wilderness of Africa?"

"A little project I've been working on," Finch said. "Maybe you've heard of it. I call it Eden Two."

Christine had heard of it, but she hadn't realized that it was located in Kenya. She had read about the project several years earlier, but she only recalled that it was somewhere in remote Africa.

In fact, she had thought the project had been canceled some time ago in the wake of engineering problems and budget overruns.

"I guess I'm a little out of it," Christine admitted. "I didn't realize you were still working on that."

Finch grinned. "Not your fault," he said. "It was part of the plan, actually. Hiding in plain sight."

"I don't follow you," Christine said.

"I've learned that the best way to undertake a massive project without getting a lot of attention is to announce the project with great fanfare and then produce nothing for the next several years. Blame budget overruns or whatever. Keep promising the moon but never deliver anything. For a while I was offering free round-trip airfare to any journalist who wanted to visit the site."

Now that she thought about it, she remembered Maria, a veteran *Banner* reporter, mentioning taking advantage of that offer. She had returned with stories of a massive boondoggle in the desert: workmen sitting idle while engineers bickered over structural concerns, problems getting materials and supplies to the remote location, and on and on. The *Banner* had done a half-page piece in their international news section predictably titled "Trouble in Paradise."

"Eventually," Finch went on, "the journalists stopped showing up altogether. When we issued a press release announcing that we were finally breaking ground, it got almost no coverage. And when we really *did* break ground, eighteen months later, not a single respectable news organization covered it. We issued nearly two hundred press releases over the next three years detailing our progress in excruciating detail and got almost no coverage. Three weeks ago, to celebrate the impending completion of the project, I fired our entire marketing department. Everyone in the civilized world has heard of Eden Two, but the only thing anybody could tell you about it is that it was a colossal failure. And since that was exactly what I was hoping for, the project has phenomenal success."

"So," Christine said, "what is it, exactly? Some kind of enclosed garden, right?"

"Eden Two," Finch announced proudly, "is a two-thousand-hectare completely self-sustaining ecosystem in the middle of the lifeless African desert."

Christine's brow furrowed.

"I know what you're thinking," said Finch. "Why would someone create a gigantic self-sustaining ecosystem in the middle of the desert?"

"Actually," Christine said, "I was wondering what a hectare was."

"Intellectual curiosity," said Finch, who evidently hadn't heard her. "Or maybe hubris. Yes, probably hubris, now that I think about it. Still, you have to admit that it's impressive."

Something about Finch's flippant amorality reminded her of Mercury. An evil version of Mercury. It took her a moment to make room in her brain for this notion, because she wasn't entirely certain that *Mercury* wasn't the evil version of Mercury. Up to this point she had thought of Finch as an even eviller version of Harry Giddings.

"You'll have to come see it sometime," Finch said. "Now that it's too late to...that is, now that it's practically finished. Not yet though. First we have to go to Mbutuokoti for this spirit talking bullshit. It's going to be fantastic."

"Right," Christine said. "Mbutuo..."

"Mbutuokoti."

"Does this mountain have a nickname, maybe?" Christine asked. "I don't seem to have your knack for the local language."

"It's easy," said Finch. "*Mbutuo* is 'mountain.' And *koti* means something like 'heaven.' Well, not heaven precisely. It's the Tawani word for 'emptiness' or 'void.' The Tawani cosmology is interesting because it posits that heaven is actually the realm of the minor deities. The greater spirits live in a great empty void above heaven. *Koti* is the name for that void."

"Then *koti* is outer space," said Christine.

"Well, not precisely," replied Finch. "Their notion of the void is rather primitive, but I suppose 'space' is as good a translation for koti as any."

"So," Christine mused, "we're making a pilgrimage to Space Mountain?"

SIXTEEN
Circa 2,000 B.C.

Uzziel leaned back in his chair, touching his fingertips together and frowning. "I don't know how you always manage to get mixed up in this nonsense," he was saying. "What were you doing at the planeport anyway?"

"I'm fine; thanks for asking," said Mercury. "My neck hardly hurts at all."

Mercury had regained consciousness in the planeport waiting area of the Courts of the Most High. Evidently someone had transported him back to the Courts and then left him sitting on a bench next to his own head. A Good Samaritan had stopped by and stuck his head back on. It would have reattached on its own eventually, but it might well have taken days. Angels don't die, but they can definitely be slowed down by decapitation.

Once his head was firmly attached, Mercury had made his way to Uzziel's office in the hopes that Uzziel might have some idea what exactly had happened at the planeport. But Uzziel was, as usual, in the dark. Evidently planeport security had covered the whole thing up. There was no word of the attempted abduction of Michael (or was it Michelle?) on Angel Band or on any of the internal Court frequencies. Whatever that had been about, the higher-ups at the planeport didn't want anyone to know about it.

"Do they know who attacked you?" Uzziel asked.

"No word from planeport security. Just a random decapitation. It happens. Planeport ruffians."

"I heard something about a V.I.A. coming through the planeport. Your little misadventure didn't have anything to do with that, did it?"

"V.I.A.?" replied Mercury. "Nope. Hadn't heard anything about that. I was just minding my own business, following up a lead on this whole flooding business..."

"Oh, right. What did you find out?"

"Nothing, actually. I'll keep asking around. Somebody has to know something."

"Forget it," said Uzziel. "I need you back in Babylon. Tiamat's up to something again."

"Tiamat's harmless," replied Mercury. "Well, not harmless exactly, but her primary concern seems to be building ziggurats. And she's not even doing that these days, what with the flooding. Shouldn't we be keeping an eye on Lucifer?"

"We are," said Uzziel. "But we already know Lucifer's a bad apple. Tiamat's an unknown quantity. I don't trust her. She doesn't suspect anything, does she?"

"Nah. She still thinks the Civilization Shepherding Program assigned me to help her run Babylon. She has no idea I'm with the Apocalypse Bureau."

"Just don't *you* forget who you work for," admonished Uzziel.

"I'm sure you'll keep reminding me," replied Mercury.

Uzziel smiled. "Only until the end of the world."

Mercury gave a pained smile and excused himself.

Generally unflappable, Mercury was starting to get irritated. He had stuck his neck out to help an archangel in trouble, and all he had to show for it was a doozy of a neck ache—and he still had no idea who or what was behind the rain. He could go back to Babylon as instructed, only to sit in a damp tent and be berated by Tiamat, or he could spend some more time trying to get to the bottom of things. Or the top, as it were.

Outside the Apocalypse Bureau building, he stopped and looked up. Just down the way was the Seraphic Administration Building, a seven-story structure whose top disappeared among the clouds. That wasn't a figure of speech: the top of the building was constantly shrouded in a layer of thick white clouds. The Courts of the Most High was essentially a small city, filled with buildings that housed the various departments that ostensibly ran the Universe. There were seven levels to the Courts, organized hierarchically. At the bottom were the paper pushers and service personnel; on the second level were low-level supervisors, researchers, and analysts; and as one went higher, one began to find oneself in the rarified air of those who did little to no actual work.

Most buildings didn't even rise to the seventh level; Uzziel's office, for instance, was on the top floor of the Apocalypse Bureau, an impressive structure that nevertheless had only four floors. In those buildings that had five or more levels, only seraphim were allowed above the fourth level, and they generally needed an escort to go above level three. It still chafed Mercury that to gain access to the top floor he needed to get "approval" from Uzziel's receptionist.

The offices of the archangels, he knew, were on the top floor of the Seraphic Administration Building. *Up there are answers,* he thought. *I should just fly up there and demand an explanation. Michael, or Michelle, or whoever, owes me that much.*

"You'll never make it," said a gravelly voice behind him.

Mercury turned. A tall, hooded angel stood before him. He removed his hood to reveal a thin, stern face and locks of curly blond hair. "I'm Malchediel," he said.

"Michael's bodyguard," Mercury said. "I saw you at the planeport."

Malchediel nodded. "Michael thanks you for your assistance. And asks that you refrain from trying to contact him again."

"Does 'he'?" said Mercury. "And what happens if I just fly up there and introduce myself?"

"You'll be decapitated again, for one. Hidden in those clouds is a squad of heavily armed seraphim just itching to slice and dice an uppity cherub who doesn't know his place."

"Look," said Mercury. "I'm not going to cause any trouble. I just want some answers. Can I just talk to Michael for two minutes? I did get my head hacked off in an attempt to foil her—*his*—abduction, after all."

"And someday he will return the favor," said Malchediel. "But I'm afraid I can't let you talk to him. What I can do is give you some advice."

"Ooh!" exclaimed Mercury. "Being given advice is my second-favorite thing!"

"Your first favorite being…"

"Not being given advice."

"Of course," said Malchediel. "But this is advice worth heeding. You're not going to find the answers you want up there." He waved his hand in the direction of the Seraphic Administration Building. "If you want to know why it's raining, go back to Babylon. Look around you."

"Super," said Mercury. "I'll get right on that."

"Also, I have this," said Malchediel, handing Mercury a small envelope sealed with wax. "Good luck."

With that, Malchediel shot into the sky and disappeared in the clouds.

Mercury opened the envelope. Inside was a business card with the seal of the archangel Michael. On the flip side had been written:

The rain comes from above.

—M.

"Wonderful," said Mercury. "Riddles." Michael and Malchediel couldn't even get their stories straight. Was he supposed to look around him or look up? Maybe, he thought, the answer is in my heart. He shoved the card in his pocket and trudged back to the planeport. Tiamat would be waiting.

SEVENTEEN

In the morning, Horace Finch and Christine arose before dawn to join the elders of the tribe on their climb up Mbutuokoti. The elders, a group of twenty men, had feasted on a concoction of milk and cattle blood the previous night and fasted in the morning in preparation for the climb. Christine and Finch snacked surreptitiously on packets of jerky he had brought with him.

Mbutuokoti, it turned out, was a dormant volcano that arose incongruously from the plain to the north of the encampment. The hike from the village to the base of the slope took nearly two hours. After a brief respite, the group began to ascend the side of the volcano. The climb was steep but not overly arduous; even in her weakened state, Christine was able to keep up with the men. She was aided in this by the fact that the men were carrying heavy bundles of bark and sticks on their backs and several of them were attempting to coax a stubborn goat up the rocky path along with them. Christine didn't know what they needed the goat for exactly, but neither she nor the goat saw this little excursion having a goat-friendly ending.

They reached the crest of the mountain by midmorning. Before them lay an oval crater, about three hundred yards across at its narrowest point and nearly fifty yards deep. The bottom of the crater was made of smooth black rock that was veined with dozens of crevasses that spread out from its center.

The group clambered down the side of the crater and made its way to the center of the crater's floor. They had to take a meandering route to avoid the crevasses, many of which were wide enough to fall into. Finch seemed particularly interested in the crevasses, stopping frequently to shine his flashlight into the depths. Christine stopped next to him and peered into the crack, but could see nothing but walls of rock disappearing into darkness many yards below.

Upon reaching the center of the crater floor, the elders immediately began a complex set of rituals to prepare them for communing with the spirits. Christine and Finch stood awkwardly to the side. Finch admitted that he didn't really know what to expect; this was the first such pilgrimage the Tawani had undertaken since he had been among them, and they hadn't been very forthcoming with details. Only Tawani elders were privy to the arcane wisdom of communing with the spirits; the rest of the tribe would have to be content with receiving their spiritual guidance secondhand. As for pink-skinned strangers, they could tag along if they liked, but it was clear that they would receive little more deference than the goat.

After nearly an hour of dances, prayers, and chants, the twenty men encircled the goat and the shaman produced a knife. Two of the men approached the goat with cords to bind its legs. As tension mounted, Christine could no longer take it. She screamed.

Her unexpected outburst had the effect of panicking the goat and distracting several of the men. The goat took advantage of their lack of attention and darted between the legs of a particularly tall, bowlegged elder. It ran across the crater's floor for a good twenty yards before vanishing abruptly into a crevasse. The men turned to face Christine in unison, howling incomprehensible curses at her. "Oh come on," Christine protested. "It's not all my fault. You're just looking for someone to blame."

The next hour was spent trying to retrieve the goat, which bleated pathetically somewhere in the blackness below. Finch lowered a flashlight on a length of nylon rope he had brought along, but the goat remained hidden among the twists and turns of the rock walls.

"How important is the goat, really?" Christine finally ventured. "Can't we do the rest of the ceremony without it?"

"For your sake, I'm not going to translate that," Finch replied. "They just might oblige you."

Christine was afraid to ask what he meant. Eventually one of the men volunteered to be lowered into the crevasse on the rope. Finch made a loop at the end of it and the man put his foot through it and lowered himself into the fissure. He was one of the smaller of the men, but the Tawani were tall, gangly people, and it was clear he wasn't going to get very far.

Finch began, "Maybe I should…"

Christine stepped forward. "I'll do it," she said. "It is *partly* my fault the goat fell in, and in any case, I'm the smallest. I'm the only one who has a chance to get down there. You guys are all knees and elbows."

As she approached, the men became agitated, apparently convinced that she wasn't through wreaking havoc with their ceremony.

"It's OK," Finch said to the men. "She's just trying to get your goat."

"Nice," said Christine. "How long have you been saving *that* one?"

Finch tried to explain to the men in their own language what she had said. Christine could tell his grasp of the language was rudimentary; he spoke slowly and often struggled to find the right words. Still, it was amazing what he had picked up in one month with the tribe; evidently he was something of a linguistic genius, having already mastered Japanese, Hindi, and several Slavic languages in addition to his native English. After a few moments, the man in the crevasse reluctantly climbed out and handed the end of the rope to Christine.

"Are you sure you want to do this?" asked Finch. "You haven't been feeling well. I think I could probably fit down there."

Christine was a bit taken aback by Finch's chivalry. He didn't seem like the type. She said, "Thanks for the offer, but I'll do it. I feel better with you up here. I don't completely trust our hosts."

Finch opened his mouth to protest, but Christine had already slipped her foot through the loop in the rope and began lowering herself into the crevasse. Finch grabbed the rope and indicated for the Tawani to anchor the other end.

Gradually they lowered Christine into the crevasse. At first the opening was almost impossibly tight, but after a few feet it opened up into a wider chasm. She heard the goat bleating not far away, but it was difficult to pinpoint the source. Stopping on a small ledge that sloped downward, she shone the flashlight around her. She still couldn't see the bottom of the fissure, but a cavern opened in the rock wall below her. Shining the light into the opening, she thought she saw, for just a split-second, something moving inside. It was possible, she thought, that the goat had hit the ledge and bounced across the crevasse, landing on the floor of the cavern. She hoped so, at least, because otherwise it probably lay wedged somewhere in the blackness below.

She shouted to Finch to give her some slack, and he responded by letting down some more rope and making a stupid pun that she mercifully couldn't hear. Kicking off against the crevasse wall, she swung to the far side and landed just within the cavern. "More rope!" she hollered up the crevasse, and the rope slackened some more. Shining the flashlight into the cavern, she was suddenly met by two glowing green eyes. After a momentary start, she realized she had found her prey: it was the errant goat.

The animal lay on the rocky floor of the cave, barely moving. Christine approached it slowly, speaking in low, soothing tones. The goat appeared stunned and frightened but unhurt, and it actually seemed happy to see her. That changed when she slipped the rope off her foot and slipped it around the goat's horns, tightening the loop quickly and wrapping the rope around a few more times for good measure. She gave the rope a jerk and it slithered across the floor until it became taut. The goat bucked and bleated, but it didn't have a chance against the men dragging it to its doom above. It was dragged, scraping and kicking, to the cavern opening, and then it lifted headfirst off the ground.

"Sorry about that," Christine said sincerely. "There just isn't any other way." She watched the goat recede against the blue sky as if being carried by some celestial dumbwaiter.

Pointing the flashlight further down the narrow cavern, she saw that it opened up again a few feet past where the goat had been lying. While the goat made its slow, clattering ascent to the heavens, she walked gingerly to the opening. Once through, she looked around and gasped.

The chamber was maybe thirty feet across, and a domed ceiling rose about twenty feet above. In the center of the room stood a simple stone pedestal, on which rested a nearly spherical object that glittered in the flashlight's beam. It was a glass apple.

EIGHTEEN

For some reason it didn't really surprise Eddie to hear that Tiamat was herself in the dark about who actually wrote the Charlie Nyx books. Lucifer, who had created the character known as Katie Midford and masterminded the whole Charlie Nyx phenomenon, would no doubt have played the matter as closely to his chest as possible. He wouldn't have given Tiamat any more information than she absolutely needed in order to play her role.

Still, Eddie was at first skeptical regarding whether Tiamat would have hired a mortal (and a young, attractive, female mortal at that) to locate the real author of the books. This skepticism, however, dissipated after only a few minutes with Cody Lang. In addition to being handy with a Glock, Cody knew her stuff. In fact, Cody seemed to know just about everyone's stuff. She was a walking, talking, Glock-toting encyclopedia of what she referred to as "the secret history of Los Angeles." Whether or not she actually had any idea of who the mystery author was, it wasn't difficult to imagine a paranoid, power-mad schemer like Tiamat falling for her spiel. She was Rasputin to Tiamat's Tsarina. To Eddie it sounded like a load of nicely-dressed-up bollocks.

"*Chinatown* was a completely sterilized version of L.A.'s history," she was saying. "They foisted that little fairy tale on the public to keep people from looking into what really happened here. Give 'em a happy little story about water rights and incest and they'll eat it up. If only it were so simple!" She chuckled and shook her head, downing the rest of her drink. "Want another?" she asked Eddie, who had barely touched his drink. Eddie shook his head and she made herself another.

"And the so-called 'General Motors streetcar conspiracy,'" she went on. "What a joke. I mean, sure, GM, Firestone, and the lot wanted to get rid of the streetcars and replace them with buses. But that was going to happen anyway—and it did happen, even in cities where the conspirators had little or no influence. The only reason anybody took notice was that in Los Angeles they pushed a little too hard. Which prompts the question, 'why?' Why did they work so hard to get rid of the streetcars in L.A. when they were on their way out anyway?"

Eddie shrugged. "Water rights and incest?" he ventured. He didn't have a clue what Cody was talking about. What did China-town have to do with streetcars and General Motors? And what did any of it have to do with the mysterious author of the Charlie Nyx books?

"Ha!" Cody replied. "No, I'm afraid the truth goes much deeper than that. Now you're probably wondering what any of this has to do with Essie," she said.

"Actually, yes," Eddie said. "I was starting to…wait, with what?"

"Sorry," Cody said. "I've developed my own jargon for this case. Essie is my code name for the author of the Charlie Nix books. From the Latin, *scriptor Carolingus*, meaning 'Charlie's author.' Abbreviated S.C., or 'Essie' for short."

"Of course," replied Eddie. "That makes perfect sense."

Cody went on, "The truth is, I don't know yet how it's all connected. I just know it is, somehow. Do you know how many corporations were indicted in the conspiracy to form a transportation monopoly in Los Angeles in 1947? Nine. In the Bible, the number nine represents divine justice and the end of human endeavors. There were six parent companies named in the indictment: Firestone, Standard Oil of California, Phillips, General Motors, Federal Engineering, and Mack; and three subsidiaries: National City Lines, Pacific City Lines, and American City Lines. Yellow Truck & Coach, which had been absorbed by GM by the time of the trial, was also involved. That's ten companies. Seven individual executives of these companies were also named as defendants. Revelation speaks of 'a beast rising out of the sea having *ten horns and seven heads.*' Is it such a stretch to conclude this beast is the petroleum-automotive complex, with its offshore drilling platforms and fleets of oil tankers?"

Eddie did think it was a stretch. He was starting to think, in fact, that Cody Lang was a few streetcars short of a fleet. She was like some kind of idiot savant, exhibiting a startlingly detailed grasp of eclectic facts that had nothing whatsoever to do with what she and Eddie were ostensibly talking about.

"I just knew when I took this case that this was going to be the big one," she said excitedly. "The one that finally connects all the dots. I mean, look at you, for example."

"Me?" replied Eddie doubtfully. He was now only half listening, as he was busily trying to think of some way of extricating himself from this situation.

"Yep," said Cody. "You and the other demons. It took me a while to figure out, but in the end there was no other explanation."

"Explanation for what?"

"The mysterious Katie Midford and her unquestioning minions. No simple waitress from Bellflower could inspire that kind of loyalty, not to mention straight-up fear, no matter how rich she had become. And I knew she was no writer because she admitted as much when she hired me. So who was she, and where had she come from? I did some research and found out that there had indeed been a woman named Katie Midford who had waited tables for several years before the Charlie Nyx books came out. But before that there was nothing. I mean, I found records of several Katherine Midfords who were about the right age, but further investigation revealed that none of them was *the* Katie Midford. In other words, this woman had just appeared from nowhere, waited tables for just long enough to establish a backstory, and then became the famous Kate Midford, the genius behind the Charlie Nyx phenomenon. Something just wasn't right, you know? And then there was the sunbathing."

"Sunbathing?" Eddie asked, confused.

"Yeah," Cody replied, finishing her drink. "She was always lying out by the pool, but her skin was too pale and firm to have spent much time in the sun. I never saw her put on any sunscreen, but she was always white. And although she was supposedly in her late forties, she didn't look that old. I mean, she did, but the oldness seemed sort of artificial, like she was a twenty-five-year-old wearing a middle-aged person costume. Something was just off about her. At first I thought maybe she was a vampire, but that didn't jibe with the sunbathing. That only left one explanation: she was a demon. Once I figured that out, I realized that they were all demons, Katie and her whole cadre of sycophants. Once a person knows what you guys look like, you're surprisingly easy to pick out. Anyway, it doesn't particularly matter to me, but I do like to know who I'm working for."

Eddie stared dumbfounded at her. Had she really deduced that Katie and her minions were demons simply from Tiamat's habit of sunbathing? It was a ridiculous leap of logic, and yet she had come to exactly the correct conclusion. An oft-repeated truism on the Mundane Plane stated that even a broken clock was right twice a day. Was this the rare instance where Cody's tortured reasoning led her to a conclusion that coincided with reality? Or was there some logic to her madness after all? He found himself wondering what else she had figured out.

"So," he asked, "did you ever find out who real the author is?"

Cody frowned. "No. Essie remains a mystery. All I really had to go on were a few cryptic e-mails she sent from an anonymous account."

"'She?'"

"Sorry, I tend to think of Essie as a she, but in reality I don't even know that much. Even the handful of e-mails Essie sent seemed to have been forwarded by a third party. The guy who set up this deal really didn't want Midford and Essie talking to each other directly. There were a few clues in some of the e-mails, but none of them led anywhere. They may actually have been red herrings meant to put me off the trail. In any case, I guess I'll never know."

"You're not working on it anymore?" Eddie asked.

"Of course not," she replied. "Like I told you, Midford owes me twenty Gs already. Well, minus about three hundred dollars in booze I've gone through over the past few days. The only thing I've been investigating lately is the disappearance of Katie Midford, and that's been an unqualified failure. My only lead was a cabin she supposedly owned in the San Bernardino Forest, but it was destroyed in that wildfire. So here I sit, trying to drink my way even on this damn case."

Realizing this discussion had gotten him nowhere, Eddie got to his feet. "Well," he said, "I should be going. Got a meeting with my publisher in an hour and I need to go to the hotel and change my shirt." He fingered the bloody bullet holes.

"Good luck with the meeting. I hope your new publishing friends aren't too disappointed when you can't produce the manuscript."

"I'll come up with something," Eddie said with feigned confidence. "These things have a way of working themselves out." He moved to leave the room.

"*Panton in suus vicis*," Cody said quietly.

Eddie turned. "What did you say?"

"It's Latin," Cody said. "It means—"

"I know what it means," Eddie said. "'Everything in its time.' Where did you hear it?"

"Just something I say," she said. "It's carved into my father's tombstone. Does it mean something to you?"

"It's a quote, from a man named Saint Culain," answered Eddie. "He was a little-known medieval scholar who believed there were no such things as coincidences."

"That's true," Cody said. "Everything is connected."

"No," said Eddie, shaking his head. "He literally didn't believe in coincidences. He thought no two events ever occurred at exactly the same time."

"That's crazy," Cody replied.

"Yeah," Eddie agreed. "Most people think so. Well, most people have never heard of him, but the few who have pretty much agree that he was insane. He's a hobby of mine, though. I've always found him fascinating."

"Demons have hobbies?"

"Most don't," Eddie admitted. "But I've had a lot of free time on my hands over the past few decades. I ran across Saint Culain while I was doing research on the Ottoman Empire."

"Research on the…"

"Long story," Eddie said.

"Funny," said Cody pensively. "I never knew it was a quote."

"Maybe your father was a St. Culain fan."

"I wouldn't know. He died when I was just a kid. And it's not like he was around much before that. He was always gone on business trips. My mother died when I was a baby, so I was essentially raised by a series of Mexican nannies. *Pobrecita!*" she exclaimed with mock pathos. "Anyway, sob story over. The point is, I always think of *panton in suus vicis* as a sort of cynical joke. The man who never had time for anything puts 'everything in its time' on his tombstone. Funny stuff."

"I suppose he would have been around if he could…" started Eddie uncertainly. Human relations were a bit of a mystery to him, and he wasn't sure of the appropriate response.

"Ha!" Cody barked bitterly. "The year before he died, he completely missed my birthday. He was out of the country, of course, but I didn't get a card, or a phone call, or anything. And when he comes home: nothing. Two months go by before he says to me, 'Hey, I completely forgot your birthday, didn't I?' Then he promises me that my next birthday will be the best ever. *Unforgettable*, he said. You know what he did for my next birthday?"

Eddie shook his head.

"He died!" Cody announced. "He was piloting a small plane over the San Bernardino Mountains, and it crashed. April 29, 1993. Couldn't forget it if I tried."

Eddie's brow furrowed. "You say your father died on April 29, 1993? Are you sure?"

Cody glared at him. "Did you hear what I just said? He *died* on my *birthday*. Yes, I'm sure."

"I'm sorry," Eddie said. "It's just…Saint Culain died on April 29, 993 AD. Exactly one thousand years earlier."

"Bullshit," declared Cody.

"Um, what?" asked Eddie.

"I said *bullshit.* There was no April 29, 993."

"Oh, right," agreed Eddie. "Before 1582, Western Civilization used the Julian calendar instead of the Gregorian. We angels adopted the Gregorian a bit earlier."

"Really?" Cody asked. "When?"

"One," said Eddie. "Of course, we didn't call it the Gregorian calendar. That would have been silly. The point is, your father died exactly one thousand years after the death of Saint Culain. Don't you find that at all remarkable?"

Cody shrugged. "I suppose."

Eddie was incredulous. "You just spent ten minutes drawing connections between *Chinatown*, General Motors, and the book of Revelation, and yet you don't find it remarkable that *your own father just happened to die exactly one thousand years after the man who spoke the words that are engraved on your father's tombstone?*"

"Coincidences do happen," said Cody. "And they don't all have some hidden meaning."

"But you have to admit…"

"Look, drop it, OK? I don't give a shit about this Saint Culain. Or my father, for that matter. He didn't have time for me when he was alive, and I don't have time for him now. I haven't even been to his grave for fifteen years."

"He's buried here? In Los Angeles?"

"Just down the highway," said Cody. "Used to be Buena Park Cemetery, but they moved it to make room for a shopping center a few years back."

"Wait, so he's not there anymore?"

"Oh, no," replied Cody. "They moved the cemetery, but my father's still there. He's too stubborn to get out of the way for a Bed, Bath & Beyond. Don't you have somewhere to go?"

Eddie sighed heavily. He had been strangely exhilarated at the thought of finding a missing piece to Cody's puzzle. But maybe it was just a meaningless coincidence. In fact, maybe they were all meaningless coincidences. Sure, Cody had figured out the truth about Katie Midford, but that could have just been a lucky guess. An occasional glimpse of insight didn't mean one wasn't delusional.

"Yeah, I'd better get going," said Eddie. "Meeting with my publisher."

"What are you going to tell them?" Cody asked.

"I'll come up with something," he muttered.

NINETEEN

Christine's surprise at seeing the apple sitting there innocuously on a pedestal momentarily edged out her horror at the realization of what it was: an anti-bomb. There was no doubt about it. It was the exact same size and shape as the ones she had seen tucked away in a secret safe on the Floor, Lucifer's staging ground for his abortive invasion of Earth—and also the same as the one that had imploded Anaheim Stadium. The apple's color appeared to be different and it was missing the trigger mechanism she had seen on the other anti-bombs, but other than that it was the same. She wondered, if this one couldn't be triggered manually, what would set it off. A timer, maybe. She held her ear to it, thinking she might hear a ticking noise, but heard nothing but Horace Finch calling to her from up above.

She picked up the apple, belatedly wondering if it was on some kind of motion-sensitive trigger. She gritted her teeth and held it away from her face, as if maybe that would offer some protection against a device that could level a small city. When nothing happened, she shrugged and slipped the apple into her pocket.

She called to Finch to lower the rope. He did so, and then hoisted her back to the floor of the crater.

By the time she emerged into daylight again, the goat was already dead, its throat slit by the shaman's knife. Its headless body hung upside down from a tripod made from three short poles, its blood draining into a clay bowl beneath it. When the bowl filled up, one of the Tawani removed it and put another in its place. Ten bowls had already been filled this way. Christine shuddered. Respect for cultural differences was all well and good, but this was revolting.

"What took you so long?" Finch asked. "I thought you'd fallen to your death."

"Sorry," said Christine. "Just doing a little…what's it called? Exploring caves."

"Spelunking," Finch said.

"Yeah, spelunking," said Christine. "Our scapegoat over there found a cave. I thought maybe it exited out the side of the mountain somewhere, but it was a dead end."

"Hmm," replied Finch, regarding her suspiciously. Christine placed her hand over the round bulge in her pocket.

Not far from the exsanguinating goat, several elders were drawing figures with its blood on pieces of flat bark that they had carried with them up the mountain. When a man had finished drawing on a piece of bark, he would place it on top of a roughly goat-sized rectangular framework that had been constructed out of sticks. Soon the bark was piled nearly a foot high. Other men were collecting dry grass from the crater floor and stuffing it in a gap underneath the framework. While they worked, dark clouds began to gather overhead.

When the goat had been drained of nearly all its fluids and the wooden framework had been packed with fuel, the animal was placed on top of the bark pile, its severed head positioned awkwardly a few inches away from its neck. As a breeze picked up and the clouds threatened rain, Christine momentarily hoped that maybe the men would be unable to get the fire started—but this hope was dashed when one of the elders produced a disposable lighter. He brushed the flame against the dry grass, and in seconds the pyre was engulfed in flames.

"What's with the drawings on the bark?" Christine asked Finch.

"Prayers to the gods," Finch replied. "They use those pictograms to communicate."

"Communicate what?" Christine asked.

Finch shrugged. "Their hopes, fears, orders for Chinese takeout, whatever. Even if the gods did exist, they'd have a hell of a time interpreting that mishmash of symbols." He shook his head dismissively. "Primitive African bullshit."

"You really missed your calling as a tour guide," Christine observed.

As the fire grew, the clouds overhead continued to darken. Lightning flashed among the clouds, and thunder rolled behind.

Flames began to caress the goat's carcass, and the elders, encircling the pyre, chanted and raised their hands to the heavens. The goat's hair caught fire, letting off thick blue smoke and an odor that smelled so bad Christine was surprised she had never heard the phrase "it smelled as bad as burning goat hair." Mercifully after a few minutes the hair was gone and the goat began to smell more appetizing. Unfortunately this only made matters worse. It was now well past noon and Christine was getting hungry.

"I don't suppose we're going to get any goat-burgers out of this deal," Christine said, as the meat began to sizzle and pop.

"'Fraid not," said Finch. "The goat is a sacrifice to the gods."

"Seems to me," Christine reflected, "there's a fine line between a sacrifice to the gods and a nice mountaintop barbecue."

"True enough," said Finch. "But unless you want to be sacrificed next, I recommend we stay on the right side of that line."

Christine stood sadly by, her stomach growling, as the goat burned to a crisp. It seemed unfair that after she had already made the sacrifice of rescuing the goat and watching it drained of its fluids she wasn't even allowed to eat any of it. "Stupid gods," she muttered, as the smoke wafted toward the heavens.

A sudden flash of lightning streaked from the clouds, striking the rim of the crater with a deafening BOOM! Christine immediately began apologizing profusely to gods she had scorned mere seconds earlier. As the saying goes, there are no atheists on mountaintops during thunderstorms.

The gods responded by pelting the mountaintop with rain.

"Are we safe here?" Christine asked worriedly, once she had done her best to appease the gods.

Finch snorted. "The odds of being struck by lightning are—"

Lightning tore through the sky again, blasting a nearby boulder to pieces. BOOM!

Christine ran. After a moment's hesitation, Finch followed. A glance backward indicated that the elders remained transfixed on the altar. The rain was now coming down in torrents.

As she approached the crater's edge, there was a third BOOM!, even louder than the first two. The earth shook beneath Christine's feet and she fell forward onto her palms. She was showered by a blast of hot air and fiery debris. After a moment, a flaming goat head crashed into the ground in front of her and rolled several feet before coming to a halt. It stared vacantly at her, its eyes filled with orange flame. She had to hand it to these primitive African gods: that was one of the creepiest things she had seen in a while.

Brushing the ashes from her hair, Christine turned to see what had happened. It was a grisly sight: the third lightning bolt had struck the altar, exploding it and electrocuting the Tawani elders. Their corpses lay face-up on the ground surrounding the charred altar site, their arms and legs splayed widely so that they looked like paper dolls arranged neatly in a circle. At the center of the circle was a charred impression in the ground—a crater within a crater. A wisp of smoke arose from its center.

As Christine made to get to her feet, the ground shook again and a narrow crack that ran through the center of the crater floor began to widen. A sudden blast of smoke shot up from below.

"Get up!" yelled Finch. "Mbutuokoti is erupting!"

Christine staggered to her feet. "Erupting?" she protested. "I thought it was dormant!"

They moved as quickly as they could across the shaking ground to the edge of the crater. The split in the crater floor continued to widen.

"That's how these things work," Finch said. "They're dormant until they erupt. Then they're not dormant anymore."

Seconds after they reached the crater wall, the entire crater floor began to collapse, massive chunks of earth and rock simply disappearing into an abyss below. As each piece fell, a blast of sulfurous hot air shot up from below. Christine and Finch climbed frantically toward the crater rim.

"Mbutuokoti hasn't erupted for over seven thousand years," Finch went on in between breaths. "But in geological terms that's nothing. The odds that it would erupt—"

"Oh yes," snapped Christine. "*Do* tell me the odds. You have no idea how reassuring that was with the lightning."

They reached the rim of the crater just as the entire floor collapsed.

"The heat of the magma is liquefying the rock," Finch explained, as they began their uneasy descent down the rocky slope.

"Magma?" Christine asked. "Is that like lava?"

"Same thing," Finch replied. "It's called magma until it…"

A massive jet of bright orange lava suddenly shot upward from the crater. It must have been a hundred feet tall.

"…erupts," Finch finished. "Run!"

But Christine was already running as fast as she dared. She was taking giant strides down the hillside, her eyes locating a solid footing a tenth of a second before each leap. The rain persisted, impairing her vision and making the rocks slippery. Finch was right behind her, so that if she slowed down he would careen into her, knocking both of them down. Softball-sized globs of semi-hardened lava began to strike the rocks all around them, breaking into oblong, orange-hot splatters on the steep ground. One hit by one of those, Christine thought, and I'm as dead as that goat.

About halfway down Mbutuokoti, just when Christine began to think she might just survive this little adventure, her foot slipped and she tumbled headlong down the slope.

TWENTY
Circa 2,000 B.C.

By the time Mercury was back in Babylon, his luck had apparently changed: the rain had stopped and the sun was shining. It appeared that the flooding, if not exactly over, was not going to get any worse. Even more remarkably, Tiamat appeared to be in a good mood.

"Mercury!" she exclaimed. "Perfect timing. I need you to get started on the plans for the next ziggurat."

Mercury was dumbfounded. "The next…You realize that most of Babylon is underwater, right? We've lost tens of thousands of people, and most of the survivors are either starving or sick or both. Maybe we should take some time to regroup before starting another ziggurat."

"No!" Tiamat snarled. "I want the plans ready so that as soon as this one is done, we can start making bricks for the next one."

"You want to finish this one?" Mercury asked. "I thought it was in the wrong place."

"I'm fairly certain it is," said Tiamat. "But there's no way to know for sure until it's done."

"Great," replied Mercury. "I'll mention that in my next pep talk to the guys."

"Excellent," replied Tiamat, oblivious to his sarcasm. "But first, I need you to go find Nabu. Or the raft, at least. I can't deal with any more whining about people being hungry. We need to find some food."

"Still no word from Nabu, eh?" Mercury asked.

"Nothing," grumbled Tiamat. "It's been six days. That was our best raft, too. Nabu better be dead, or he's going to be in big trouble. If he ever comes back, I'm going to tie a brick around his neck and throw him off the ziggurat."

Mercury thought for a moment. "Couldn't we, you know, just *make* food?"

"Mercury, you know that's against the rules. We're not allowed to use miracles to interfere in a society's development."

"Really?" asked Mercury dryly. "You're going to start quoting the rules now?"

"Look, I can't just start miraculously providing food to people. It sets a bad precedent. Now stop arguing with me and go find Nabu before I lose my temper."

Mercury bit his tongue and walked away through the huddled masses who begged him for a scrap of bread. He was tempted to bring a few loaves into being, but Tiamat was right: you couldn't just start doing miracles for people. Where would it stop? He reached the edge of the ziggurat and made his way down to the water, some twenty feet below. He glanced up to make sure no one was watching, and then used a small amount of interplanar energy to warp the sunlight around his frame, making himself near invisible. He leaped into the air toward the mountain peaks in the distance.

He skimmed low and fast across the water's surface, just a barely noticeable variation in the current. Once he was too far out to be identifiable from the ziggurat, he dropped his camouflage and soared higher into the sky. It took him less than an hour to reach the foothills, and only a few minutes longer to spot Nabu and his crew picking berries on a hillside.

He alighted a few hundred yards away and walked up.

"Nabu!" he exclaimed. "What a surprise!"

"Mercury?" Nabu said incredulously. "How did you…?"

"Got lost," said Mercury. "I was looking for my dog, and I wound up here."

"I didn't know you had a dog."

"Well, that would explain why I can't find him. So, how goes the food hunt? About to head back?"

Nabu shook his head sadly. "We've barely found enough to keep ourselves alive. Mostly berries, a few nuts. We saw a deer yesterday, but couldn't get close enough to spear it. It's bad, Mercury. Real bad."

"Hmm." Mercury said. "Don't worry; we'll figure something out." He clambered up the hillside a few hundred yards and stepped out onto a narrow outcropping from which he could see most of the way around the peak. Except for a few other hilltops and the mountain range in the distance, water covered the land as far as he could see. The hillsides didn't look very promising as far as food was concerned.

Casting his eyes out across the sea, he spied something unexpected: a boat of some kind. As he watched, it grew gradually larger: it was moving slowly toward him.

"Hey, Nabu!" Mercury called down the slope. "Get up here!"

Nabu and his men clambered up after Mercury.

"Check it out," Mercury said. "A boat. Come on!"

He scrambled down the hillside in the direction of the boat. It looked like it would make landfall on a shallow slope about a half mile away. They sprinted most of the way, with Mercury in the lead, but when they got there they realized the boat was still several hundred yards out. It was bigger than they had realized: it was nearly five hundred feet long, with a pitched roof covering most of the boat.

Mercury whistled. "Holy crap, that's a big boat."

Nabu and his men mumbled agreement. None of them had ever seen a boat even a quarter of that size. As it drifted closer to the shore, they saw a man with long, gray hair standing on the deck, peering out at the hilltops.

"Hey!" called Mercury. "Over here!"

The man waved and yelled something to someone else on the boat. Another man, burlier and brown haired, appeared and hurled what appeared to be an anchor over the deck railing. There was some more movement on the boat, and Mercury realized they were lowering a small rowboat to the water. When the rowboat was afloat, the two men climbed down some sort of rope ladder into it and began to row toward Mercury.

After some time, the rowboat neared the shore, and the younger, brown-haired man leaped out, guiding the boat to dry ground. The older man stepped gingerly onto the hillside.

"Hey, dudes," said the old man. "I'm Noah, captain of the *Rainbow Warrior*. This is my son, Japheth. What's happening?"

"Hi," said Mercury. "I'm Mercury. Nice boat. How many people you got on that thing?"

"People?" asked Noah. "Just eight adults, plus the grandkids. Immediate family only, man."

"Eight people?" asked Mercury, incredulous. "You could carry a small city in that thing."

"Yeah, most of it is taken up with the animals," said Noah.

"Animals? What animals?"

"Well," said Noah, frowning a bit, "like, all of them."

As Noah spoke, a large raven sailed quietly out of the sky and alighted on his shoulder. In its beak was a leaf.

"Shoo!" Noah barked at the bird, waving it off with his hand. "Get back on the boat, you stupid bird! Man, if I ever have to do this again, I'm leaving the damn ravens off the boat."

"You think something like this is going to happen *again*?" asked Mercury.

The raven, circling in the air above them, cawed at them in response.

"Shut up!" yelled Noah, waving his arms wildly. "Back. On. The. Boat!"

"Seems pretty unlikely we'd ever have a flood like this again," Mercury went on.

"Maybe," said Noah. "Never say never."

"Caw-caw-CAW!" cawed the raven.

"Is that bird *saying* something?" asked Mercury.

"Yeah," said Noah, glaring at the bird. "He's telling me to *leave the damn ravens behind next time*."

"Caw-caw-CAW!" cawed the raven.

"I swear he's trying to say something," said Mercury. "Like 'here's the shore.'"

Japheth shook his head. "Sounds like 'where's the boar?' to me."

Noah began screaming and running in circles, trying to scare off the bird. Finally the raven gave up and flew back to the *Rainbow Warrior*. "Level four!" it seemed to caw.

Japheth smiled weakly. "My dad is a bit eccentric," he said. He glanced at Noah, who was bent over with his hands on his knees, panting wildly. Japheth surreptitiously held his thumb to his lips and tossed his head back, sticking his tongue out and rolling his eyes wildly.

"We're on a mission," proclaimed Noah, when he had recovered. "We're saving the animals. You see, God is fed up with humanity's violent ways, so he sent a flood to wipe us out. I mean, not us. You."

As he spoke, another bird—this one a pigeon—landed on his shoulder. In its beak was some sort of branch.

"*Et tu*, pigeon?" cried Noah, slapping crazily at the bird.

"Woooooooo!" said the pigeon, dropping the branch on the ground and flapping into the air.

"Seriously, I think those birds are trying to tell you something," said Mercury. "Maybe they want you to know that the flood waters are receding, and that it's safe to land the *Rainbow Warrior*."

"Woooooooo!" said the pigeon, as it flew off.

"Idiot birds," grumbled Noah. "They don't know shit. Obviously the flood can't be over yet, because every living thing hasn't been wiped from the face of the Earth. I was promised the flood waters would cover the mountains to a depth of fifteen cubits."

"Fifteen cubits!" exclaimed Mercury. "Wow. You know, I'm pretty sure there isn't enough water on Earth for that. Are you sure God didn't say that the water was going to rise fifteen cubits altogether?"

"Well, that wouldn't kill every living thing on the face of the Earth, would it?" asked Noah, sneering at Mercury. "So we're staying on the *Rainbow Warrior* until I get a definite sign the flood is over."

As he spoke, a giant, beautiful parrot alighted on his shoulder. "Noah!" warbled the bird. "I am the LORD your God. The flood is over! Land the boat already! You want a cracker? That's a good girl. Tell him, just like that. Don't forget the first part. I am the LORD your God!"

"Dammit, Japheth," said Noah. "What did I tell you about teaching the parrot to blaspheme?"

Japheth held up his hands innocently. "But I didn't—"

"That's enough out of you, parrot! Back to the boat!"

The parrot flew off dejectedly.

"As I was saying," Noah continued, "God is wiping out humanity because of their wicked violent ways. We're going to be the sole survivors. Gotta stay on the boat until it's over."

"Hmmm," said Mercury, taking this in. "So just to be clear, God abhors violence so much that He decided to drown millions of people in a horrific flood, is that it?"

"Yep," said Noah.

"Well, it's nice He thought to save the animals," said Mercury. "Say, you don't happen to have any extra food on board, do you?"

"Sorry, man," said Noah. "Brought just enough for the animals. I finally increased our rations the other day when the rain stopped. My kids have literally been at each other's throats."

As if on cue, there was a scream from the boat. "Dad!" called a shrill voice from somewhere below deck. "Shem is trying to cut me with a carving knife again!"

Noah turned back to the boat. "Shem!" he hollered, "What did I tell you about eating Ham?"

The caterwauling on the boat seemed to stop. Noah turned back to Mercury. "I'm sorry, I should get back to the boat. My kids can be real assholes sometimes. No offense, Japheth."

Japheth forced a smile.

"Maybe we could trade with you for some food," Mercury said. "We'd kill for a sheep or two."

"No way," said Noah. "I can't spare any sheep. Maybe some grain. What do you have to trade?"

"Well," said Mercury. "We've got plenty of bricks. Possibly some ore."

"Bricks?" snorted Noah. "I'm living on a boat, man. What would I need bricks for? I might settle for some wood."

"No wood," said Mercury. "Sorry."

"Then I guess we have nothing to talk about," said Noah.

Out of the corner of his eye, Mercury noticed Nabu and one of his men very quietly pushing the rowboat off the shore. Nabu, catching his glance, put his finger to his lips, and then cocked his head toward the boat and made an eating motion.

Noah made to turn back toward the rowboat.

"Wait!" cried Mercury. "I forgot! There's something you need to see!"

Noah eyed him skeptically.

"Like what?" said Japheth.

"Snipe!" Mercury announced. "Two of them!"

"What's a snipe?" asked Noah.

"Why," Mercury replied in mock disbelief, "you've never seen a snipe? They're great, beautiful, flightless birds. Quite a sight to see, although between you and me, not the brightest fowl around. I'm a bit surprised that any of them survived the flood this long. My goodness, those could be the last two snipe on earth! Think of that! But as you say, you've got things to do. Those monkey cages aren't going to clean themselves."

Noah and Japheth exchanged glances. "We may have a few minutes," said Noah.

Nabu and his partner had hopped onto the boat and were paddling stealthily out to the ark.

"Great!" exclaimed Mercury. "They're just over here." He marched up the hillside with Noah, Japheth, and the other men in tow. As they walked, Mercury continued to express astonishment that they had never seen a snipe, going into great detail about the snipe's gorgeous plumage and its spectacular and often suicidal mating rituals. By the time they had reached the crest of the hill, Noah and Japheth were jittery with excitement. To think, they had taken the *Rainbow Warrior* to sea without a pair of snipe!

"OK, the snipe were in that grove of trees down there," said Mercury. "We'll need to split up. Noah and Japheth, you take your men around to the left and wait. The rest of us will flush them out from the right. Let's do this!"

Noah and Japheth took off excitedly to the left. When they were out of sight, Mercury led the men back the way they had come. Nabu and his partner were furiously paddling the rowboat back to shore. On the deck of the ark, several people were screaming curses at them. The rowboat was stacked high with sacks of food.

"Nice work, Nabu!" Mercury exclaimed. "OK, everybody in the rowboat."

The men did as they were instructed. The boat was so weighed down that its lip barely protruded from the water.

"Hey," said Mercury, examining the contents of the rowboat. "What's this?" The carcass of an animal, the size of a large sheep, lay nestled among the sacks. A single horn protruded from its forehead.

"Dwarf unicorn," said Nabu proudly. "They're good eatin.' They had two of them on the boat, so I figured they could spare one."

"Good thinking," replied Mercury.

They pushed off from the shore as Noah and Japheth bounded over the ridge. "You sons of bitches!" Noah howled. "Come back here with my boat!"

But the rowboat was already too far out to be caught. While the men paddled, Mercury lay back in the boat and relaxed. So God had sent the flood to wipe out all the wickedness on the Earth, had He? Well, that was one possibility.

TWENTY-ONE

Christine awoke in what appeared to be a hospital bed. The clock on the nightstand next to the bed said 7:36 a.m. The oversized gown she was wearing read *Property of Nairobi Medical Center.* An oxygen mask was strapped to her face. Her right ankle was wrapped in a bandage and suspended several inches off the bed.

She pulled off the mask, brushing a cloud of dust from her hair in the process. Her arms and legs were scraped and bruised, but she seemed to have avoided major injury. She tried to sit up but was hit by a combination of pain and déjà vu that forced her to lie down again. Add lightning and volcanic eruption to my list of miraculous survivals, she thought. She half expected Harry Giddings to call and tell her to fly back to Los Angeles. The only thing that was missing in this little reenactment of her Israel experience was the metallic briefcase she had been given by General Isaakson.

This line of thought prompted another panicked realization: she had no idea where the glass apple was. If she was right about it, the apple was potentially even more dangerous than the Attaché Case of War. It wasn't something she wanted falling into the wrong hands. She looked frantically about the room before seeing the apple resting innocuously on a window ledge. How nice, she thought. A piece of decorative tchotchke with the destructive power of a small nuclear device. She would have to get the apple out of here and somewhere safe as soon as she could. Somewhere like the inside of a mountain in the middle of the Kenyan wilderness, for example. She shook her head at her stupidity. Why hadn't she just left the damn thing where it was?

As she pondered this, the door to her room opened. It was Horace Finch, looking only slightly less banged up than she. He was carrying a vase containing an enormous bouquet of flowers.

"Hey, you're awake!" he exclaimed. "Here, these are for you." He set the vase down on a small table between Christine and the window. He went on, "I wasn't sure either of us was going to survive the local medical care. I pulled some strings and got you a private room and a doctor with a medical degree from UCLA. He's a morphine addict with a history of credit card fraud, but beggars can't be choosers."

"You pulled strings? What string do you have access to in the Nairobi Medical Center?"

"Well, technically I offered to buy them a helicopter. They wanted mine, but I'm rather fond of her, so I told them I'd order one more suited to their needs."

"You have a helicopter?"

"Of course," Finch replied. "How do you think we got here? Once I managed to get us shielded under a boulder, I called my pilot back at Eden Two. He got to Mbutuokoti in twenty minutes. He dropped the rescue harness, I strapped you in, and we were off. Half an hour later we were in Nairobi."

"Being an eccentric billionaire has its advantages, I suppose," said Christine.

Finch nodded absentmindedly and walked to the window. "Nice view," he said. "They told me this was the best room in the hospital. Not that that's saying much. I've been to Taco Bells with better hygiene procedures."

He turned to face her again. "By the way, I didn't mention the thing with the goat and the thunderstorm and the volcano. No point in complicating matters with absurd, non-medically-relevant details. I told them you were in a spelunking accident."

"Ooh, kinky," replied Christine.

Finch looked at her uncomprehendingly, and then shook his head, evidently deciding it was better not to ask. "Anyway, get some rest," he said. "I've got to make some phone calls, but I'll be back later."

Christine nodded and Finch left the room. She lay back in bed and closed her eyes. She had almost drifted back to sleep when she heard a muffled *whup-whup-whup* in the distance. A helicopter, she thought. She sat up, unhooked her ankle from the sling, and hopped awkwardly to the window just in time to see a bright yellow helicopter with the Finch logo emblazoned on the side disappearing into the sunrise.

"Son of a bitch," she muttered. "Where does he think he's going?" And then she realized what had happened. She looked down at the empty windowsill, which had been obscured from her view by the flowers. The glass apple was gone.

TWENTY-TWO

Eddie's meeting with the lovely but demanding Wanda Kwan went better than he expected, which wasn't saying much. He assured her that the manuscript was coming along perfectly well, but when pressed for details, all he could muster were some vague promises about water rights and incest. Wanda seemed a bit troubled by this dark turn in what was ostensibly a series of adolescent fantasy books, but she brightened when he promised her six explosions, seven outfit changes, three chapters taking place at the Charlie Nyx Travel Plaza and Family Fun Place, and no mention of the setting of the six previous books.

The fact was that Eddie would have promised to write the entire book in Pig Latin to get out from under the piercing gaze of Ms. Kwan. At this point he was fairly certain he wasn't going to be able to deliver anything, so why not promise them the moon? Actually, that wasn't a bad idea, he thought. Maybe I'll tell them the climax of the book takes place on the moon. They'll love that.

Driving back to the hotel from the Beacon building, he spotted the Buena Vista Mall just off the freeway and, on a whim, exited and pulled into the parking lot of the massive shopping complex. If there had once been a cemetery here, there was no indication of it now. Had Cody been screwing with him?

Wandering around the mall parking lot, he questioned several shoppers before finding an elderly woman who remembered the cemetery. Her husband had died of a stroke some twenty years earlier and rested in peace for over a decade before being moved to Fullerton to make room for a Burger Giant. Eddie thanked her, offered his condolences, and headed toward the Burger Giant, which was adjacent to Bed, Bath & Beyond. If Cody was telling the truth, then her father's grave was around here, somewhere.

There was no indication of any grave marker, just acres of concrete and bland stucco-and-concrete-block buildings. The complex housing Bed, Bath & Beyond and Burger Giant was a long, narrow stretch of stores. Eddie walked around the entire structure and found nothing indicating the presence of a gravesite. He circumnavigated the structure once more, this time looking for any subtle markings on the pavement, thinking that perhaps they had simply paved over top of the grave. But if there really was a human being buried under the parking lot, somebody would have left a marker of some kind, wouldn't they? And Cody had definitely said that her father had a tombstone. Of course, she didn't say whether her father's tombstone had been removed along with the rest of them. He found nothing.

Standing at the rear of the structure near the service entrances, he appraised it once more and noticed something a bit odd. Most of the building was covered by a flat roof, with eaves that extended some three feet past the stucco walls. But near the center of the structure was a section, maybe fifty feet long, that appeared to have no roof. Some sort of open-air courtyard?

A single door presented itself in this section of the building. Eddie approached it and looked around to see if anyone was watching. The area was deserted except for a couple of men unloading some boxes a hundred or so yards away. They seemed to take no notice of him.

The door was locked, but this presented no difficulty for Eddie, as the lock's tumblers miraculously decided to line up just as he turned the handle. He pulled the door open and slipped through.

Inside was one of the strangest things Eddie had ever seen, and having been around for several thousand years, that was saying something. It was, quite simply, a gravesite. Ensconced within this featureless strip mall was a miniature park, covered by a lush, well-manicured lawn. Directly in the center of the lawn was a small wooden gazebo that rested on a granite base about three feet high. Engraved on the base, facing the door Eddie had just entered, were the words:

COLIN LANG
LAID TO REST APRIL 29, 1993

PANTON IN SUUS VICIS

"Well," said Eddie. "It appears I've found the Beyond department."

He approached the gazebo and stood for a moment, staring at the inscription. "Hello, Mr. Lang," he said to the unresponsive stone. "Nice to make your acquaintance. Figures that the one human being with whom I have something in common would be dead."

As an angel, Eddie had a hard time wrapping his brain around the concept of mortality. How could a person *be* one moment, and then *not be* the next? Presumably their souls continued on after death in some way, but in all his centuries he had never bumped into one on any of the Heavenly planes. As far as anyone could tell, the man named Colin Lang had simply ceased to exist, while his temporal remains rotted under a suburban strip mall. Eddie felt a bit let down. He wasn't sure what he had hoped to find, but there were clearly no answers here—about the Charlie Nyx manuscript or anything else.

"Well, I suppose I should let you get back to things," said Eddie. "I had an idea you might be able to help me out with something, but I can see you're busy, so I'll just see myself out." He turned and walked back to the door.

"Oh," he said, turning back to face the monument. "Cody says hi."

As Eddie reached for the door handle, he was greeted by evidence of life beyond the grave. Actually it was not so much from *beyond* as from *under*. For just a second there was a deafening sound like a jet airplane taking off, which caused Eddie to turn back to the gazebo just in time to see something the size of a Volkswagen crash through it from underneath, shoot some twenty feet into the sky, and then fall to the grass a few feet from him. It appeared to be a metal box, about seven feet on each side, now badly dented and misshapen from the fall. Clouds of smoke and debris poured from the hole in the ground.

Eddie stood aghast, evaluating the scene. He noticed, on the side of the box nearest him, a sort of metal bracket, as if the box were a vehicle designed to travel along a track. After a moment, he heard a sound like a person groaning coming from inside.

With angelic grace, Eddie leaped onto the edge of the box and peered down, noticing that the top—or at least the side of the box that was currently facing up—was a sliding metal gate, the sort that used to be used on elevators. Lying inside the box, half hidden by the gate, was the form of a person. He or she was not moving.

Eddie pulled aside the gate and leaped into the box. The figure was a small man with dark skin and a slight frame. He was banged up and barely conscious. Blood streamed from a gash on his forehead.

Sirens wailed in the distance, and Eddie heard someone banging on the door to the hidden courtyard. There were going to be a lot of awkward questions if he didn't get out of here quickly.

"Mr. Lang!" Eddie shouted at the man. "Can you hear me?"

The man groaned almost imperceptibly.

"I'll save you, Mr. Lang! Your daughter is going to be so excited to see you!"

Eddie's assumption that the mysterious man in the box was Colin Lang, while not entirely rational, can to some extent be blamed on the fact that he had not yet had a chance to fully process the events of the previous several seconds. His mind had been forced to make a transition from a purely theoretical consideration of life after death to a very real and pressing real-world situation in which a man in a steel box had been forcibly ejected from a gravesite occupying a spot of real estate that should by all rights have been a Jamba Juice. It was simply too much for him to take in.

Eddie ran his hands over the man, manipulating interplanar energy to patch up the worst of his wounds. He heard voices outside and what sounded like the jingling of keys. Lifting the man's limp body over his shoulder, Eddie leaped on top of the box. Glancing behind him, he saw the door handle turning.

Eddie crouched and then leaped with all his strength, soaring over the courtyard toward the Burger Giant next door. Uniformed men poured through the door underneath, looking about the area, bewildered. Fortunately, none of them thought to look up.

Eddie was a bit out of practice with flying, and he landed off balance on top of the Burger Giant. Losing his footing, he skidded across the gabled roof and fell to the concrete patio in front of the restaurant, with the limp body of the small-boned-but-sur-prisingly-heavy-presumed-to-be-the-once-thought-dead-Colin-Lang squarely on top of him.

They had landed on the side of the mall opposite most of the hubbub, but there were still plenty of civilians around to gawk at the site of two men falling to their presumed death from the roof of Burger Giant.

"We've got to get out of here, Mr. Lang!" said Eddie to the once-again-unconscious man, as he hoisted him over his shoulder.

"We're OK!" Eddie declared to the openmouthed crowd of onlookers. "My friend is just tired! From being on the roof!"

Eddie smiled in what he hoped was a reassuring manner and took off running. He ended up running around in circles in the parking lot for a good five minutes, with the hapless unconscious man draped over his shoulder, because he couldn't remember where he had parked the BMW. Eventually he found it, stuffed the small black man into the passenger seat, and drove off.

He couldn't wait to get back to Katie Midford's house and show Cody that he had recovered her father from his own grave, a bit bunged up but definitely alive. "Cody is going to be so happy you're alive, Mr. Lang. She's really great, by the way. Beautiful girl. Tall, blond and, well, I suppose *feisty* is the right word. I don't mean to be disrespectful."

He glanced over at the small, swarthy man with short, tightly kinked grayish-black hair who was slouched unconscious in the seat next to him. He hardly seemed old enough to have a daughter Cody's age. Nor white enough to have a daughter Cody's color.

Eddie reached over and once again harnessed a small amount of interplanar energy to heal the worst of the man's wounds. As the cuts sealed, the man stirred and moaned.

"Between you and me," said Eddie, "I'm pretty good at spotting a narrative thread, but I'm frankly at a bit of a loss as to how this all ties together. I mean, how is it possible that you're even alive, first of all?"

The man blinked and grunted something incomprehensible.

"Don't worry," said Eddie. "We'll get it all sorted out. Cody—your daughter, Cody, that is—will probably be able to piece it all together. She's got sort of a gift for that, I think. Why, she's got this theory about, um, streetcars and Charlie Nyx and the petroleum inferiority complex that would just blow your mind. I mean, I'm not sure I get all the nuances, but Cody…"

"Cody?" the man groaned softly, holding his hand to the bruise on his head. "Who is Cody?"

"Oh, no!" exclaimed Eddie, turning the corner onto Katie Midford's street. "You have amnesia! Do you remember your name?"

"Of course," said the man. "Jacob. Jacob Slater. Who the hell are you?"

"Hmm," said Eddie, concerned. "Let's try for best three out of five. Do you know what year it is?"

"I've got some idea," replied Jacob. "But before I let you in on that little secret, why don't you tell me who you are and what you have to do with all of this."

"All of what?" Eddie asked.

"You know, the CCD and the…" It occurred to Jacob that as an employee of the FBI, he was bound by Bureau protocol and a confidentiality agreement he had signed when he started this assignment. He had no idea whether these bonds extended to his knowledge of a secret particle accelerator beneath Los Angeles, but he figured it would be wise to err on the side of caution.

"What's a CCD?" Eddie asked. "I just went to see your grave because Cody said...I mean, your daughter Cody, she said that you died a thousand years to the day after Saint Culain, and I thought that it was a strange—"

"I don't have a daughter," said Jacob.

"Hmmm," said Eddie. "Wait, so you're not Colin Lang?"

"Who?"

"Colin Lang!" Eddie exclaimed. "That was his grave you just popped out of!"

"Grave?" Jacob asked. "I wasn't in a grave." He thought for a moment. "Was I?"

Eddie nodded. "I can see how you would be confused. They buried you in a strip mall."

"Look," said Jacob. "I wasn't buried. I'm not dead. And I'm not this Colin Lang, whoever that is. My name is Jacob Slater. I work for the FBI. The last thing I remember was being in a tunnel under some church. Now are you going to tell me who you are and what's going on here?"

Eddie nodded. "Sure," he said. "My name's Ederatz. Eddie for short." He paused and bit his lip before going on. He had to take this man's word for it that he wasn't Colin Lang. But did it really matter who he was? Normally Eddie wouldn't tell someone he had just met who he really was, but Jacob had a disarming way about him. He possessed a sort of pained earnestness that one only found in mortals, and only a very few mortals at that. Besides, Eddie's quest for the seventh Charlie Nyx book had led him directly to Jacob. If Jacob knew something about the final book, then there was no telling what else he knew. Maybe he was already fully aware who Eddie was, and he was simply testing him with these questions. Eddie didn't dare risk lying.

He continued, "I used to work for the Mundane Observation Corps. The seraphim had me assigned to report on the decline of the Ottoman Empire, but I was stuck in Cork. I made a deal with a cherub named Gamaliel to get extracted from this plane by misleading Harry Giddings about the Apocalypse, but that plan fell through with the implosion in Anaheim, so when this chick from the Finch Publishing Group came to me, looking for the seventh Charlie Nyx book, I figured—"

"The *what* in Anaheim?" Jacob interjected.

"Huh?" replied Eddie.

"What did you say happened in Anaheim?"

Eddie's brow furrowed. "You haven't heard about the Anaheim Event? It's been all over the news for six weeks. Where have you been, under a rock?"

Jacob gritted his teeth. "I know about the Anaheim Event," he said. "I want to know what *you* know about it. What hasn't been on the news."

"Oh," said Eddie. "Well, let's see. The implosion was the work of a cherub named Izbazel, a servant of Lucifer. He was trying to kill Karl Grissom, the Antichrist. Slight overkill, if you ask me, using an anti-bomb to implode a stadium full of people. And the clincher is, he missed! Karl got away and is safely ensconced on the Infernal Plane."

Jacob's mind did its best to remove the patently absurd parts of this account and ended up holding onto only "implosion" and "anti-bomb." It occurred to him that he would have dismissed these two words as well if he hadn't used them himself in an official briefing only a few hours earlier.

"How did you know it was an implosion?" he asked.

"Oh, the M.O.C. knows everything," said Eddie. "I mean, eventually. Sometimes it takes them a while to piece everything together, but it's pretty much common knowledge what happened in Anaheim."

"Common knowledge," repeated Jacob dimly.

"Oh," said Eddie, "Not on Earth. You mortals are still in the dark, as usual. But in Heaven, everybody knows about the implosion. OK, we're here."

Eddie had pulled the BMW into Katie Midford's driveway.

"Where is here?" asked Jacob, rubbing his head and peering out the window at the palatial residence.

"Katie Midford's house," said Eddie.

Jacob started, "OK, well, I think I'll just call a cab and…" He trailed off as he noticed the statuesque young blond who had just emerged from the front door. His heart quickened. "Who…is that?" he asked.

"That's Cody," said Eddie. "So she's not your daughter?"

Jacob shook his head slowly. "God, I hope not," he said.

Eddie exited the car and Jacob followed.

"Who's the runt?" asked Cody, as they approached.

"Well," replied Eddie, "he's not your father, if that's what you're thinking."

TWENTY-THREE

Once Horace Finch was safely at his residence within the Eden Two dome, he locked the doors, shuttered the windows, and then set about summoning a demon.

Summoning a demon is neither as simple nor as difficult as is often portrayed in popular media. The actual summoning process is straightforward: you simply draw a sigil representing the demon's name on a flat surface[9] and then repeat the demon's name several times.

The difficult part is actually getting the requested demon to answer. These days nearly all demons have summoner ID, which allows them to determine who is attempting to summon them, and they tend to ignore unsolicited summonings. Additionally, many demons are on Lucifer's official Do Not Summon list, and attempting to summon them may incur the wrath of the Infernal Communications Commission.

Finch, however, had had contact with this particular demon in the past, and had some reason to believe that he would pick up. In point of fact, his "demon" was still technically classified as an

---

9 Sand is recommended over more permanent media such as spray paint, because you run the risk of irritating the demon by not adequately "hanging up" after the call if you are unable to completely erase the sigil. The demon may hear a faint buzzing sound for days after the summoning, and in extreme cases may wreak vengeance upon you for this annoyance to the ninth generation. Also, sand is generally cheaper.

angel, but that would be rectified when Heaven found out what this particular angel had been up to. Merely responding to a summoning was a severe breach of Heavenly protocol; angels were not allowed any contact with humans that hadn't been approved through the proper channels.

After several repetitions of the name, a ghostlike image appeared above the sigil.

"What is it, Finch? I've got a lot of work to do here."

"I apologize, my lord," said Finch. "I thought you would want to know. *I found it.*"

"You found it? The apple?"

"Indeed," said Finch. "After thirty years of searching, I finally found it! And right in my own backyard, of all places!"

"Didn't I tell you?" said the figure. "It was between the two streams, just as the prophecy foretold."

"Yes, exactly," said Finch. "I had been looking in the wrong place the whole time. The two streams weren't the Tigris and the Euphrates after all. They were—"

"Yes, yes, I know," said the figure. "Just as I told you. Everything is in place. Have you taken care of the CCD in Los Angeles?"

"I have, my lord," said Finch. "Blew the whole business to kingdom come. Even if those fools in Anaheim manage to dig down to the tunnels before the new CCD is up and running, they will find nothing but rubble. Nothing to connect Los Angeles to me or the Order."

"Good. How goes the problem with your scientist?"

"He's still resisting," said Finch. "But I think I can change his mind. If not, I've got a backup plan."

"Someone else to activate the CCD? I thought there was only one person on Earth who was familiar enough with the design."

"So did I," said Finch. "But it turns out there may be one more. A man named Jacob Slater, who studied under Alistair Breem. He seems to know quite a bit about the CCD. In fact, he was apparently in the CCD shortly before we destroyed it. Our agents reported that he only escaped because he had some help. Supernatural help."

"Angels?"

"One angel, at least," said Finch. "That's the main reason I'm calling. I have every confidence in my operatives, but even my best men are no match for an angel. I'm going to need some help retrieving Slater."

"Say no more," said the figure. "I will take care of it. My minions will deliver this Jacob Slater into your hands."

"Excellent," said the Finch, rubbing his hands together. "Soon the secrets of the Universe will be ours!"

TWENTY-FOUR

Christine took the first flight back to Los Angeles. She had debated trying to find Finch at the Eden Two site, but she would have had to charter a flight to get there and she had no guarantee Finch would be there. And even if he were, what would she do, knock on the door and ask for her apple back? Finch must have some idea what the apple was; otherwise, why would he have stolen it and disappeared like that? No, if she was going to keep him from doing something stupid or malicious with the anti-bomb, she needed to pull rank on Horace Finch. She needed angels on her side. For the first time she found herself hoping the interplanar portal in her breakfast nook was still working. If it was, she could find her way to the planeport and maybe get a hold of Uzziel or someone else in the Heavenly bureaucracy who would know what to do about the missing anti-bomb.

She took a cab from LAX to her condo in Glendale. It was unrealistic, she knew, to expect that she could get away with never setting foot in the ill-fated condo again, but she hoped to at least make it to Labor Day, when she would need her fall wardrobe. She stood in front of the door, took a deep breath, and opened the door. She was unprepared for what she found inside.

"Hi!" shouted a small, wiry man from the kitchen. "Man, am I glad to see you. Did you get ketchup?"

Christine stood dumbly in the doorway. She shook her head.

"Oh, and before I forget," said the man, "your sandwich grill appears to be missing. I've looked *everywhere*."

Another man, who had been sitting at the table in Christine's breakfast nook reading her newspaper, stood up and approached her with his hand extended. "Sorry about my dumbass friend," he said. "He's not the brightest angel in the choir." He shook Christine's hand. "I'm Ramiel," he said. "The idiot eating all of your SpaghettiOs is Nisroc."

Nisroc waved politely from the kitchen. "I forget," he said. "Microwave first or can opener first?"

"Can opener, you moron. And use a friggin' bowl this time. I swear to God, you're going to burn this place down yet. Pardon my French." Ramiel was slightly taller than Nisroc, and he sported the thick-necked, crew-cutted look of a high school wrestler. Christine instantly hated him. She wasn't as certain about Nisroc; he seemed well-meaning if a little dim.

She was so shocked by their unapologetic presence in her condo that she forgot to be upset at the intrusion. "You're angels," she said at last. "What are you doing here?"

"It's not by choice, I'll tell you that," Ramiel said. "What a dump. The only selling point of the whole place is the linoleum."

Sure enough, the linoleum remained in the breakfast nook, looking as pleasant and innocuous as the last time Christine saw it. It really was a welcoming pattern, she thought.

"The portal," she said flatly. "It's still here."

"Well of course it's still here," Ramiel replied. "Do you know how convenient it is to have a portal in the middle of Glendale? Thanks to Lucifer's brilliant scheme, Los Angeles is a twenty-minute commute from the planeport, *max*. The powers-that-be weren't about to mothball such a useful portal."

"You make it sound like Lucifer's grand plan was to improve interplanar mass transit," Christine said. "As I recall, he was trying to nuke this whole plane."

"Hey, you can't make an omelet without breaking a few eggs," Ramiel replied.

"Break the eggs!" exclaimed Nisroc, slapping his forehead with his palm. "I wondered about the crunchiness."

"You still haven't answered my question," Christine said. "What are you two doing here?"

Before Ramiel could answer, Nisroc announced excitedly, "We're being punished!"

"*You're* being punished," Ramiel said. "*I'm* performing a vital function in the service of Lucifer."

Christine shrunk away from Ramiel. "Wait, you work for Lucifer? You're *demons*?"

"*He's* a demon," Nisroc said. "I'm still an angel. Well, I was on my way to becoming a demon, but now I'm doing penance to get my old job back. And don't let Ramiel scare you; he's OK, except before he's had his coffee in the morning. We've been assigned to watch your condo."

"Assigned by whom?"

"Heaven and Hell, respectively," replied Ramiel. "It's a joint mission. We're supposed to prevent any unauthorized use of the portal."

Further inquiry revealed that Nisroc and Ramiel were the angels responsible for the earthquakes in Southern California that had reconfigured the transplanar energy channels, thereby creating an interplanar portal in Christine's breakfast nook. When Lucifer's plan to send an army of demons through the portal to wreak havoc on the Mundane Plane failed, Ramiel had returned to the Infernal Plane and Nisroc had fallen on the mercy of Heaven, claiming that he wasn't fully aware of the gravity of what he had done. The Council of Independent Planes had decided that while they worked out the legal implications of Lucifer's violation of the Apocalypse Accord, the portal should remain open and Heaven and Hell should each send a representative to ensure that no unauthorized use of the portal occurred. As this job consisted of sitting in Christine's apartment all day and keeping an eye on her linoleum, there weren't many volunteers from either side. Eventually Nisroc and Ramiel, who were each in a fair amount of hot water with their respective bosses, were drafted for the job. Neither of them had left her condo for six weeks.

"Also," Nisroc said, "I have instructions for you. From Uzziel."

"Uzziel?" Christine asked. "Mercury's boss?"

Nisroc nodded. "He said to tell you..." Nisroc trailed off uncertainly. He looked at Ramiel.

"Good lord, you're useless," Ramiel grumbled. He turned to Christine. "You're supposed to step on the portal. You'll be transported to the Floor, where you'll be met by an escort who will take you to Uzziel."

"What does Uzziel want with me?" Christine asked.

"I don't know," Nisroc said. "Uzziel didn't tell me. He just came here a few days ago and said that if a pretty woman with brown hair and a nose that was a little too pointy showed up, I was supposed to tell you to step on the portal. That's basically it, I think." He looked to Ramiel again, who rolled his eyes.

"Hmph," said Christine. "OK, I'll do it, not because Uzziel summoned me, but because I happen to have something to discuss with Uzziel."

Ramiel shrugged. "Whatever floats your halo," he said.

Christine took a deep breath and stepped onto the linoleum.

"Oh, one more thing!" Nisroc exclaimed as the portal began to glow beneath her. "Get ketchup!"

TWENTY-FIVE
Circa 2,000 B.C.

A few weeks after the waters began to recede, Mercury stood on a hilltop north of Babylon, overlooking the aftermath of the flood. Tiamat had instructed him to determine the state of the surrounding territories so that she would know how much of the labor force she would have to expend on defense. The deluge had been nearly as bad as Noah had suggested: very few signs of civilization remained anywhere in the region. The Egyptians and Babylonians had survived, albeit with significant losses, but nearly everyone else had been wiped out.

His eye alighted on something that looked a bit like an upside-down hut on a rocky hillside further to the north. As he stared at it, trying to figure out why somebody would build such a bizarre structure, he realized that it was Noah's boat, the *Rainbow Warrior*, having run aground when the hill was still an island. He leaped into the air, soaring toward the boat. It was much farther away than he had thought; as he got closer, he was struck again by just how gigantic Noah's boat was. Had he really built that thing with just the help of his three sons? Noah may be a little crazy, Mercury thought, but he's got to be the greatest carpenter the world will ever see.

Passing over the valley between the two hills, he noticed a pair of large round boulders that looked remarkably like a couple of grazing elephants. The illusion was impressive even before one of the boulders reared its neck, stuck its prehensile trunk in the air, and made a sound like a trumpet.

"Wow," said Mercury, rubbing his eyes. You didn't see a lot of elephants in the Middle East. Presumably this pair came from Noah's boat, but where did he find them in the first place?

Mercury zoomed down to take a closer look. Not far from the elephants were several small garden plots and a smattering of pens holding various domesticated animals. A number of men and women worked at various tasks: chopping firewood, feeding animals, building fences, and the like. A gaggle of small children raced around the encampment, shouting and playing games, their shouts echoing off the hillsides. Up the hillside, closer to Mercury, was a plateau on which rested a number of tents of varying sizes. Obviously the *Rainbow Warrior* had come to rest on the hillside, across the valley and its crew—Noah's extended family— had settled here. They had pitched their tents on the plateau as a defensive measure: the area would be difficult to reach from the rocky hillside above, and any invader approaching from below would have to make his way through a maze of corrals populated by geese, dogs, donkeys, and other animals that didn't take kindly to being disturbed. Of course, they hadn't planned on being visited by an angel.

Mercury landed on the plateau and made his way to the tents. He hadn't specifically been looking for Noah, but now that he had found his camp, he was determined to have a talk with him. The last time they had met, Mercury had been too preoccupied with survival to give much thought to this Noah character, but over the past few weeks he had done some thinking, and something didn't sit right. However eccentric Noah was, it was undeniable that he had somehow known the flood was coming—known it for quite some time, in fact. After all, how long would it take to build a boat like that? Decades, probably. If Noah was insane, he happened to be just the right kind of insane at just the right time to ensure his family's survival. And if he wasn't insane, well, then he was certainly worth talking to. In fact, he was probably worth talking to either way. As hard as it was to believe, this peculiar mortal had figured out—or had been told—something that even the highest tiers of the Heavenly bureaucracy were in the dark about.

As Mercury neared the first tent, he came across a small boy sitting alone on the ground. His legs were splayed at right angles in front of him, and in between his knees sat a wooden crate. The boy was peering between the slats of the crate and occasionally poking something inside with his finger.

"Hey, buddy," said Mercury amicably. "What's in the box?"

The boy looked up for a moment and then, apparently unimpressed with this stranger, resumed his study of the crate.

"Hello?" said Mercury.

The boy made no reply.

Mercury studied the child. He was maybe eight years old, his skin dark with some indeterminate combination of suntan and dirt, his dark brown hair long and ratty. Presumably he was the offspring of one of Noah's sons.

"Should you be out here by yourself?" asked Mercury. "There could be..." He was going to say "wild animals," but he wasn't sure what constituted a "wild animal" to a kid who has just spent half a year living in a massive waterborne zoo. "Anyway, wouldn't you be safer with the other kids?"

Still the boy said nothing.

Mercury kneeled across from him and peered into the crate. Inside was a very frightened-looking rabbit.

"Your rabbit doesn't look too good," said Mercury.

"She's going to have babies," said the boy, in a monotone.

"Oh," said Mercury. "And you're going to take care of them when they're born?"

The boy laughed. "I'm going SQUASH them."

Mercury stared at the boy in alarm. "I'm sorry, did you say you were going to—"

"SQUASH!" the boy squealed. He was clenching a stone in his fist. "SQUASH SQUASH SQUASH!"

The rabbit was now pressing its body as tightly as possible against Mercury's side of the crate. It was obviously terrified.

"Now, look here," said Mercury. "There's no call to—"

"SQUASH SQUASH SQUASH SQUASH SQUASH SQUASH SQUASH SQUASH SQUAH SQUASH SQUASH SQUASH SQUASH SQUASH SQUASH!"

"Stop it!" cried Mercury. "What the hell is wrong with you? Do you know how much trouble your grandfather went through to save this rabbit? What is your name, young man?"

"I'm Canaan and my dad is Ham and he's going to SQUASH you!" the boy screamed.

"I can assure you that's very unlikely," said Mercury.

"SQUASH! SQUASH SQUASH SQUASH SQUASH SQUASH!"

"OK, that's quite enough," Mercury snapped. "Now, we're going to let this poor little thing out of the crate…" He lifted the crate and the boy howled. Canaan tried to grab the frightened creature, but Mercury seized both of his wrists with his unnaturally long fingers and hoisted the boy into the air. The rabbit darted into the nearby brush as Canaan continued to scream.

"Dad!" the boy shrieked. "Dad! This man is hurting me! My dad is going to SQUASH you. SQUASH SQUASH SQUASH—"

"Wow, I bet you're TIRED!" exclaimed Mercury, and suddenly the boy's eyes rolled back in his head and he went limp. Mercury set him down on the ground.

"Good grief," he muttered. If the purpose of the flood was to wipe out humanity's violent streak, then God or whoever was responsible had seriously dropped the ball with this little sociopath. "Hey!" Mercury yelled to the heavens. "You missed one!"

He continued down the path to the tents. As he passed the largest of the tents he heard a voice emanating from inside. Someone with a deep, gravelly voice was singing—loudly and off-key. The song went:

Who built the Ark?
Noah! Noah!
Who built the ark?
Brother Noah built the ark.

Old man Noah build the Ark,
He built it out of hickory bark.
He built it long, both wide and tall.
With plenty of room for the large and small.

Who built the Ark?
Noah! Noah!
Who built the ark?
Brother Noah built the ark.

In came the animals two by two,
Hippopotamus and kangaroo.
In came the animals three by three,
Two big cats and a bumble bee.

Mercury peeked inside the tent. Noah was inside, sprawled naked on a pile of pillows. His left hand held a wine jug and his right hand rested in his lap. He seemed to be performing a sort of puppet show in time with the music, except that he had no puppet, per se.

"Oh, jeez," Mercury muttered to himself, as he closed the flap of the tent. "It's bad luck just seeing something like that." He shuddered and made his way down to the farm area.

"Excuse me," he said to a young man chopping wood nearby, "I was wondering if you could give me a hand?"

The man turned with a start to face Mercury, gripping his axe defensively.

"No need for that, friend," assured Mercury. "I'm unarmed, and I mean you no harm. I'm just here to talk—"

"How'd you get up here?" the man demanded.

"I, uh, walked," he said. "Didn't you see me a few minutes ago? Walked right past you. I guess you were too busy chopping wood to notice."

"Hmm," said the man.

Mercury went on, "I just came by to have a word with your dad, Noah."

"You know my father?"

"Oh, sure. I used to be his gopher."

"His gopher?"

"Yeah. That was our little joke. I'd ask him what kind of wood he was using on the boat, and he'd say, 'Gopher wood.' And I'd say, 'Gopher wood, what's that?' And he'd say, 'Stop asking stupid questions and gopher wood.' Ah, good times. You're probably too young to remember."

"Huh," replied the man, uncertainly.

"Anyway, Brother Noah seems to be, ah, indisposed."

"Oh, hell," spat the man, dropping his axe and wiping his sweaty brow with the back of his hand. "What's he up to *now*?" He stomped up the path to the tents, with Mercury in tow.

"I'm Mercury," offered Mercury.

"Ham," replied the man, without slowing his stride.

"Ah," said Mercury. "I met your son a bit ago. Charming boy." Ham muttered something unintelligible.

As they approached the big tent, they heard singing, even louder and more off-key now:

Who built the Ark?
Noah! Noah!
Who built the ark?
Brother Noah built the ark.

In came the animals four by four,
Two through the window and two through the door.
In came the animals five by five,
The bee came swarming from the hive.

Who built the Ark?
Noah! Noah!
Who built the ark?
Brother Noah built the ark.

In came the animals six by six,
The elephant laughed at the monkey's tricks.
In came the animals seven by seven,
Giraffes and the camels looking up to heaven.

Ham peeked inside the tent, and then slapped his hand over his mouth and bent over, his broad shoulders shaking uncontrollably. At first Mercury thought he was sobbing, but when he turned around, he could see that Ham's face was contorted with laughter. Unable to restrain himself, Ham ran from the scene and keeled over, rolling around on the ground hysterically. He was laughing so hard that he couldn't breathe. Tears poured down his cheeks. His whole body was wracked with paroxysms of glee. Clearly his father's booze-addled, musical puppet show was, bar none, the funniest thing that he had ever seen. Mercury followed Ham away from the tent and stood by, waiting for him to recover from his fit of laughter, but the episode showed no signs of waning. Every so often, Ham would look to be on the verge of losing consciousness, and then take a giant gulp of air and continue laughing.

After about five minutes of this, Mercury began to feel profoundly uncomfortable. He had rather hoped that Ham would pull the curtain on the puppet show and let Noah know he had a visitor—not exaggerate the incident to epic proportions. When a pair of hyenas wandered over to see what the fuss was about, Mercury decided enough was enough.

"Hey!" he said, kicking Ham lightly in the ribs. "Do you feel that this is appropriate behavior, given the circumstances?"

Ham's reddened eyes opened and he gasped several times for air. "You know what?" he said, "You're right! Where are my manners?"

"That's more like it," said Mercury. "Now if you wouldn't mind—"

"I've got to tell Shem and Japheth!" Ham exclaimed, jumping to his feet. He ran back down the path to find his brothers.

"What in the name of…" Mercury mumbled in disbelief. He looked to the heavens. "Really?" he asked. "*This* is the family you decided to save?"

After a minute or two, Ham returned, followed closely by his two brothers.

"Hey," said Japheth, regarding Mercury. "You're the bastard who sent us after those snipe—and stole our dwarf unicorn."

"'Stole' is a strong word," said Mercury. "I *borrowed* your dwarf unicorn."

"Borrowed? So you intend to give him back?"

"I did intend to," said Mercury. "But then he died. And was eaten. By me. Look, let's not dwell on who borrowed who's unicorn, and who intended to let whom die from starvation. The important thing is that we're all alive and well now, and that we've learned from this flood that killed almost everybody on earth that violence doesn't solve anything."

"Hmph," grunted Japheth. "We'll let my father decide about that." He walked up to Noah's tent and peered inside. The singing had ceased. "He's passed out," said Japheth.

"Oh, man, you missed it!" exclaimed Ham. "He was doing this thing with his—"

"What the hell is wrong with you?" snapped Shem. "He's your *father*, you friggin' pervert. Now go get me a blanket."

Ham grumbled something and stomped off. After a moment, he returned with a wool blanket, on the corner of which was written CANAAN.

"What the hell is this?" Shem asked.

"What?" Ham asked. "I'm not using *my* blanket."

Shem gave Ham a smack upside the head. "Go back to chopping wood, dickhead."

Ham sulked off.

Shem and Japheth each took a corner of the blanket and walked backwards into the tent, trying to avoid seeing anything that would scar them for life. Shem tripped over something, crashing to the ground with an expletive. Noah grunted and the two brothers high-tailed it out of the tent.

"OK," said Japheth. "He's covered up. You can go in and talk to him if you want, but I don't expect he'll be in a very good mood."

"Thanks, guys," said Mercury.

"And don't try anything," said Japheth. "We'll be waiting right over here."

"No worries," replied Mercury. "We're just going to have a little chat."

"Good luck with that," said Japheth, with a wry smile. He and Shem sat down on some nearby rocks. "Man, this is getting embarrassing," Mercury heard Japheth say.

"Tell me about it," replied Shem. "Promise me that if I ever get that drunk, you'll cut my foreskin off."

"Damn, brother. What is it with you and foreskin? Sometimes I worry about you."

Mercury entered the tent.

Noah still lay on the pile of pillows, but his genitalia were mercifully now covered. He was holding up a corner of the blanket. Squinting at it, he slowly read aloud: "CANAAN."

"Nice kid," Mercury said.

"Was he in here?" Noah asked.

"Well," replied Mercury. "Actually, yes. He was here."

"Man, that kid gives me the creeps. I think I'm going to curse the little psycho. That'll teach him. God, my head is killing me."

Mercury studied the old man. He looked worn out, like an athletic champion a few hundred years out of his prime. Probably he had spent his whole life preparing for the flood, and now that it was over, he had no idea what to do with himself. Some people just weren't cut out for retirement.

"Here, I think I can help," said Mercury, reaching his hand out to touch Noah's head. "I'm not really supposed to do this— you know, interfere with the natural consequences of excess—but I think I can make an exception for you."

At his touch, Noah instantly brightened. His headache was gone. "Who are you?" Noah asked, amazed. "Hey, you're the guy who took our unicorn."

"Yeah, sorry about that," replied Noah, taking a seat on the ground across from Noah.

"No worries. We barbecued the other one. They're good eatin'. And between you and me, I didn't mind have two fewer horny animals on that boat. So who are you? An angel?"

"Actually," said Mercury, "I am." He wasn't sure why he was being so candid with this guy; there was just something about Noah that made you trust him.

"So you were sent by God to take that unicorn?"

"Well," said Mercury. "God sometimes gives us angels a little leeway in our assignments."

"But He sent you here? Is He calling me home?"

"Uh," replied Mercury. Boy, Noah's earnestness was a double-edged sword. "Not exactly," Mercury went on. "Actually, I'm here for a sort of, uh, debriefing."

Noah clutched the blanket around his waist.

"What I mean," Mercury hurriedly continued, "is that after these sorts of, uh, cataclysmic events, we like to follow up with our prophets and ask them a few questions about their experience, to ensure quality of service."

"Quality of service?" Noah asked dimly.

"Right," said Mercury. Noah noticed that he was now holding a clipboard that he hadn't remembered seeing before. "So first of all, on a scale of one to ten, with one being very unsatisfying and ten being very satisfying, how would you rate your overall experience as a prophet of the Almighty God?"

"Um," said Noah. "I guess maybe a seven?"

"Great," replied Mercury. "And how likely—again, on a scale of one to ten, with one being very unlikely and ten being very likely—how likely would you be in the future to volunteer to be a prophet of the Almighty God?"

Noah frowned. "Um, maybe a four? It's just that I'm a little tired, and it was my understanding that the whole world would be wiped out by this flood..."

"Yes, yes," said Mercury. "We'll get to that. How thorough would you say the instructions you were given were? Again, on a scale of one to ten."

"About an eight, I guess. I had to improvise a bit with the planking on the bow, but other than that..."

"Excellent. And how did God primarily communicate with you? The options here are: A) Vegetation that seems to burn but is not consumed; B) Talking animal; C) Angel or angels; and D) Mystical vision slash voices in head."

"Well, D, I guess."

"Great. And how well was the reason for the calamity explained to you, with one being not very well at all, and ten being very well explained?"

"The reason for the calamity?"

"You know, why God decided to send the, uh...Let's see, flood, was it?"

"Oh. Um, well, I'm not sure. See, I'd have given this one a ten a few weeks ago, but now I'm not sure."

"Go on."

"Well, like I said, it was my understanding that God sent the flood to wipe out humanity, because of their wickedness. But obviously some of the Babylonians and Egyptians survived, so I guess I don't see the point of the boat."

"You did save a lot of animals that might otherwise have died off," reminded Mercury.

"Yeah, I suppose," admitted Noah. "But if people are the problem, I don't get why God didn't just send some kind of plague that only kills people and leaves the animals alone, you know? And why did God create people in the first place? Shouldn't He have known they were going to turn bad? And...can I say something off the record here?"

"Sure," said Mercury, setting down his clipboard.

"Frankly," Noah said, "I don't understand why he picked *me*. Why *my* family? I'm nothing special, and my kids, they can be real assholes, as I believe I've mentioned."

"Oh, I don't know," said Mercury. "They helped you build the boat, didn't they? And they kept it upright even during the worst of the storm. That's pretty impressive. Yes, I'd say that you produced some decent seamen."

"That's nice of you to say," said Noah. "I guess Shem and Japheth are OK, but there's no getting around the fact that Ham is kind of a dick. And that kid of his? Canaan? Seriously, that boy is not right in the head. Of all the millions of people on the Earth, why spare *him*?"

"Hmmm," replied Mercury thoughtfully. "You're absolutely certain God told you that He was sending the flood because of mankind's wickedness?"

"Pretty sure, yeah. He said, 'I am going to put an end to all people, for the Earth is filled with violence because of them. I am surely going to destroy both them and the Earth.' Not a lot of gray area there."

"Hmmm," said Mercury again. "And there was no mention of any specific group of people, or any particular sort of activity that he objected to? Other than, you know, just the general violence and wickedness?"

Noah stared at him, uncomprehendingly. "I'm not sure I follow you."

"Well, for instance, did He mention the Babylonians at all? Maybe a particular building project they were working on?"

Noah frowned and shook his head.

Mercury sighed. He wasn't getting anywhere with this fellow. "All right," he said, getting to his feet. "I think I have everything I need..."

"Hang on," Noah said, standing to face him. Suddenly he was filled with vigor and determination. He was a good five inches shorter than Mercury, but he had a sort of ineffable presence that made Mercury feel like he was being looked down on. "Every-thing *you* need?" Noah growled. "What about what *I* need? How about a pat on the back? A thank-you card? *Something*?"

Mercury put out his hand. "Noah, on behalf of the angels in Heaven, I hereby thank you for a job well done."

Noah folded his arms across his chest and spat.

"See here," said Mercury. "It's not your place to question the ways of Heaven."

Noah regarded him sternly, and then a smile began to creep across his face. He tossed his head back and laughed.

"What's so funny?" Mercury asked.

"What's so funny," said Noah, chuckling, "is you. I have to hand it to you, Mercury, you have succeeded in cheering me up. I demand answers, and God sends me an angel who is even more in the dark than I am. As confused as I am about my place on Earth, I now at least have the consolation of *not being you.*"

"Oh yeah?" replied Mercury indignantly. "Well, for your information, God didn't send me at all. I came here totally of my own volition."

Noah chuckled again. "Sure you did, Mercury. But hey, don't let me keep you. I'm sure you've got lots of important things to do—of your own volition, of course."

Mercury started to reply, but his thoughts wandered to Tiamat. She would be expecting him back soon. He was also late for his weekly report to Uzziel. And he was still no closer to finding out the cause of the flood.

"We'll have to continue this discussion later," said Mercury flatly. Turning to exit the tent, his eyes were greeted by a brilliant display of colors.

"Wow, look at that!" Noah exclaimed.

"It's just a rainbow," Mercury stated. "Water vapor in the sky refracting different wavelengths of light at different angles."

Noah smiled and shook his head. "You know, for an angel, you're not very bright," he said. Then he turned to Shem and Japheth, who stood by expectantly. "Gather everyone around," Noah said. "I've got an announcement to make."

"Oh no," said Japheth. "We're not building another boat, are we?"

"Goodness, no," said Noah. "We're done building boats. Today we start rebuilding civilization. Today is a good day!"

Mercury shook his head and took off toward Babylon. It turned out that Noah was nuts after all.

TWENTY-SIX

Jacob was so exhausted from nearly being blown up and buried hundreds of feet under Anaheim that, although he didn't entirely trust Eddie, he was relieved when Cody invited him into Katie Midford's house for a drink. The three of them sat in Katie's living room, sipping Scotch.

"I'm Cody Lang, by the way," said Cody, holding out her hand. "Actress slash private investigator."

Jacob shook her hand. "I'm Jacob Slater. I'm a blast…" He trailed off, not sure how much he should say.

"I'll be the judge of that," said Cody. "So are you a friend of Eddie's?"

"Um, not exactly," said Jacob.

Eddie interjected, excitedly recounting how he had rescued Jacob from the strip mall gravesite.

Cody glared at Eddie. "You…went to my father's grave? What gives you the right?"

"Did you hear what I said?" Eddie asked, incredulously. "I found him inside of a metal box that just happened to shoot twenty feet into the air from underneath the gazebo marking your father's grave, *while I was standing there*. Between you and me, I've never seen the point of dwelling on fate or destiny, but obviously I was *meant to be there* when this happened. Clearly Jacob here is the key to the mystery of the seventh Charlie Nyx book!"

Cody snorted and shook her head.

Jacob cleared his throat. "Um, the what?" he asked.

"The seventh book! The final book in the Charlie Nyx series!" exclaimed Eddie. "I told you everything I know about the implosion and the Lucifer and the Antichrist, so now you can tell me about book seven!"

Jacob shrugged helplessly. "I'm sorry, I don't know what you're talking about. Who is Charlie Nyx?"

Eddie laughed. "Who is Charlie Nyx! Seriously, it's OK. You can tell me. I was *meant to know*."

"Seriously," said Jacob. "I don't know what you're talking about. I've never heard of Charlie Nyx. You say he wrote a book?"

Now Cody began to laugh—a harsh, bitter laugh. "Listen, you knucklehead," she said, holding out her drink and pointing her index finger at Eddie. "He doesn't know anything. He's just some guy. You were apparently destined to meet the one person on the planet who hasn't heard of Charlie Nyx. Congratulations. You're never going to find that book, OK? Neither am I. We're wasting our time. Now I'm going to finish my drink and then see if I can still get a walk-on part in that shitty Michael Bay movie they're filming downtown."

Jacob forced a smile. "Sorry," he said sheepishly.

Eddie sighed. Was it true? Was his quest doomed to fail? "But if I can't deliver the manuscript," he said, "my career is over. I'll have nothing to do but sit and wait for the Apocalypse. Which probably won't be that long, but still."

Cody threw back the rest of her drink and stood up. "I've got an idea, Shakespeare," she snapped. "How about if you actually *write* something, rather than trying to make your fortune off someone else's work? I hear that a lot of writers break into the profession by *writing*." She grabbed her bag and walked to the door. "Nice to meet you, Jacob. I don't recommend hanging out with this loser for very long. You'll end up just like him."

She reached for the door handle, but before her hand touched it, the door swung open on its own. Standing on the other side were two men. The man on the left was tall, muscular, and good-looking; the one on the right was smaller and had a shifty look about him.

"Who the hell are you?" demanded Cody, her right hand hovering over the opening of her bag.

"Easy, chickie," said the smaller man. "We don't intend you any harm. We're here for your guest." He waved a gun in Cody's direction and she stepped slowly back into the house.

"You," pronounced Eddie coldly as his eyes met those of the tall man.

"Hey, Eddie," said the man. "Finally made it out of Cork, eh? Congratulations."

"No thanks to you," Eddie said.

"You know these guys?" Cody asked.

"I know the linebacker," said Eddie. "Name's Gamaliel. He used to be one of Tiamat's minions. I can only assume his sidekick is Izbazel. Nice to see you boys working together again. Like Sonny and Ricardo."

Cody gave Eddie a puzzled look. "I think you mean Sonny and Cher," said Cody.

"The point is…" began Izbazel.

"No, he means Lucy and Ricky Ricardo," replied Gamaliel. "You know, from *I Love Lucy*."

"Lucy and Desi," corrected Jacob. "Ricky was the name of the kid. The couple was Lucille Ball and Desi Arnaz."

Cody shook her head. "Lucy was her character's name, too. They named the kid after his dad on the show, Ricky Ricardo, played by Desi Arnaz. The name of the couple on the show was Lucy and Ricky."

"Anyway, the point is..." Izbazel said again.

"I wasn't talking about *I Love Lucy*," snapped Eddie. "I was talking about *Miami Vice*. You know, Sonny Crocket and Ricardo Tubbs."

"Ricardo Tubbs?" Gamaliel asked incredulously. "Who even remembers something like that? Not one in fifty people would get that reference."

"He's right," Cody said. "You can't say 'Sonny and Ricardo.' That's like saying 'Batman and Jeff.'"

"Fine," exclaimed Eddie. "Whatever. They're a pair, OK?"

"THE. POINT. IS!" shrieked Izbazel. The room fell silent and all eyes turned toward him. For a moment, he forgot himself what the point was. "Oh!" he eventually said, trying to retain his hold on the group. "The point is this: we're taking Slater."

"Right," said Gamaliel, nodding.

"Me?" asked Jacob. "What do you want with me? I don't even know what any of you are talking about! I never even heard of Charlie Knox!"

"Eddie, do your chocolate bullet thing," Cody said.

"Oh yes," said Izbazel, mockingly. "Please. Do your chocolate bullet thing."

Eddie held up his hands. "I can't," he said. "They aren't letting me get a handle on the energy channels. I can't overpower a pair of cherubim, even if it is Scarecrow and Mrs. Robinson here."

"Fine," Cody spat. "God forbid you pull your own weight for once." She had used the fraction of a second that attention was focused on Eddie to slip her hand into her bag, and before anyone knew what was happening, she had fired four shots, tearing holes in the bottom of the bag. Izbazel and Gamaliel staggered backward. She had hit each of them twice in the gut.

"Eddie!" she shouted. "Chocolate bullets!"

But Eddie, having sensed the break in the pair's hold on the energy channels, had already seized his opportunity. Izbazel squeezed the trigger again and again, but nothing happened. "Damn you, Eddie!" Izbazel screamed.

"Run!" Eddie yelled. "I'll hold them!"

Jacob got up from the couch and ran past Cody into the kitchen. She fired four more shots into the would-be abductors and then followed on his heels. Eddie waved his hand and the couch leaped from the ground and flew toward Izbazel and Gamaliel, pinning them against the wall.

Eddie followed up the couch with an easy chair, three lamps, and a bookcase. He manipulated the mysterious energy streams to hurl every bit of furniture he could find at them. But within seconds, he could feel himself losing his grip on the stream. The pile of furniture exploded into ten thousand pieces, revealing two very pissed-off cherubim.

"You're out of your league, Eddie," Izbazel said. He gave the barrel of his gun a kiss and then leveled it Eddie. "Shoulda stayed in Cork." He fired over and over, emptying the clip into Eddie. Eddie stumbled backwards and crumpled to the floor, unmoving. "After Slater!" Izbazel barked.

"I'm on it," Gamaliel said, sprinting after Jacob and Cody. He caught up to them in Katie's garage. They had gotten into Katie's Porsche 911 and Cody was gunning the engine. The garage door was very slowly sliding toward the ceiling, but when she saw Gamaliel, she threw the car into gear. It squealed backward, the bottom of the garage door catching the convertible canopy and tearing it clear off. "Duck!" Cody yelled, too late to do any good. The garage door clipped the top of Jacob's head and he fell forward, smacking his forehead on the dash. After that, he didn't move.

The car peeled into the street and Cody slammed on the breaks, throwing it into first gear. She punched the accelerator and the car engine roared but didn't move. She punched it again. The car howled, but still refused to budge.

"Whoops," said Gamaliel, striding toward the car. "Looks like a drive train problem. The good news is that it's probably covered by your warranty. The bad news is that this isn't."

Flames shot from the engine compartment.

"Uh-oh," said Gamaliel. "Engine fire. I'd run if I were you."

Cody cursed and got out of the car. "Sorry, Jacob. Nothing I can do." She ran.

Gamaliel opened the passenger door and pulled Jacob's limp body from the car. Hoisting the small figure over his shoulder, he walked back toward the house. Behind him, the Porsche exploded, knocking Cody to the ground.

Izbazel emerged from the house and rejoined Gamaliel on the way to a Chrysler parked down the road. They dumped Jacob in the backseat and then got in the front. Izbazel got behind the wheel and they pulled away, honking politely at Cody as they passed.

"Well, shit," said Cody, pulling herself to her feet.

Eddie stumbled out the front door and made his way to Cody. "What do you think they wanted with Jacob?"

"How would I know?" asked Cody. "I don't even know the guy. I don't know those two demons either, for that matter."

"Jacob works for the FBI, I guess. Seemed very interested in the Anaheim Event. Not very helpful in terms of the Charlie Nyx problem, though. I know, I know, I should just forget about it."

"Hmm," said Cody. "About that…sorry I kind of lost it back there. I may have been projecting a bit. I'm starting to think I'm wasting my time with all this conspiracy stuff."

"No, you're right," Eddie replied. "That book was never going to work anyway. The Finch people have put so many restrictions on it, I might as well just start from scratch. Maybe I will. Hole up in the hotel for a couple of weeks and see what I can come up with. It will probably be shite, but at least it will be my shite."

Sirens wailed in the distance.

"Sounds like a good plan," said Cody. "We'd better get out of here. We're going to have a hard time explaining the gunfire and the exploding Porsche. Not to mention the fact that we're both technically trespassing. We'll take the Beemer. I'll drive."

"Fine," said Eddie, tossing Cody the keys. "I've been running from sirens all day. Ironic, isn't it?"

They got in the car.

"How is that ironic?" Cody asked.

"Because in Greek mythology, the Sirens lured men to their doom. But I hear them and I run away. Ironic."

Cody snorted. "Fucking writers."

Eddie smiled.

TWENTY-SEVEN

Christine found herself back on the miserable gray plane known as the Floor. This time, however, it was even more depressing than the last, as the plane appeared to be completely deserted. The portal was located in a sort of warehouse area; steel shelves packed with boxes containing God-knew-what filled a spacious, dimly lit room. She called out several times but there was no answer. She knew that somewhere, not far away, there was another portal that would take her to the planeport, but even with her impeccable sense of direction she wasn't certain she could find it.

She made her way to a door that she was fairly certain was the one she had followed Nybbas through the last time she was here. Opening the door, she found herself in the cubicle maze that had once been the center of Lucifer's efforts to corrupt humankind. It was completely deserted, prompting Christine to wonder what had happened to the thousands of demons who had toiled away like diabolical telemarketers, tempting mortals to give in to their baser instincts. No doubt a few of them had gotten jobs producing reality shows on TV.

Christine threaded her way through the cubicle maze, with its Formica desks littered with dusty old computer monitors and headsets, trying to retrace the path she had taken before. Let's see, she thought. Left at the "Corruptor of the Month" board, right at the poster of the lone mountain climber selling "PERSISTENCE," left at the cartoon of the two nerds in hell, with the one nerd saying to the other, "Hot enough for ya?" And...I'm completely lost.

She found herself in an unfamiliar array of cubicles, staring at a sign that read: "There is no 'I' in team, but there are two in PERDITION. Lucifer is WATCHING."

Great, now what? she thought. Try to find my way back to the warehouse portal or press on and possibly get even more lost? Damn it, I know it's around here *somewhere*.

She was startled by a voice behind her. "Enjoying your little excursion?" it said. "Good grief, you mortals should be required to wear tethers."

She turned to face the source of the voice, but she realized with a sinking feeling that she already knew who it was: Perpetiel, cherubic escort and kibitzer *par excellence*. The pudgy, near-naked angel buzzed over the cubicles toward her, flapping his small, birdlike wings. "Don't you know the left-hand rule?" he asked, condescendingly.

"The left-hand rule?" Christine asked.

"For navigating mazes," Perp explained. "It would come in handy in a situation like this. Did you know that there's no biological difference between a puma, a cougar, and a mountain lion?"

"Yeah, you told me that one before," Christine said.

Perp seemed taken aback. "Before when? I just got here."

"The last time we met," said Christine. "In the planeport."

"I think I would remember if we met before," said Perp. "Speaking of which, did you know that people are more likely to remember you if you wear the same outfit every day?"

"I did know that," said Christine. "You told me that one as well."

"Really?" Perp asked. He seemed genuinely confused. "You're sure it was me?"

"Pretty sure," said Christine. "You were wearing the same outfit."

"Huh," replied Perp. "Do you know how to make mock hollandaise sauce?"

"I think so," said Christine. "You told me that one, too."

"Ooh!" Perp shouted excitedly. "Can you tell me? Because I've forgotten. This way!"

Perp buzzed off over the cubicles, and Christine did her best to follow him, darting left and right to avoid obstacles in her path. Perp didn't seem terribly concerned with whether she was keeping up; the only way she could keep him in sight was to occasionally shout one of the steps in making mock hollandaise sauce. He would then stop for a moment, say something like, "Stir constantly until thick and smooth, yes!" and then dart away again.

At long last they reached the second portal and Christine collapsed in exhaustion. "Need…a minute," Christine gasped, lying on the floor, covered in sweat. Perp observed her piteously. "I suppose you have a newfound respect for escort angels who work for tips," he sniffed. "Not so easy, is it?"

Christine gritted her teeth. "If the cats aren't sleeping on the radiator," she gasped, "turn down the heat."

"Hey!" Perp exclaimed. "That's mine! You're stealing my tips!"

"Yeah," said Christine. "And I'll keep…stealing them if you… don't slow down and…shut up."

"Hmph," Perp grunted. "Then I won't take you where you need to go."

"Yes, you will," Christine retorted. "Uzziel sent you…down here to get me. You'll be in trouble if you…return empty-handed.

When ants travel in a straight line, expect rain…When they scatter, expect fair weather."

"OK, OK," grumbled Perp, pressing his hands over his ears. "Just stop it! Stop taking my tips!"

Christine smiled and got to her feet. "Good," she said. "Let's go see Uzziel."

They went through the portal to the planeport and then walked to the portal that went to the Courts of the Most High, where Uzziel's office was located. Perp led Christine sullenly across the dazzling, azure-skied plane to a great crystal pyramid-shaped building in front of which a sign announced "Apocalypse Bureau."

"Well, I suppose you can make it from here," Perp sniffed.

"Yes," Christine said. "I think so. Um, thanks, Perp. Oh, and one more thing: I was wondering if you could tell me how to get red wine out of cashmere."

"Ha!" replied Perp. "You and every other mortal!" With that, he zipped away.

Christine walked up the granite steps into the lobby of the Apocalypse Bureau's headquarters and told the receptionist she was there to see Uzziel. After some discussion about whether she had an appointment and whether she thought she could just walk in off the street and expect to see a very busy seraph with a lot of Very Important Concerns to attend to, she was told to take the elevator to Level Four, where Uzziel's office was located. She walked up to a door bearing a golden plaque that read "Deputy Assistant Director Uzziel" and knocked. After a moment, a tall man with a devilish smile opened the door.

"Do you have an appointment?" he asked.

Christine nearly fainted again. It was Mercury.

TWENTY-EIGHT

Eddie and Cody took the BMW back to Eddie's hotel.

"I suppose you'll go home now," said Eddie, as they stood in the Wilshire's lobby. "Move on to the next case."

"Not sure there's going to be a next case," Cody replied. "I meant what I said back at Katie Midford's house. I think my obsession with the so-called 'secret history of Los Angeles' may have more to do with my own issues than anything else. I've seen a lot of weird stuff as a PI, but in the end, none of it ties together. I need to move on to a more realistic job."

"Like acting," Eddie said, with a straight face.

"Ha!" Cody exclaimed, not realizing Eddie was serious. "At least with acting, you're *supposed* to play make-believe. You're not trying to get at any ultimate truth. You just make shit up."

"I always thought that good art was its own sort of truth," Eddie mused.

Cody grinned. "Fucking writers," she said. "I'm going to get a drink." She strode to the bar and Eddie followed.

After they had each tossed back a couple of gin and tonics, Cody announced that she was going to the ladies' room. Eddie nodded and beckoned for another drink. As he lifted the third drink to his lips, a familiar voice spoke behind him.

"You've gotten a bit off track," it said.

Eddie spun around on his barstool, a look of shock on his face. "You!" he gasped.

A balding middle-aged man wearing wire-rimmed glasses and a frumpy suit stood before him. He had met this man once before, at Cob's Pub, in Cork. "How's the report coming?" the man asked.

"Oh," said Eddie. "It's, ah, done, basically. I have it in the car. Do you want to see it?"

"Not necessary," said the man. "I have faith in your abilities. I assume you constructed a compelling story, with likable characters and a satisfying resolution?"

"Well," said Eddie. "I don't mean to toot my own horn..."

"Why not?" asked the man. "Whose horn would you prefer to toot?"

"Um," replied Eddie uncertainly. "I'm sorry?"

"You should be," said the man. "Why are you tearing around Los Angeles trying to find a nonexistent book when you've got a perfectly good one of your own?"

"The publisher wasn't interested in a book about angels," Eddie explained. "They said maybe after the final Charlie Nyx book..."

The man sighed. "Eddie, your book *is* the final Charlie Nyx book."

Eddie scowled. "No," he said. "This is the book about Mercury and Christine and the Apocalypse, remember? The seventh Charlie Nyx book is still out there somewhere."

"No, it's not," said the man.

"How do you know?" asked Eddie.

"Because I wrote the other six," said the man.

"*You* wrote them?" Eddie asked in disbelief. "Wait a minute. Who *are* you?"

"I've gone by many names, Eddie. You probably know me best as Culain. *Saint* Culain if you're nasty."

"What?" Eddie gasped. "No. No, that's...absurd! You were supposed to be..."

"I was supposed to be what?"

"And Culain...he's been dead for a thousand years!"

"Hmm, yes," said the man, nodding. "Every identity has to end eventually. Especially the higher profile ones."

"So...what? You're an angel?"

The man shook his head. "Just a man. A man who's been around for a long time."

Eddie was speechless. Who was this man who had commissioned the writing of Eddie's account of the near-Apocalypse? Where had he come from? How did he know so much? And who was he working for? Eddie's shock was turning to anger.

"You...told me you were above the archangels," Eddie said at last. "You lied to me. You're just...a *man*."

A wry smile crept across the man's lips. "It's true that I'm a man. As to who's above whom, well, that depends on your understanding of the hierarchy of the Universe. The fisherman is above the fish, but it's not the fish who follow the fisherman."

"Wonderful," Eddie grumbled. "Riddles. The fact is, you tricked me."

The man laughed. "Tricked you, yes. The way you tricked Harry Giddings into proclaiming the Apocalypse. Got him killed, too. Along with a hundred and forty-four thousand other people. But I'm sorry, I interrupted your tragic story of being deceived into writing a best-selling novel. Go on."

"I'm not going to sit here and take the blame for that antibomb going off in Anaheim," Eddie retorted.

"You can take the blame wherever you like," said the man. "The hotel has room service, in case you'd like to enjoy the blame in your suite."

"What do you want from me?" Eddie demanded.

"Eddie," the man said pityingly, "I don't want anything from you. Focus on what I've *given* you: a riveting story about the end of the world. I even put the Finch Group on your trail, so you'd have an in when it came time to publish it. What are you waiting for? I thought you wanted to be a writer, not some kind of second-rate muckraker. No, worse than that: a plagiarist. A common thief. I had higher hopes for you, Eddie."

"Hey, Eddie," said a woman's voice from behind them. It was Cody. "Making friends at the bar, I see. Who's the…" She trailed off as they turned to face her. Her face went pale.

"No…" she whispered. "It can't be. You're…dead."

"You know this guy?" Eddie asked. "He's a bit of a pain in the ass. He's been going on about how I'm supposed to publish this book that I…"

"Hi, sweetheart," said the old man warmly. "It's really good to see you."

When Cody spoke again, it was a barely audible whisper, consisting of a single word.

"Dad?"

TWENTY-NINE

Jacob awoke to find himself strapped into a plush leather chair, the hum of jet engines filling his ears. To his right was a small oval window that showed only an endless expanse of blue. The small table in front of him bore coasters featuring the logo of the Finch Corporation.

He could only assume that something truly horrible was happening to him. He had never seen a movie in which a government scientist regains consciousness on a private jet miles above the ocean because his friends had noticed he was getting a little burned out and thought he could use a surprise jaunt to Bermuda. His suspicion that nefarious agents were at work in his present situation was bolstered by the fact that the last thing he could remember was being in a mysterious tunnel hundreds of feet underground.

He sighed and stared out the window. A fluffy wisp of cloud drifted past. This is nice, he thought. Nice plane ride. Nice plane.

"Can I get you something to drink?" asked a uniformed flight attendant who had approached his seat.

"Sure," said Jacob. "Diet Coke?"

"Pepsi OK?"

"It'll do."

The flight attendant smiled and walked away.

Jacob stared out the window some more. My head hurts, he thought. Should have asked for some aspirin.

After a moment, the flight attendant returned with his Pepsi.

"Thanks," said Jacob, taking the drink. "Also, I'm sorry; could I get some aspirin?"

"Tylenol OK?"

"It'll do."

The flight attendant smiled. "Would you like to know where you are?"

"Airplane, right?" said Jacob.

"Yep," she replied.

"Good enough," said Jacob.

The flight attendant smiled and walked away.

Jacob looked out the window again. He didn't see any reason to rush things. Clearly he had been kidnapped and taken aboard an evil tycoon's private jet to be flown to a secret hideout to be used as a pawn in some sort of malevolent scheme, but there would be plenty of time for that.

After a few minutes, an older, balding gentleman in an expensive gray suit walked up and sat down in the chair across from him. He handed Jacob a small paper packet. "Tylenol," he said. In his other hand, he held a brown accordion folder that appeared to be stuffed to capacity.

Jacob smiled, tore open the packet, and downed the pills with a sip of Pepsi. He returned to staring out the window.

"My name is Gardner Vasili," said the man. "I suppose you're wondering where you are."

"Airplane," said Jacob, still absently staring out the window. "The stewardess told me."

"Right, but aren't you a bit curious..."

"Let me ask you something," said Jacob. "Do you know who I am?"

"Of course," said Gardner Vasili. "Jacob Slater. Forensic blast expert for the FBI We've devoted quite a lot of resources to…"

"OK," said Jacob. "I was just checking."

"Checking?"

"Yes," said Jacob. "I wanted to make sure this wasn't a case of mistaken identity. It would be embarrassing if we got to the secret hideout and it turned out that I wasn't who you thought I was."

"What secret hideout?"

"You are taking me to a secret hideout, right?" asked Jacob.

"In a manner of speaking."

"Fine. So you don't think I'm someone named Lane or Lang?"

"No. Should I?"

"No, it's just that I have a vague memory of someone calling me 'Mr. Lang.' It may have been a dream. Also, do you know anyone named Cody?"

"I don't believe so."

"Me neither," said Jacob. "Could I have another Pepsi?" He held out the empty glass.

"Now look, Mr. Slater," said Gardner Vasili. "I have certain things I need to explain to you."

"Knock yourself out," said Jacob, tossing an ice cube from the bottom of the glass into his mouth. He crunched the ice loudly in his teeth and appraised the dapper gentleman who was patiently waiting for the noise to die down so that he could explain whatever nefarious goings-on were in fact going on. Jacob wasn't sure if it was the knock on the head or if he was finally completely fed up with being manipulated by powers beyond his understanding, but he had no interest in hearing the man's explanation. As a scientist and investigator, insatiable curiosity was an occupational hazard, but Jacob had reached a point where he simply didn't want to know any more.

It was also true that he was enjoying being in a position of power for once. Most people in Jacob's position would probably have exploded in anger at being abducted and taken aboard a private jet to be whisked away to a secret lair for nefarious purposes, but explosions were, ironically, not in Jacob's nature. His anger had driven him to show no emotion at all, and his impassivity was clearly bewildering his captor. Jacob knew the feeling: having expected an explosion, the man was greeted instead with an *implosion*, and was at a loss about how to proceed.

"Mr. Slater, if I may..." began Gardner Vasili, as Jacob finished off the ice cube.

Jacob picked up the glass again and made to toss another ice cube in his mouth.

Gardner Vasili deftly swept in and intercepted the glass en route.

"Diet Pepsi, please," said Jacob, with a smile.

"*Mister Slater*," Gardner Vasili began again. "I work for Horace Finch. You've heard of Horace Finch?"

Jacob made no reply.

"Horace Finch is, at last reckoning, the twenty-sixth richest person in the world. He owns the Finch Group, which owns the Charlie Nyx franchise, the Charlie's Grill chain of restaurants, and the *Beacon*, among other properties."

Jacob sighed. Gardner Vasili was obviously not going to leave him alone—let alone get him another Diet Pepsi—until he had fully explained the nefarious goings-on to his heart's content.

"I know who Horace Finch is," said Jacob. "Now can you just tell me what he wants with me so that I can get another drink and enjoy the rest of the flight?"

Gardner Vasili smiled. "Mr. Finch has need of your expertise."

Jacob frowned. "Horace Finch needs a forensic blast specialist?"

"Not that expertise," said Vasili. "Your other area of expertise."

Jacob tried to think what he knew about other than explosions. "Horace Finch needs me to make lasagna?"

"Very funny, Mr. Slater. No, Horace Finch needs your help getting his CCD online."

Jacob's brow furrowed. "Has he tried Viagra? I could forward him some e-mails."

"You don't seem to appreciate the gravity of the situation, Mr. Slater. Playing dumb isn't going to help you. We have surveillance video of you in the Los Angeles collider minutes before it was destroyed. We suspected you knew something after your performance at ACHOO, but when you showed up in the CCD, we knew you were our guy."

Jacob was beginning to think this was a case of mistaken identity after all. They obviously knew who Jacob was, but had completely misinterpreted his actions. Seeing him poking blindly around the elephant, they had somehow come to the conclusion that he was an elephant tamer.

"The HeadJAC briefings are classified," Jacob said. He hadn't yet decided whether it was in his interest to confess that he knew virtually nothing about the "collider" under Los Angeles, so he decided to play coy.

"You underestimate Mr. Finch's reach," said Gardner Vasili.

"Got it," said Jacob. "No Viagra."

"We'll be on the ground in four hours," said Gardner Vasili. "I suggest you use that time to familiarize yourself with the design. We've made some upgrades to the original." He tossed the accordion folder onto Jacob's lap, got up, and walked back to the cabin.

To Jacob's credit, he sat and stared aimlessly out the window for another three minutes and twelve seconds before cracking and excitedly pulling the stack of papers from the folder. The cover page read:

TECHNICAL SPECIFICATIONS FOR CCD-II
CHRONO-COLLIDER DEVICE
WEKTABA, KENYA

Chrono-collider device? thought Jacob. He had done two years of graduate work in physics and had never heard of such a thing. As far as he knew, Wektaba, Kenya, was not at the forefront of research into quantum mechanics.

He paged through the papers but couldn't make heads or tails out of most of it. Particle accelerators, he knew, were designed to create high-velocity collisions between the smallest particles of matter known to humankind. The idea was to observe the way the particles reacted in an attempt to discover the basic principles underlying the fundamental questions of the nature of space, time, and matter. The Large Hadron Collider in Europe, for example, had been built with the intention of testing various predictions of high-energy physics, involving many particles whose existence was purely theoretical. Such collisions could be dangerous; a certain fringe element had even suggested that activation of the LHC might destroy the world.

Jacob concluded that either a great deal had happened in quantum physics since he left the field, or whoever had written this document was further out on the fringe than even those doomsayers. The purpose of the CCD was, as far as he could tell, to isolate a particle called a chroton. The CCD would fire a tightly focused beam of energy at a small amount of matter in an attempt

to free some of these chrotons, and then somehow channel the chrotons into some sort of specially designed receptacle. It wasn't clear from the documentation what this receptacle was, exactly. If he weren't being held captive on an insane billionaire's private jet, he would have suspected that the whole document was an elaborate joke. It was the sort of thing that would have had his old mentor, Alistair Breem, in stitches.

One mystery was solved, however: he knew where the plane was going.

THIRTY

"Mercury, what the hell are you doing here?" Christine demanded.

Uzziel, seated behind a massive oak desk, replied smugly, "He turned himself in."

"Yes, Uzziel," Mercury said. "I turned myself in. Or, to put it another way, you couldn't catch me." He turned back to Christine. "Come on in," he said cheerfully. "Uzziel needs your help to trump up some charges against me."

Uzziel motioned to two chairs facing his desk and they sat. "Trump up charges?" Christine asked.

"Hardly," said Uzziel. "I'm being more than fair with Mercury. I simply need you to corroborate certain elements of the official report having to do with Mercury's unauthorized creation of an End Times cult in Berkeley, his failure to assassinate the Antichrist as instructed, his misuse of Heavenly resources for his own purposes..."

"His own purposes!" exclaimed Christine. "He saved the world! He...that is, *we* foiled not one but *two* demonic schemes to take over the Mundane Plane!"

"Yes," Uzziel agreed, "but the way he went about it was entirely underhanded. And, I might add, he also foiled thousands of years of planning for the Apocalypse."

"Forgive me if I don't shed any tears over that," said Christine. "Forget it, Uzziel. I'm not helping you railroad Mercury."

"You may not have any choice," said Uzziel. "If you won't voluntarily cooperate, the Iscaya can subpoena you and..."

"Iscaya?" Christine asked.

"Independent Seraphic Senate Commission on Apocalyptic Irregularities in the Execution of the Apocalypse Accord," replied Uzziel. "ISSCAIEAA. Iscaya."

"Of course," said Christine. "Carry on."

"Look," said Uzziel. "There's no need to make this into an adversarial situation. I understand the value of what you and Mercury did, but the bureaucracy has to be appeased. We've got to document everything and put the best possible face on it, and maybe if we can find someone to blame, what do you call it...?"

"A scapegoat," Christine replied.

"Right, if we can blame it on those idiots in Prophecy for not reigning in Harry Giddings or somebody in the Mundane Observation Corps for losing track of whoever was feeding him bad information, then maybe Mercury can get by with a slap on the wrist and a transfer to another department. Maybe T and C."

"Transport and Communications?" Mercury snorted. "You'd have me patting down tourists at the planeport? When I turned myself in, you agreed to do everything you could to help me keep my job in Apocalypse."

"Be realistic, Mercury," said Uzziel. "You know I appreciate your talents, but there's going to be a shakedown once Iscaya releases its findings, and without some serious leverage, you're not going to survive the purge."

"Leverage?" Christine asked. "What kind of leverage?"

"Well," said Uzziel, "Anything we could offer them showing that Mercury is a valuable member of the Bureau..."

"Come on, Uzziel!" Mercury protested. "I've got six thousand years of service under my belt. I think you can—"

"I wasn't finished," Uzziel snapped. "If we can demonstrate that you're a valuable member of the Bureau who is able to put aside his own personal agendas for the greater good of Heaven, then we might have a chance of saving your job."

Mercury stared blankly at Uzziel.

"I think," said Christine, "he means that you need to follow orders for once."

Mercury looked sick. "Ugh," he said. "Really?"

"Really," said Uzziel. "Remember, there's no *I* in 'team.'"

"And there are two in 'perdition,'" added Christine.

"Er, yes," said Uzziel. "Unfortunately, I have no assignments for you right now. Everything is up in the air now that the Rapture fell through. And Lucifer's been very quiet since his plot to renege on the Apocalypse Accord was uncovered. Other than retrieving the two Attaché Cases of the Apocalypse, there isn't much to do. And I've already got my most capable agents on that."

"Your most capable agents!" Mercury snorted. "I hope you've got pestilence insurance, Christine."

"I've seen some of your agents, Uzziel," Christine replied. "One of them is in my condo trying to figure out how to make SpaghettiOs. You and I both know that Mercury is the only man...er, cherub for this job."

"You know I'm not one to brag," Mercury added, with a straight face, "but she's right, Uzziel. If you want those cases retrieved safely, I'm your cherub."

"No way," said Uzziel. "My job is at risk here, too, you know. If the Council finds out I've assigned *you* to an important task like this..."

"The Council cares about results," Mercury retorted. "By the time they find out I'm on the case, so to speak, we'll have the Cases back in our possession."

Uzziel shook his head, stony faced.

"What if," Christine asked, "I provided you with some intelligence about another serious danger on Earth…the Mundane Plane? Something potentially even bigger than the Cases?"

"A bigger threat than the Attaché Cases of the Apocalypse?" asked Uzziel. "Like what? I've looked into the reports of M. Night Shyamalan remaking *The Greatest Story Ever Told*, and it's just a baseless rumor."

Christine considered her options for a moment, then spoke. "An anti-bomb," she said. "Like the one that went off in Anaheim."

"Impossible," said Uzziel dismissively. "The anti-bombs have been under constant guard since the Antipocalypse, and they are all accounted for. Well, except for the one that imploded Anaheim."

"Well, you'd better re-count," said Christine. "Because I had one of your little glass apples in my pocket yesterday."

"No, no," said Uzziel. "It may have looked similar to your mortal eyes, but it couldn't have been an anti-bomb. Did it really look just like the ones you saw on the Floor?"

"Well," Christine said, beginning to doubt herself. "It was missing the trigger mechanism at the top. Also, it was a different color. But I'm telling you, it looked just like—"

"What color was it?" Mercury asked.

"It was darker," Christine replied. "The others were sort of a translucent rose color, but this one was more like crimson. It was almost completely opaque."

Mercury cast a fearful look at Uzziel. He asked, "You saw one of these on the Mundane Plane? On Earth?"

Christine nodded.

"No..." said Uzziel again. "It can't be."

"It sure sounds like it, Uzziel," said Mercury. "I don't think Christine would make up something like that."

"What?" Christine asked. "What is it?"

"An anti-bomb darkens in color as it ages," Mercury said. "When it's young, say for the first several hundred years, it's that rosy color. Over the next few thousand years, it gradually gets darker and darker until it's a dark crimson. That's how you know it's, well, ripe."

"Ripe?" asked Christine.

"Yes," answered Uzziel. "What Mercury is saying is that if what you saw really was an anti-bomb, it could detonate at any moment. There's no need for a trigger with a ripe anti-bomb. The slightest shock could set it off."

"Jeez, I was carrying that thing in my pocket while running down the side of a volcano in the middle of a thunderstorm," Christine said.

Mercury winced. "Yeah, I wouldn't recommend that," he said.

"Thank God it's somewhere in remote Africa," Christine said. "At least, it was the last time I saw it."

Mercury and Uzziel exchanged worried glances. "We'd better tell her," Mercury said. "She has a right to know."

Uzziel nodded. He went on, "The other thing about anti-bombs is that they get more powerful as they ripen. A fully ripe anti-bomb is roughly a thousand times as powerful as a young one like the one that destroyed Anaheim Stadium. If what you saw really was an anti-bomb, it won't matter where it is when it goes off. If it's anywhere on the Mundane Plane, it will create a shockwave that will be felt across the globe. Earthquakes, tsunamis, tornadoes...it will make that Anaheim implosion look like a firecracker. Er, an imploding firecracker."

"Then we have to stop it," Christine exclaimed. "We have to retrieve the anti-bomb and get it somewhere safe...some other plane where there aren't any people."

"Yes," replied Uzziel. "But first you have to tell us where it is."

"I'll tell Mercury," said Christine. "Not you."

"Mercury doesn't have the resources to deal with a ripe anti-bomb, Christine," said Uzziel. "Just tell me where you saw it, and I'll dispatch someone to retrieve it."

"No way," said Christine. "I don't trust you."

"Please, Christine," Uzziel chided. "This isn't the time to be bargaining for Mercury's freedom. There are larger matters at stake. Earth itself is on the verge..."

"Yes, Earth is on the verge of destruction. Again," Christine said. "And if it's destroyed, what do you think is going to happen to your precious Apocalypse Bureau? Not to mention Prophecy Division and probably a hundred other branches of the bureaucracy that I've never heard of. As much as you angels look down on us mortals, your whole bureaucracy seems to be built around manipulating and controlling us. When there aren't any mortals to push around anymore, what's going to happen to you?"

Uzziel shifted nervously in his chair. "Well, we always knew that Mundane history would someday come to an end," he said. "We've been assured that when that happens, our resources will be redirected to other—"

"Yes, I'm sure there's some kind of plan in place," Christine said. "There always is. But if I'm not mistaken, your plans all revolve around the orderly execution of the Apocalypse, and this missing anti-bomb isn't part of the plan. If it goes off, it will short-circuit all your grand plans. There's no telling what will happen to you then. Maybe God, or these 'Eternals' that I've heard about, will decide that angels aren't all they're cracked up to be. Maybe He, or They, will just erase you all from existence."

Uzziel was noticeably troubled by this line of thinking. "I'll tell you what," he said. "If you tell me where the anti-bomb is, I'll assign Mercury to retrieve the Cases. I can't have him dealing with an anti-bomb; it's too sensitive. But if I can convince the higher-ups that we're dealing with a crisis even bigger than the missing Attaché Cases, they probably won't make an issue out of Mercury being assigned to retrieve them."

"I'll take it!" Mercury exclaimed, obviously relieved to be assigned to anything other than Transport & Communications.

"You do realize that if you fail," Uzziel went on, "you'll be blamed for any havoc caused by the Cases, on top of all of the other charges against you. We're talking about a whole new level of trouble you'd be in. They'd annihilate you."

"Annihilate?" asked Christine.

"Angels don't die," Uzziel replied. "But they can be annihilated. Wiped out of existence. *Erased*, as you put it."

"Oh," said Christine quietly. "Well, maybe if you have someone else…someone whose wits aren't strained by a can opener…"

"No, I want to do it," said Mercury. "Damn the consequences. I can't let those Cases run rampant on Earth. I mean, think of all the snowmen."

"All right, if you insist," said Uzziel. "But don't say I didn't warn you. Now tell us where this supposed anti-bomb is, Christine."

Christine told them everything she knew about the glass apple and Horace Finch. They had heard of Finch, of course; as one of the richest men on the Mundane Plane, his fame had even reached Heaven.

"It's no wonder we had no record of a missing anti-bomb," Uzziel said. "That thing has probably been sitting inside that mountain for seven thousand years. We had no idea there were any of that vintage left."

"I should have just left it alone," Christine moaned.

"If you had, it would have detonated eventually," Mercury said. "That volcanic eruption would have set it off for sure."

"Yeah," Christine said, "except that I got the feeling we were sort of the *cause* of the eruption. I mean, I know it sounds crazy, but it seemed like the goat sacrifice angered the gods or something. Otherwise, how do you explain the fact that the volcano just happened to erupt during the ceremony, after being dormant for seven thousand years?" She looked at Uzziel. "Unless somebody in Heaven had something to do with it."

Uzziel shook his head decisively. "No way," he said. "There's no chance somebody could have gotten away with an unauthorized miracle of that scale in the current political climate. I've got to get three signatures before I scratch my ass these days. Figuratively speaking."

"In any case," Mercury went on, "it's good you retrieved it. It would have detonated eventually, maybe tomorrow, maybe a hundred years from now. An overripe anti-bomb can be set off by the slightest tremor. Better we know about it now when we actually have a chance to stop it."

"I'll see that it's taken care of," said Uzziel, pulling a file folder from his desk drawer. He handed the folder to Mercury. "Here's all the intelligence we have on the missing Cases. Pestilence was last spotted at the World Health Organization's headquarters in Switzerland. The information on Famine is a little more sketchy, but I'd suggest starting with Pestilence. If we get any more info on Famine, I'll send you an update over Angel Band."

"Great," said Mercury. "Open a portal and we'll grab that baby."

Uzziel shook his head again. "It'll take too long to get authorization for the portal. I'm telling you, the days of opening up a quick temporary portal to the Mundane Plane are over. You're going to have to use the Megiddo portal. It's only a few hundred miles from there to Switzerland anyway. Better get moving."

Christine and Mercury made their way back to the portal that would take them to the planeport. Christine considered returning to the Floor to take the portal back to her condo, but for some reason she couldn't peel herself away from Mercury. It wasn't beyond the realm of possibility that she felt some small amount of affection for him, but she was fairly certain that her primary motivation was her lack of faith in the good intentions of angels. Mercury was certainly clever, but he wasn't the most empathetic cherub; she still wasn't convinced that his idea of saving the world completely jibed with her own. If, on the off chance he were presented the choice between saving all of the human beings in the world or all the snowmen, for example, he might not necessarily make what she would consider the appropriate choice. As for Uzziel, she didn't trust him not to pull the plug on the Mundane Plane tomorrow if he thought it would make an effective Power-Point Presentation. In any case, it seemed to her that at least one human should be around to keep tabs on the angels, and no one else was volunteering.

"So you turned yourself in," Christine said, as they walked. "I wouldn't have expected that."

"Yeah, well, I've been thinking," said Mercury.

"Thinking about what?"

"Oh, you know, angel stuff. My place in the Universe."

"Really."

"Yeah, and I was thinking, I've been playing the system for, like, six thousand years now, getting by on my wits, trying to find a way out..."

"A way out? Of what?"

"Of...I don't know, everything. It's different for angels, you know. You people, you putz around for a few decades trying to figure out what the hell is going, you fail, and then you die. But for us, man, it just goes on and on, you know? It's like one of those movies based on a *Saturday Night Live* sketch. You've got like two minutes of solid material but it drags on for two freaking hours. Except that instead of two hours, it's seven thousand years."

"Mercury, what on Earth are you talking about?"

They blinked through the portal to the planeport without even pausing in their conversation. This interplanar travel stuff was becoming old hat to Christine.

"Immortality," answered Mercury. "It sounds great on paper, but holy crap does it not live up to the brochure. Angels are supposed to find some sense of purpose in their place in the Heavenly bureaucracy, but that's never really worked out for me. So I do what I'm told, more or less, but I rebel in a hundred different little ways. But then it occurred to me, you know, that maybe the reason I wasn't content with my place is that I never really accepted my place to begin with. I never really committed to my job, you know? So I thought, OK, I'll turn myself in, throw myself on the mercy of the court and whatnot, and then do my best to fulfill my God-given purpose."

"Your God-given purpose?"

"Yeah, you know, my job. My place in the Divine Order. You said yourself that I'm the most capable agent in the Apocalypse Bureau. Maybe if I really apply myself, I can get promoted to management in a few hundred years. And after that, well, who knows?"

They turned down the concourse that would take them to the portal to the Mundane Plane.

Christine frowned. "Mercury, it's true that I've grown to appreciate your talents, but honestly, I don't think climbing the corporate ladder is your thing. Ambition for ambition's sake is a dead end. You're never going to find contentment that way. There's always going to be someone higher than you."

"Then what? I can't run forever, and I can't keep halfheartedly committing myself to my job at the Bureau. I've got to have *something*. Some reason to go on."

"Of course you do. We all do. But has it occurred to you that maybe your discontentment with your situation is itself an indication of your purpose, your true place in the Divine Order? You act like your only options are to flout the bureaucracy or to give in to it, but what if you're supposed to do both? What if your existence is supposed to be in the tension between doing what you're told and doing what you feel like doing? I mean, it has to be, doesn't it? If you were just a tool of the bureaucracy, you might as well be a machine, or a robot, rather than an angel. And on the other hand, if you just gave in to whims at every instant, you'd just be an animal, living your life on instinct. It seems to me that for angels, and human beings, too, life is a constant state of tension between the robot and the animal."

"Huh," Mercury said. "So God wants me to be some kind of half-robot, half-animal, like those Transformers that can turn into dinosaurs."

"Yes, or you could remain a complete jackass, like you are now. What I'm saying is that you shouldn't feel like you're not fulfilling your Divine Purpose just because you ruffle the feathers of some Seraphim once in a while."

They had reached the portal to Megiddo.

"Ladies first," said Mercury.

Christine stepped onto the shining pattern, with Mercury close behind.

THIRTY-ONE
Circa 1,800 B.C.

Even after the floodwaters had begun to recede, problems with the ziggurats persisted. On the first day back to work on the almost-finished ziggurat, Tiamat was summoned to the Courts of the Most High for an emergency meeting of the Seraphic Council. When she returned after three days, she seemed irritable but also somewhat relieved. She had suspected (not without reason) that she was being summoned to answer for her numerous violations of the bylaws of the Seraphic Civilization Shepherding Program, but this worry turned out to be misplaced. The Council, it seemed, had bigger problems to worry about.

"Can you believe that?" she asked Mercury. "The archangel Michael abducted by agents of Lucifer. Man, that has got to be embarrassing for Heaven."

"So what happened?" Mercury asked. "Did they get her, I mean him, back?"

"Oh, they got him back," Tiamat replied, evidently not having noticed Mercury's slip. "But there will be Hell to pay."

"Meaning what, exactly?"

"Sorry, it's classified," answered Tiamat smugly. "I shouldn't even have told you about the abduction. Anyway, Lucifer struck a deal with Heaven. I didn't think they were going to go for it, but in the end, the Council caved. I voted no on the deal, for the record. I figured it served Michael right for getting nabbed. The Council shouldn't be negotiating with Lucifer in any case. Although the guy's got balls, I grant him that much."

"Hm," Mercury answered. Damned seraphim and their secret schemes. He had half a mind to tell Tiamat that he knew all about the abduction, but he knew it would accomplish nothing. Better to keep that information to himself.

The real problem, Tiamat went on, was that the overseers of the Seraphic Civilization Shepherding Program had decided that some of the participants in the program were maintaining too high a profile on the Mundane Plane. They were threatening to scrap the program if Tiamat and some of the other angels didn't start acting more like shepherds and less like despots.

"What we need," Tiamat announced, "is a figurehead."

Up until this time, Tiamat's strategy had been to manipulate local princes, often pitting them against each other in an effort to keep any one of them from becoming too powerful. As long as she was the linchpin between the warring provinces, the local rulers were willing to kowtow to her demands—and these days, she didn't demand much other than a steady supply of slave labor to build ziggurats.

Her superiors had evidently decided, however, that this was no way to build a civilization, and she had to admit that the constant bickering between the provinces had grown tiresome after three hundred years. She had been tempted on numerous occasions in the past simply to assert her authority over the whole area,[10] but she knew Heaven would never let her get away with

---

[10] The SCSP charter granted her influence over the Eastern wing of the Fertile Crescent, a narrow but highly desirable strip of land in between the Arabian Desert and the Zagros Mountains, stretching from the Persian Gulf to the terminus of the Euphrates, a few hundred miles from the Mediterranean.

it. What she needed was someone who could rein in the rival princes but still owed his allegiance to her.

They found their figurehead in the form of an ambitious young Amorite prince named Sumu-Abum. Tiamat received an unquestioning oath of loyalty in exchange for her assisting Sumu-Abum in vanquishing the rival provinces and creating a unified Babylonian Empire.

The plan worked well at first: Sumu-Abum focused on military victories while Tiamat continued to build ziggurats. But Sumu-Abum's attempts to unify Babylon were hampered by rumors that he was receiving assistance from the wicked Tiamat. It was Mercury who suggested a solution.

"What we need," he said, "is a redirect. As much as I hate to say it, Sumu-Abum needs to declare his allegiance to Marduk."

"Marduk!" Tiamat spat. "We've almost gotten people to forget about that idiot, and now you want to make our handpicked figurehead the president of the Marduk fan club?"

"Think about it," said Mercury. "Right or wrong, Marduk is popular. He evokes thoughts of a golden age, when Babylon was guided by a benevolent god. And you, well..."

"I *what*?" Tiamat demanded.

"I'm just saying, it's easy to idealize the past. Marduk's not around, so people don't blame him for all their problems. They associate Marduk with everything good that happens, and they associate you with everything bad that happens. What we need to do is convince them that Marduk is somehow indirectly working through Sumu-Abum. That way, we solve the problem of your affiliation with him, and every action he takes is lent an air of divine provenance."

As much as she hated Marduk, Tiamat had to admit it was a sound plan. And Mercury turned out to be right: once

Sumu-Abum started claiming to be an agent of Marduk, consolidation of the kingdom became much easier. After Sumu-Abum died in an unfortunate gardening accident, Tiamat selected a new king, Sumu-la-El. Tiamat stuck with the agent-of-Marduk strategy with great success through five kings. The sixth, however, ended up being a bit of a handful.

"Hammurabi's all right," Mercury insisted. "He just has too much energy."

Hammurabi had, over the course of a few years, conquered nearly all of Mesopotamia, and now was anxious to move into Phoenicia, to the west. Tiamat opposed the idea, as Phoenicia was too distant to be a reliable source of laborers for the ziggurats, and in any case she had no shortage of workers these days. Further, she felt that the need to defend the Phoenician territories would stretch the Babylonian military too thin, making them vulnerable to attack from the Hittites and Assyrians.

"The guy needs a hobby," said Tiamat.

"He has one," replied Mercury. "He collects city-states."

"He needs a hobby that's not going to get Babylon overrun by Hittites," said Tiamat. "Can you get him to take up the lyre or something?"

Mercury sighed. "I'll see what I can do."

The next day, Mercury met with Hammurabi, who excitedly related his plans for a surprise attack on the Phoenicians.

"Surprise?" asked Mercury doubtfully. "I think you may have lost the element of surprise at the Battle of Elam, where you yelled, "Next stop, Phoenicia!""

Hammurabi rubbed his beard thoughtfully for a moment, and then crossed out the word SURPRISE in front of ATTACK.

"Good thing the clay wasn't dry yet," he said.

"Hmm," replied Mercury. "Have you considered your legacy?"

Hammurabi appeared puzzled. "What do you mean? I'm going to take over the entire Fertile Crescent. I'll be the greatest emperor the world has ever known!"

"Well, sure," said Mercury. "But then what?"

"What do you mean, 'then what?' I'll be the most powerful man in the world! I'll be immortal!"

"Mmmm no," said Mercury. "I'm pretty sure it doesn't work like that."

"Well, not literally immortal, like you and Tiamat. But still, I'll be famous *forever*."

"Listen, Hammy," said Mercury. "Talking as someone who *is* literally immortal, you've got to believe me when I say that the point of life isn't just getting more and more and more. Quantity doesn't equal quality. Whether you have all of eternity at your disposal or the entire world at your command, there's no shortcut to finding meaning or purpose. I mean, there's no question that you've done well as the king of Babylon; you're head and shoulders above every other ruler in the area. But what does it all mean in the end?"

Hammurabi frowned, regarding his ATTACK plan glumly. He knew that Mercury was a master manipulator, but somehow it didn't matter. It didn't matter that Mercury probably didn't believe a word he was saying; what mattered was that Hammurabi believed it. What *does* it all mean? he wondered. What *is* my legacy going to be?

"So what do I do?" he asked in desperation.

"I think you need to spend some time reflecting," said Mercury.

"Reflecting?"

Mercury nodded. "You've been all go, go, go ever since you became king. Maybe it's time to just sit and think for a while. With any luck, your purpose will come to you." He added hurriedly, "Just make sure you run it past me before you do anything."

"OK," said Hammurabi. "Thanks, Mercury."

After that, Hammurabi disappeared for three days. Mercury was about to tell Tiamat that he had solved their problem when Hammurabi showed up at his door bearing another clay tablet.

"Check it out!" Hammurabi exclaimed, holding the tablet for Mercury to see. "I call it 'Hammurabi's Code.'"

The tablet read:

WHY CAN'T WE ALL JUST GET ALONG?

Mercury smiled faintly. "Not really much of a code, is it?"

Hammurabi frowned. "You don't like it? I spent three days on that."

"It's a fine sentiment," admitted Mercury. "But it's kind of whiny, isn't it? I mean, it doesn't sound like something a *king* would say."

"Hmmm," said Hammurabi. "OK, let me think about it some more."

Hammurabi disappeared for another three days. When he reappeared, he was bearing a tablet that read:

BE NICE TO EVERYBODY

"Wow," said Mercury. It was all he could do to keep himself from telling Hammurabi to go back to conquering neighboring provinces. "It's a bit more assertive, I guess. Still, I don't think that's the stuff that a legacy is made of."

"Well, hell," grumbled Hammurabi. "Then I just don't know. How about 'Treat others the way you would like to be treated'?"

"The thing is," Mercury said, "I like the idea of a code, but I don't think you're going to be able to do this in one sentence. Think of this as the legal foundation for your empire. You're going to need a few more concrete rules."

Hammurabi nodded, wheels turning in his head. "Got it!"

He disappeared for six weeks.

"OK, check this out," he exclaimed upon his return. He handed Mercury two clay tablets, filled with writing. "Ten commandments!"

Mercury looked over the tablets. "This isn't bad," he said. "I like how you establish your authority with this first one. But I still think you need more."

"More?" Hammurabi asked. "Really?"

"Well, for example," said Mercury, "what if slave strikes the body of a free man? What happens in that situation?"

"Well, obviously you'd cut the slave's ear off."

"Hmm," Mercury replied. "Yeah, see, I wasn't getting that from this. I mean, you know it and I know it, but it's not explicitly spelled out in your rules. Or how about this: A man strikes a pregnant woman, causing her to miscarry and die. Then what?"

"The assailant's daughter is put to death, of course," said Hammurabi.

"Again, not really evident from these ten rules," said Mercury, frowning at the tablets. "Like I said, it's a good start, but if this is supposed to be some kind of code of conduct, you're going to need to eliminate some of the ambiguity."

Hammurabi sighed. "Fine," he said, and trudged away.

This time he was occupied long enough for the workers to make significant progress on the latest ziggurat. Tiamat was giddy with enthusiasm, convinced that they were finally building in the right spot—whatever that meant. "A few more years," she could be heard mumbling under her breath. "A few more years."

THIRTY-TWO

"I can't believe stupid Uzziel assigned us to retrieve the stupid Case of Pestilence," Mercury groused. "Doesn't he realize that we're the A-team? I mean, remember that time we averted the Apocalypse?"

He and Christine were resting in a small park in view of the unimpressive, squat building that served as headquarters of the World Health Organization. A cold breeze had picked up, and above the building, dark clouds were gathering.

"Three hours ago, you were overjoyed not to be escorting tourists around the planeport," Christine chided.

"Yeah, well, that was before I had to carry your ass across half of Europe. We nearly got smoked by those F-15s, you know."

"I told you to stay low over Israel, didn't I?" Christine said. "It's not 2,000 BC anymore, you know. They have air defenses now."

"So I've gathered. Anyway, we're here. What's the plan?"

"You're asking *me*?" Christine asked incredulously. "This is your show. I'm just here as auxiliary support."

"Right," said Mercury. "OK, here's the plan: we go into that building over there, find the Case, and take it."

"Brilliant," said Christine. "Do we know where in the building they're keeping it?"

"According to the intelligence, it should be here on the fifth floor," Mercury said, pointing at a map that Uzziel had provided.

"Security?"

"Couple of guards, maybe," said Mercury. "Shouldn't be a problem. I'll just turn their bullets to chocolate."

"Chocolate? Why chocolate?"

"We're in Switzerland, Christine. Get in the spirit of things."

Mercury set off toward the building and Christine followed. She wanted to yell at him to stop, but surprisingly, she couldn't think of a flaw in his plan. Mercury was right: a few armed guards were no match for a cherub. If the case really was in the building, there was no reason to think Mercury would have any trouble recovering it.

And once they had the Case of Pestilence, they would move on to Famine. War and Death were already back in Heaven's possession, and once Mercury delivered the remaining two, the Apocalypse would officially be averted—assuming that Uzziel did his part by neutralizing the threat of the anti-bomb in Africa.

"OK," said Mercury, as they neared the building. "You'd better wait here. I don't want to take any chances."

"Wait here?" protested Christine. "Why did I even come along, then, if I'm not even going to go inside the building?"

"Auxiliary support," said Mercury. "Just wait here. I'll be back in a jiffy."

Mercury disappeared inside the WHO building, and Christine waited anxiously on a bench some fifty feet from the entrance. Thunder rumbled in the distance, and Christine felt droplets of rain on her face.

Retrieving the Case will be a piece of cake for Mercury, she told herself. On the other hand, she thought, it would have been a piece of cake for *any* angel—a realization that prompted the question: why hadn't it been recovered before now? Uzziel could have sent any old cherub—even that moron Nisroc—to get the Attaché Case of Pestilence. Why hadn't he?

Paging through the dossier, it was fairly clear why the Case of Famine hadn't yet been retrieved. It had been sighted at the headquarters of a small biotech company in South Africa, but had disappeared after the hubbub with the runaway corn. The company, which bore the unwieldy name AfroGeniTech, was privately owned, but was suspected by the M.O.C. to be a front for one of the big Western biotech firms. The section of the dossier speculating on the current whereabouts of the Case of Famine had mysteriously been redacted with a black marker almost beyond coherency, but Christine's eyes were drawn to a brief note in the margin. It read:

EH?

"My God," she whispered, looking up from the dossier. But her pondering was cut short by the sight of two figures striding toward the building. "Oh shit," she mumbled, and did her best to bury her face in the dossier.

There was no doubt about it: it was Izbazel and Gamaliel, two very bad demons. She had been under the impression that the two had been through a falling out, but now apparently they were working together again. When Christine first met them, they had been working for Lucifer, but then it turned out that Gamaliel was secretly working for Tiamat, Lucifer's chief rival. The fact that Izbazel and Gamaliel were together again meant...what? They were both working for Lucifer? Or they were both working for Tiamat? Or, God forbid, Lucifer and Tiamat had teamed up?

The two cherubim passed Christine by without a glance, disappearing into the WHO building. They were evidently not after her. Presumably they were here for the Case of Pestilence. Or Mercury. Or both.

I have to warn Mercury, she thought.

Christine had pulled her hair back for the flight from Israel,[11] which was probably part of the reason Izbazel and Gamaliel hadn't recognized her. She removed her sunglasses from her purse and put them on. Not much of a disguise, she thought, but she didn't have time to come up with anything better. She took a deep breath, got to her feet, and walked boldly to the door.

Pretending to be enthralled by something on the screen of her phone, she went through the revolving door and strode into the lobby. Standing some ten yards directly in front of her, facing the elevators, were Izbazel and Gamaliel. As she came in, their heads turned to face her, and for one sickening split-second she forgot entirely how to breathe, walk, and keep her heart beating. Her mind went completely blank with fear.

But in the next instant, they turned back to face the elevators, and momentum carried her into her next step. Her heart started beating again, and once she had managed to take three more steps without collapsing into a quivering pool of jelly on the marble floor, she started breathing again. Altering her course to avoid the elevators, she walked to the door behind the reception desk labeled "STAIRS."

---

11   Mercury had shielded her from the three-hundred-mile-per-hour winds as best he could, but a cherub flying at top speed can't fully compensate for variations in air pressure. The effect is equivalent to riding in a convertible sports car on the Autobahn.

The door swung shut behind her and she sprinted up the stairs to the fifth floor. She had to get to Mercury before he got on the elevator with the Attaché Case.

The door opened to a nondescript hallway lined with doors marked only with numbers. She recalled from the intelligence dossier (which she had stuffed into her purse) that the case was supposed to be in room 501. She was at 521 now, and the numbers decreased down the hall. Rounding a corner, she came upon the elevators, and it occurred to her that she didn't know whether Izbazel and Gamaliel were simply waiting in the lobby for Mercury to return, or whether one or both of them were on their way up to intercept him. She hadn't had the time or the presence of mind to determine whether the elevator's UP button had been lit up.

515, 514, 513. She ran down the hall, on a quest for the door that read 501. A few yards past the elevators, she heard a sound that nearly made her forget how to walk again.

DING!

"Oh no," Christine gasped. The hall went on for another fifty feet: there was no way she could get out of sight before the cherubim emerged from the elevator.

She tried the nearest door. Locked. She tried the next door: also locked. Behind her, she heard the doors sliding open. Sweat was now pouring down her face, blurring her vision. Looking desperately down the hall, she spied a door that seemed to be asking, "SO?" She wiped the sweat from her eyes and looked again. The door's placard read: 507.

Launching herself at the door, she pulled down the door handle and shoved. It belatedly occurred to her that if the door had been locked, she probably would have knocked herself unconscious, but mercifully it opened. She fell inside and the door swung closed behind her.

For some time she lay facedown on the cold vinyl floor, breathing as quietly as she could without passing out from lack of oxygen. At last she got up and surveyed her surroundings.

She was in a supply closet, dimly lit by fluorescent light. Boxes of staples, Post-it notes and other office supplies filled the metal shelves that lined the walls. One shelf was taken up entirely by metallic briefcases that superficially resembled the Four Attaché Cases of the Apocalypse. Clearly these were not the actual Cases; they were slightly smaller and the corners were more rounded. To allay her suspicions, she opened one of them, finding only a molded foam insert that seemed to be designed to hold test tubes. Presumably the cases were intended for transporting scientific samples. The actual Case of Pestilence was probably still in room 501.

Taking a deep breath, Christine very slowly opened the supply room door and peeked out into the hallway. It appeared to be deserted.

She stepped into the hall, her heart pounding in her chest and her hands shaking with adrenaline, and walked to the last room on the floor, marked 501. As she reached to pull the handle, the door swung open and a tall figure stood before her, holding a silvery briefcase.

"Hey, Christine!" he said cheerfully. "Correct me if I'm wrong, but wasn't one of us going to wait downstairs?"

"Mercury!" she gasped breathlessly. "Gamaliel...Izbazel..."

Mercury's brow furrowed. "Wait, I know this one. List three cherubim, from smartest to dumbest."

"They're...here!" said Christine. "You...didn't see them?"

"Nope," said Mercury. "Nobody up here but us chickens. Seriously, this whole place is full of chickens. It's weird."

"They must still be downstairs," Christine said. "You can't go down there. I think Uzziel set us up."

"Uzziel working with Izbazel and Gamaliel? Seems unlikely. It would be like Sammy Hagar fronting for Van Halen."

"Sammy Hagar did front for Van Halen," Christine said.

"No shit?" replied Mercury. "Well, then we could be in serious trouble."

"What are we going to do, Mercury? If Uzziel has gone bad, you'll have no chance to redeem yourself. He's probably pinning more crimes on you as we speak."

"Hmmm," said Mercury. "Maybe. But we can always go over Uzziel's head. We just need some leverage."

"Leverage?"

"We can't just go to the Courts and charge Uzziel with treason. We need to give them a reason to listen to us."

"The Attaché Cases of the Apocalypse."

"Right. We stick to the plan. We've got Pestilence; now all we need is Famine. We bring those to Heaven and they'll have their matching set back. They'll have to listen to us. Of course, first we have to get out of here."

"Yeah, about that…" Christine said, peering down the hall. "I think I have an idea."

THIRTY-THREE

Eden Two was contained within a geodesic dome constructed of glass and steel, soaring at its zenith to the height of a thirteen-story building. Inside the dome was a rain forest that housed some ten thousand different species of plants and animals. Eden Two was, by all accounts, an impressive feat of engineering and zoology, a phenomenal waste of money, and almost certainly the most elaborate work of camouflage ever devised.

Finch's private jet landed on an airstrip that had been constructed about a mile south of the dome. Jacob was ushered by two armed men into a Lincoln Navigator that sped across an asphalt road toward the dome. The driver parked the Navigator in a garage nestled among several other plain concrete buildings a short distance from the edge of the dome, and the men escorted Jacob to an elevator that plunged more than twenty stories underground. Beneath the floor of the dome, a circular tunnel, some fifteen miles in circumference, had been constructed. The men left Jacob alone in the control room, without explanation.

Jacob experienced a sense of déjà vu. A bank of monitors displayed the views from cameras placed along the perimeter of the tunnels. Below the monitors was a vast array of complex controls.

In place of vacuum tubes and reel-to-reel tape drives there were microprocessors and flat panel displays, but other than these superficial differences, the whole setup was eerily familiar. The only difference between this facility and the one under Anaheim was that the control room here was in the center of the collider. Four doors, one in each wall, led to hallways that branched out in opposite directions to the circular collider tunnel. The collider itself seemed to be identical to the one that had almost collapsed on him earlier in the day. "It's just like the one in Los Angeles," he murmured to himself.

"To the centimeter," said a high-pitched male voice behind him.

Jacob turned to see a small man with a thick head of silvery-gray hair. He recognized the man as Horace Finch, the twenty-sixth richest man in the world.

"Why?" asked Jacob.

"Why what?" replied Horace Finch.

"Take your pick," said Jacob. "Why build a particle accelerator under Los Angeles? Why build an identical one in a remote area of Africa? Why kidnap me and bring me here? Why weren't there any pretzels on the plane?"

"Excellent questions, all," replied Finch, taking a seat across from Jacob. "To adequately answer them, I need to go back about four thousand years."

"Oh," muttered Jacob bitterly. "And I was afraid it was going to be a long story."

"Do you know what a ziggurat is, Jacob?"

"Step pyramid," replied Jacob. "They built them in ancient Babylon. They were probably monuments to dead kings or places to worship the gods, like the pyramids in Egypt."

"Correct," said Finch. "Except for the last part. Do you know what the name *Babylon* means?"

"You know," said Jacob, "I don't mean to be overly critical of your storytelling, but this would probably go faster if you didn't stop to ask me leading questions all the time."

"*Babylon* means 'gateway to the gods," Finch went on. "The founders of Babylon chose that name because they intended to use the ziggurats to connect to a higher plane of existence. The idea was to focus a mysterious form of energy on a portal that would open to the higher plane.

"It was a sound idea, but they failed. Political instability, infighting among the ruling elites, natural disasters...all of these factors conspired to prevent them from finishing the array of ziggurats that would have allowed them to break through the veil of our reality. Some say that the gods themselves intervened to keep the Babylonians from succeeding. You can hear echoes of this notion in the story of the Tower of Babel in Genesis."

Finch quoted: "Then they said, 'Come, let us build ourselves a city, with a tower that reaches to the heavens, so that we may make a name for ourselves; otherwise we will be scattered over the face of the whole earth.' But the LORD came down to see the city and the tower the people were building. The LORD said, 'If as one people speaking the same language they have begun to do this, then nothing they plan to do will be impossible for them. Come, let us go down and confuse their language so they will not understand each other.' So the LORD scattered them from there over all the earth, and they stopped building the city."

He continued, "The Egyptians had better luck getting their pyramids completed, but unfortunately for them they were building in the wrong place. There are only a few places where our reality comes close to overlapping the one above us, and Egypt isn't one of them. The Babylonians knew how close they had come, though, and they handed down their knowledge through the generations, in the hopes that someday their quest would come to fruition. It was clear that building massive pyramids or ziggurats attracted too much attention, but it was hoped that a less conspicuous means would be found to tear open the veil.

"The Babylonian priests formed a secret order, known as the Order of the Pillars of Babylon, to guard their knowledge of the higher reality. The Order eventually became very wealthy and powerful, devoting vast resources to researching the mysteries of the occult—with no success. Three millennia passed by without any breakthrough.

"It was in the nineteenth century that the order finally gave up mysticism and redirected its efforts into scientific pursuits. But after a hundred years of fruitless scientific research, the OPB was about ready to give up science as well.

"In the end, the breakthrough came in the form of quantum physics applied to the work of a little known medieval philosopher called Saint Culain. I won't bore you with the details, but Culain realized that the secret of the higher reality was bound up with the secret of time itself. Culain believed that time was made up of particles he called chrotons. Culain was never particularly respected, and his ideas fell even more out of favor when Einstein demonstrated that time was relative. Before Einstein, people thought of space and time as being a sort of inert backdrop against which events occurred. But Einstein showed that time and space are interrelated, and that they can be affected by events. The idea that space was its own 'thing,' made up of ether or some other medium, went by the wayside, and the notion that time itself was made of particles became even more ridiculous. But I don't have to tell you this; you're a physicist."

Jacob shrugged. "I'm a practical scientist, not a theoretical physicist. But I know the basics. Niels Bohr and Heisenberg and the rest of them came along and pointed out some problems with Einstein's theories. Their ideas give rise to quantum physics, which teaches that at the smallest scale, the Einsteinian rules break down."

"Exactly," said Finch, excitedly. "Basically, everything in the Universe, whether it's energy or matter, is made up of quanta. Light is made up of quantum units called photons. Matter is made up of quantum units called fermions. But then the obvious question is: what is time? And that brings us back to Saint Culain and his chrotons."

Jacob shook his head. "There are no such things as chrotons. I'm aware of the idea of quantum time, but even the nuttiest proponents of it don't believe in your chrotons."

"Nuttiness isn't really a useful attribute for determining accuracy," Finch replied, undeterred. "And the fact is, proponents of quantum time *do* believe in chrotons. They just call them something else."

It took Jacob a moment to realize where Finch was headed. "Gravitons," he said.

Finch smiled. "Exactly. The theory is that space-time is made up of elementary particles called gravitons. But gravitons are simply chrotons by another name. Quantum physicists are obsessed with gravity and frightened by time, so they call them 'gravitons.' It's like pigeons and doves."

"Pigeons and doves?"

"There's no definitive biological distinction between a pigeon and a dove. But if you were walking down the street in Manhattan and you commented on all the lovely doves picking food out of the cracks of the sidewalk, people would think you were a little nutty. Conversely, if you released a hundred pigeons at a wedding, you'd be acting in very poor taste. And yet, from the biologist's perspective, they are the same animal."

"Aren't doves white?" asked Jacob.

"There's no firm rule," said Finch, "Although it's true that pigeons used in ceremonies tend to be albinos. So if you think about it, in addition to representing peace, the dove could double as a symbol for white supremacy. Anyway, the point is that it's all a matter of context. A pigeon is a pigeon, whether or not he's invited to your wedding. Culain came up with chrotons a thousand years before anybody had ever considered the notion of a graviton, so I'm sticking with his terminology. Not to mention that 'what is time?' is a more interesting question than 'what is gravity?'

"Think about it, Jacob! What if there really is something like a chroton, an elementary unit that makes up time itself? In that case, time, rather than being something mysterious and completely out of our control, is just another building block of reality. Time doesn't have to always move forward any more than ice always has to come in cubes. If we isolate the chroton, we control time itself. Hell, we control everything. Once we can step outside of time, we've broken through to the higher reality!"

"Holy shit," said Jacob.

"I know, right?" exclaimed Finch. "Isn't it *awesome*?"

"No," said Jacob. "I meant, 'holy shit, you're insane.' And you still haven't answered any of my questions. Particularly the one about the pretzels."

"I apologize," said Finch. "I will get to your questions. Now as I mentioned, there are only a few places on earth where a doorway can be opened to the plane above us. This is due to the location of what I call meta-energy streams. Where our reality is closest to the reality above us, there is a convergence of the streams."

"This is all nonsense," said Jacob. "There's no evidence of any 'meta-energy streams.' You're mixing highly theoretical physics with mystical mumbo-jumbo."

"It may seem so," said Finch. "But first of all, you have to understand that the term 'meta-energy stream' is just a metaphor. We understand these so-called 'streams' about as well as physicists understood the atom a hundred years ago. When I was in school, I was taught that an atom was comprised of a bunch of protons and neutrons kind of glommed together, with electrons whizzing around the nucleus like planets orbiting the sun. It turns out, of course, that this is a wildly misleading model. But it was people using essentially that model who designed the atomic bomb, so I guess it was close enough for government work.

"Anyway, the point is this: quantum physics teaches us that our own observations of a phenomenon can affect the outcome of a phenomenon. What mainstream physics has not yet come to terms with is the fact that this is true not only on a micro scale, but also on a macro scale. Not only do submicroscopic particles misbehave as a result of observation, entire universes do!

"Within our reality, there are actually multiple universes. Call them 'planes,' for simplicity. Sometimes these planes bump up against each other, and sometimes they even slide over top of one another. This interplanar friction causes a release of energy—well, not energy exactly, but what I call meta-energy. You can think of this meta-energy as holding the different planes together the way fruit is held together in Jell-O. If the Jell-O vibrates, the fruit vibrates with it, and sometimes the vibrations cause two pieces of fruit to collide. Now the question is: what is making the Jell-O vibrate?"[12]

---

12   Contrary to popular belief, the gelatin in foodstuffs such as Jell-O does not come from horse hooves. Horse hooves are made of keratin. Gelatin is made from collagen that is derived from cattle bones, cattle hides, and pigskins. Now you are *that* much closer to understanding the Universe.

"No," replied Jacob irritably. "The question is more along the lines of 'what the hell am I doing here, and why aren't there any pretzels?' Seriously, I don't know who you think I am, exactly, but I don't know anything about parallel universes made of Jell-O. I'm just a guy who analyzes explosions for the FBI. That's it."

"I think you know more than you let on," Finch said. "But perhaps I have strayed too far into the theoretical. The point is that that there is a reality outside the Jell-O. If you could get outside the Jell-O, you could see all of the fruit at the same time, from any angle. All of reality, past, present, and future. You could go anywhere, do anything, at any point in history. You could see the source of the vibrations and conceivably even affect them. You could create new universes or destroy them!"

Jacob sighed. "I don't suppose you can prove any of this."

"Well, of course not," said Finch. "That's the whole point of the CCD, isn't it? The chrono-collider device is designed to instigate a high-speed collision of ions, in the hopes of releasing and channeling chrotons. The OPB built the CCD in Los Angeles back in the thirties, but they never got it to work. A shame, too, after all the work that went into it. Buying up orchards, getting rid of the streetcars, building giant amusement parks as a cover for all the massive machinery and construction…It would have been easier to build it out in the desert, but our calculations told us that southeastern Los Angeles was the perfect site for the collider."

"Because of the convergence of the energy streams," Jacob said dryly.

"Yes," replied Finch. "Er, no. Well, sort of. The streams didn't quite converge in L.A., which ironically made it an ideal spot for the CCD. Two streams came very close to meeting in L.A., which caused a near-perfect balance of the meta-energy. Los Angeles was situated between the two streams the way Babylon was located between the Tigris and the Euphrates. But as I said, the Anaheim CCD failed. And now the meta-energy streams seem to have moved, so that they now cross somewhere in Glendale, sending the whole business out of whack."

"Tragic," said Jacob.

"No matter," said Finch. "The Anaheim collider was shut down decades ago. They never did get it to work properly, and after the 1950s the area was too densely populated to conduct tests there without anyone noticing. So about twenty years ago, we started laying the groundwork for a new collider, here in Kenya. The meta-energy streams are almost as well balanced here as in L.A., and there's the added benefit that the only people within fifty miles of here are primitive tribesmen with almost no contact with the outside world. If you want to conduct secret experiments aimed at discovering the fundamental mysteries of the Universe, this is the place to do it."

"And what do you need me for?" Jacob asked.

"Ah, yes," said Finch. "The crux of the matter. You see, Jacob, I've had a bit of a personnel issue. My chief physicist has unfortunately developed some misgivings about the project, so I need someone familiar with the design of the CCD to activate the collision sequence. That's where you come in."

"Um, no," said Jacob, shaking his head. "I'm not your guy. I haven't studied quantum mechanics for ten years, and even then I was no expert. I never even heard of a chrono-collider before today. I swear to God."

Finch laughed. "Yet you happened to be inside the L.A. collider only seconds before we blew it up. And you happened to be the only one of a team of government scientists to figure out that the Anaheim Event was not an explosion but an implosion. No, Mr. Slater, I'm afraid I don't buy it."

"You don't buy it?" Jacob growled. "You kidnap me, fly me to a secret hideout in Africa, and spend ten minutes spewing out the most ridiculous metaphysical bullshit I've ever heard, and now you've got the gall to tell me that you don't buy the fact that I happened to be in the wrong place at the wrong time? You've got the wrong guy, you jackass. Even if I *could* turn on your damn collider, I wouldn't."

Finch frowned. "Hmm," he said. "Now you're starting to sound just like my last chief physicist. I guess I'll let you guys sort it out. Of course, I should let you know that I only have room on my staff for one chief physicist. The only other position I have open is lion trainer."

"You mean lion tamer."

"No, I mean trainer. The lions haven't been getting enough exercise lately. You'd be helping train them. I hope you brought some better shoes. Anyway, I'm sure it won't come to that. Come with me; I'll introduce you to Alistair."

"Alistair? You mean...?"

"Of course," Finch said. "Alistair Breem, your mentor. My ex-chief physicist. I'm sure he'll be thrilled to see you."

THIRTY-FOUR

Izbazel and Gamaliel stood waiting for the elevator doors to open. When they did, the two cherubim would grab Mercury and the Attaché Case of Pestilence and bring them both to Uzziel, who was waiting for them. Izbazel and Gamaliel had a bit of a falling out when Izbazel found out Gamaliel had been secretly working for Tiamat, but Uzziel had assigned them to this task because of their shared hatred for Mercury.

There was a sound like breaking glass somewhere up above. The two cherubim exchanged anxious glances.

"Go!" snapped Izbazel. "Check it out."

Gamaliel sprinted outside, catching sight of a figure against the darkening clouds, soaring away from a man-sized hole in a fifth floor window. The figure was carrying something square and gray, the size of a briefcase.

"Izzy!" shouted Gamaliel. "Get out here! He's got the Case! He's getting away!"

Gamaliel shot into the sky after Mercury, and Izbazel ran out into the courtyard of the WHO building. While Gamaliel pursued Mercury across the ominous sky, Izbazel remained on the ground and focused a stream of interplanar energy on Gamaliel. With the power of two angels propelling him, Gamaliel could travel twice as fast as Mercury, and soon the two were only a few feet apart.

"You're dead, Mercury!" Gamaliel shouted, grabbing hold of Mercury's ankle. Thunder rumbled in the distance.

Mercury spun in midair. "That's Achilles, dumbass," he replied, bringing the metal case down hard on Gamaliel's head.

Gamaliel howled and released his grasp on Mercury. Lightning flashed not far away, followed shortly by a deafening clap of thunder, as Mercury darted away once again.

Gamaliel chuckled to himself. "You never should have left Tiamat," he yelled after Mercury. "She's taught me all sorts of useful tricks."

"Tell me all about it," Mercury called back, soaring away across the sky.

"How about this one, for instance," shouted Gamaliel. "Mercury rises…and Mercury *falls!*" He clapped his hands and a white flash lit up the heavens.

Christine, standing on the sidewalk not far from the WHO building, looked up in horror as a bolt of lightning traced a jagged path from the clouds to the earth—straight through the metal briefcase Mercury was holding. Mercury yelped in pain and then was silent, falling limply from the sky. He landed with a thud on the sidewalk a few hundred yards away. Pieces of the briefcase spiraled to the ground after him.

Izbazel took off running toward Mercury's figure, and Gamaliel shot out of the sky, alighting next to him. They stood over Mercury's body. Wisps of smoke arose from his charred clothing.

"Had to sacrifice the Case," Gamaliel said.

"No matter," replied Izbazel. "The important thing is that we take Mercury out of play. Let's get him out of here while he's still unconscious. Uzziel will be thrilled, even without the Case."

Gamaliel picked up the body, and the three angels disappeared into the clouds.

Christine, clutching a silvery briefcase to her chest, turned and walked away.

THIRTY-FIVE
Circa 1,800 B.C.

Hammurabi ended up with 346 Rules, 218 Maxims, 412 Rules of Thumb, 86 Strong Suggestions, and 24 Helpful Hints. It took him three years. Mercury convinced him that he had maybe overdone it a bit this time around, and eventually they whittled Hammurabi's Code down to 281 laws.

By the time they were done, the ziggurat was within weeks of completion.

"This is it!" Tiamat exclaimed. "The culmination of hundreds of years of sacrifice."

Mercury nodded. "A lot of men died building all those ziggurats."

"What?" replied Tiamat. "Oh, yes. Shame about the deaths. Anyway, exciting, isn't it?"

"I guess so," said Mercury. "It would be more exciting if I knew what the purpose of the ziggurats was."

Tiamat chuckled. "Well, I suppose there's no harm in showing you," she said. "You're going to find out soon enough anyway."

"Really?" asked Mercury excitedly.

"Yep," said Tiamat. "Come with me."

She led Mercury to the drawing room. She had her servants move the furniture to the edge of the room, revealing an ornate mosaic in the center of the room. "Leave us," she snapped at the servants.

Mercury had seen the mosaic before and had noted its similarity to an interplanar portal, but had assumed that the resemblance was only for aesthetic effect.

"Do you know what this is?" asked Tiamat.

Mercury shrugged. "Looks like a portal, but obviously it won't work. The only place on this plane where the energy channels converge is at Megiddo. Building a portal here would be pointless. Besides, the pattern is all wrong. It doesn't point to anywhere in the Universe."

"True enough," Tiamat. "It points to somewhere *above* the Universe."

"What the hell does that mean?" Mercury asked. "There's nothing above the Universe. The Universe is all there is. That's why it's called the *Universe*."

"I'm not going to bicker over semantics," said Tiamat. "The point is that the collection of planes we think of as the Universe isn't all there is. There's another level of reality, above or outside of all that. The spatial metaphor you use isn't important. The important thing is that it's real. Haven't you ever wondered where the Eternals live?"

Mercury sighed. "The Eternals? Really?"

"You still don't believe in the Eternals?"

He shrugged. "To me they seem like an unnecessary complication of the Universe. When humans don't understand something, they blame the gods or the angels. When angels don't understand something, they blame the Eternals."

"Mercury, *you're* an angel."

"I'm aware of the irony," Mercury said. "My point stands. Who do you think the Eternals blame when something goes wrong? It's an endless ladder of scapegoating."

Tiamat's eyes narrowed. "Mercury, don't take this the wrong way, but shut the hell up and listen to what I'm telling you. See these stones around the edge of the portal?"

Mercury nodded.

She went on, "You probably don't remember, but three hundred years ago, these stones were a murky greenish-gray. Almost black."

"Huh," Mercury said. He did vaguely remember that, now that she mentioned it. Now the stones were a pale rose color.

"The ziggurats," she said, "channel energy that vibrates at a higher frequency than the normal interplanar energy. Call it metaplanar energy. It's undetectable even to angels, but with the right equipment, its paths can be traced. Every ziggurat I build is an attempt to get the metaplanar energy focused on this portal. Unfortunately, the channels are difficult to trace with any precision, and the slightest miscalculation can send them wildly off course."

Mercury's eyes had glazed over.

"Pay attention!" Tiamat barked. "Look, think of it like this: you have a nail. The tip of the nail is stuck in the ground. Balanced on the head of the nail is a large wooden wheel, lying on its side. Your goal is to drive the nail into the ground. You are not allowed to touch the wheel, but you have a pile of small rocks that you may place on the wheel. What would you do?"

"I'd start piling rocks in the middle of the wheel," answered Mercury.

"Right," said Tiamat. "But now let's say you're not allowed to place rocks within six inches of the center of the wheel. Now what?"

"Hmm," Mercury said. "I suppose I'd start by setting two rocks as close as I could to the center of the wheel, counter-balancing each other."

"Fine," said Tiamat. "But let's say you've miscalculated slightly, causing the wheel to tilt dangerously in one direction."

"Then I'd set another rock on the high part of the wheel to balance it out."

"And then the wheel tilts in that direction, because you've overcompensated. Or worse, you've undercompensated, and you have to place another rock near where you've just placed one, but then the wheel will be *way* off balance, so you've got to drop one on the opposite side to counterbalance your counterbalancing. It's not a perfect analogy, but you get the point. It would take a long time, but eventually, if you keep patiently placing rocks, you'll drive the nail into the ground."

"So the ziggurats are the rocks?" asked Mercury.

"Right," replied Tiamat. "And this," she said, gesturing at the mosaic, "is the center of the wheel. Except that instead of driving a nail into the ground, we're breaking through the barrier that separates our Universe from the one above it. When the final ziggurat is completed, the channels will be precisely focused on this spot. Those stones will turn completely white, and this will become a portal to the metaverse. And once I have access to the metaverse, I'll be able to transport instantly to any location on any plane. I'll be able to observe anything that happens, anywhere. For all practical purposes, I will be omniscient and omnipotent. I will rule the entire Universe, and then some!"

"Wow," said Mercury, trying not to let his voice quaver. "I always knew you were ambitious, but I had no idea..."

"I'm going to make Lucifer's rebellion look like a toddler's tantrum!" Tiamat declared. "God Himself will bow before me!"

Mercury smiled weakly. "And I'll be able to say I had something to do with it," he said.

But Tiamat, cackling madly, didn't hear him.

THIRTY-SIX

Christine was exhausted, but the faint hope that she'd be able to get some sleep in the Land Rover was dashed as soon as they hit the road. Maya was about as happy to see her as she had expected.

"...not sure what you thought you were signing up for," Maya was saying, "but you can't just up and leave whenever you feel like it. I don't have time to be driving to Nairobi and back on a moment's notice. I just get back from the Tawani camp, and then I get a call that you're in Nairobi, for God's sake..."

"I know," said Christine. "I'm really sorry, but this really is an emergency. I've got to get to the Tri-Fed facility or...some really bad things are going to happen."

"Really bad things happen here all day, every day, Christine. Living in Los Angeles, you don't really have the perspective—"

"Listen," Christine growled hoarsely. "Have you been to Anaheim? Have you seen the giant hole in the ground that used to be Anaheim Stadium? That's the kind of bad stuff I'm talking about. Except Anaheim was just a warm-up. Think of something ten-thousand times worse than what happened in Anaheim, centered right here in Kenya. That's the kind of bad stuff I'm talking about. Now shut up and drive."

Maya shut up and drove.

Christine had taken the first flight from Geneva to Nairobi, having called the Eternal Harvest facility to arrange for Maya to pick her up. Her luggage consisted of her purse and one checked bag: a metallic suitcase bearing an icon that looked like some sort of protozoan. She had hoped Mercury would be able to get away from Izbazel and Gamaliel, but they had been prepared for the possibility that he wouldn't make it. Fortunately, angels had a tendency to underestimate mortals like Christine. They hadn't even noticed her slinking away with the real Attaché Case of Pestilence.

With Mercury in captivity, it was up to her to retrieve the Case of Famine and…then what? She hadn't had time to think through her plan beyond that point. Somehow she'd have to get back to her apartment, take the linoleum portal to the Courts of the Most High, and then try to find someone in the Heavenly bureaucracy to listen to her—and hope she wasn't too late to save Mercury, not to mention the world.

Maya pulled up to the Tri-Fed facility and honked. Crispin, the pudgy man with the giant head, came out to greet them with a puzzled look on his face. Christine got out to meet him.

"Back so soon?" Crispin asked through the chain link. "I've don't have any more seed. Maybe next month."

"I don't want the golden eggs," said Christine. "I want the goose."

"The goose? I don't have any—"

"The Attaché Case," Christine said.

"The what?"

"Don't play dumb, Crispin. I know it's here. That's where all the seed comes from. After the trouble with the corn in South Africa, Tri-Fed moved it up here, where no one would be looking for it."

"I'm sorry," said Crispin. "I can't help you. I don't know anything about any Attaché Case."

"Fine," said Christine. "Here's what I'm going to do. I'm going to go back to the EH office, call up Tri-Fed, and tell them that a certain employee of theirs at Test Facility 26 named Crispin is selling their top-secret seed on the black market. How do you like them apples?"

"You're threatening to get me fired?" Crispin asked. "You know that if I give you that briefcase, I'm going to get fired anyway." The rate of his perspiration had visibly increased.

"Look, Crispin. Here's the deal: Tri-Fed isn't supposed to have that briefcase. It's dangerous. And I don't mean rusty nail dangerous, I mean *worldwide famine* dangerous. You watch the news, right? You see what's going on with that corn in South Africa. That's the sort of thing you get with these Cases."

"You can't prove that what's going on in South Africa has anything to do with Tri-Fed," said Crispin.

"Your loyalty is commendable," said Christine, "if a bit lackluster. Have you ever wondered why someone would release an unkillable, inedible strain of corn that wipes out every other form of vegetation in its path?"

"They're saying it's ecoterrorism," said Crispin uncertainly.

"Right," said Christine. "And what terrorist group might be responsible for such an insidious deed? SPECTRE? THRUSH?"

"Huh?" replied Crispin.

"This isn't a James Bond movie, Crispin. Terrorists try to sneak onto airplanes with bombs in their shoes and box cutters in their pants. They don't spend tens of millions of dollars and God-knows-how-many years developing genetically engineered strains of corn to wreak havoc on South Africa's farmland."

"OK," said Crispin. "But why would Tri-Fed release a harmful strain of corn? It isn't in their interest."

"I have no doubt their intentions were good," replied Christine. "That's the thing with these Cases. Most of the time they'll give you exactly what you want, but occasionally…well, things will go horribly wrong. I'm sure the scientists working at this facility are super smart and well-intentioned, and I'm sure they think they can weed out the problems, but they *can't*. That's the rub with the Attaché Cases of the Apocalypse. They always cause more problems than they solve."

"Cases of the *what*?"

Christine sighed. "Wait here," she said, and walked to the driver's side of the car.

"Get out," she said to Maya.

"What?"

"Get. OUT."

Maya got out.

Christine got behind the wheel, threw the Land Rover into reverse, and gunned the engine. She slammed on the brakes, kicking up a massive cloud of dust, and then threw the transmission into first gear and gunned the engine again, smashing into the gate and tearing it from its hinges. She got out of the car and trudged past Crispin to the door of the facility.

"What the hell are you doing?" Crispin yelled. "You can't…"

Christine picked up a fist-sized rock from the ground, hurled it through a window, and then spun around to face Crispin.

"Here's the deal," she growled. "You have two options. Option one: you can say that a crazy woman drove her Land Rover through that gate, broke into your office, and took the briefcase. Option two: shoot me. Please decide quickly; I haven't got a lot of time." She eyed the holster at Crispin's hip.

Fortunately for Christine, Crispin was the sort of person who was more than happy to let someone else frame his options for him. Christine had given him two, and for a moment he considered the latter. He *could* shoot her, he thought. Unfortunately, what was in the holster was only a half-empty canister of pepper spray, on account of the fact that Crispin was only one-eighth of a security guard. He pictured himself spritzing the woman with pepper right in her oddly mesmerizing face. And then he pictured the woman going ballistic and chasing him around the compound with rocks in her fists. He started to sweat even harder. He really, *really* wanted to go home.

Crispin stared dumbly at Christine, considering his options. What was the worst that could happen if he gave her the Case? He'd get fired, that was it. They'd send him back home.

Crispin lumbered back to the building. He came out bearing a silvery briefcase. Christine took it from him and walked to the truck.

"What the hell was that?" Maya asked incredulously.

"No time to explain," said Christine. "I need you to take me back to Nairobi. I need to get to Los Angeles."

"Los Angeles?" said a man's voice behind them. "Why would you want to take the Attaché Case of Famine to Los Angeles?"

Maya and Christine spun around. A strange man was approaching from behind the truck. He was tall, with angular features and sandy brown hair.

"Who is that?" Maya asked.

Christine stared, shaking her head. "I have no idea," she said, but she had a sinking feeling that the strange figure was not a man at all.

"Name's Israfil," said the man. "I work for the Bureau."

"The FBI?" asked Crispin. "I swear, I didn't know I was breaking any laws…"

"Different Bureau," said Israfil, winking at Christine. "Christine knows."

"What is he talking about?" Maya demanded.

Christine's gripped tightened on the handle of the Case.

"Hand over the Case, Christine. And don't try any funny business. Uzziel warned me about you."

Christine studied Israfil, trying to get a read on his motivations. Was he in on Uzziel's scheme, or was he just a conscientious employee of the Apocalypse Bureau who thought he was doing the work of Heaven? If he was the latter, then she might be able to appeal to his sense of propriety.

"Uzziel warned you about me, did he?" Christine asked. "Well, let me warn you about Uzziel. Do you know who Izbazel and Gamaliel are?"

"Of course," said Israfil. "Demons. They're both in Heavenly custody, I believe."

"You believe wrong," said Christine. "I just saw them in Geneva a few hours ago. Uzziel's got them doing his dirty work. He assigned Mercury to retrieve the Case of Pestilence but then sent those two to intercept him."

"Ridiculous," said Israfil.

"What if I can prove it?" asked Christine. "What if I can get you the Attaché Case of Pestilence as well?"

"You know where Pestilence is?" asked Israfil.

"I do," replied Christine. "I've stashed it somewhere safe. And I'll tell you where, but you've got to do me a favor."

Israfil frowned. "I don't like the sound of that."

"It's nothing illegal," Christine assured him. "And think of it: you'll be exposing a major defection within the Bureau and handing them *both* missing Cases. You'll be a hero, Israfil. Hell, they'll probably put you in charge of the Bureau. Trust me, there's going to be an opening soon."

"All right, what is it?" Israfil asked.

"I need you to set up a meeting for me."

"A meeting?" asked Israfil. "With whom?"

"With a friend of mine," said Christine. She pulled a card from her pocket and handed it to Israfil. It bore the seal of the Archangel Michael.

THIRTY-SEVEN

Eddie, Cody, and the mysterious man claiming to be Saint Culain had retired to Eddie's suite. Cody had nearly fainted at the sight of the man, and Eddie decided that whatever was going to happen next, it would probably just as well happen in the comfort of his private suite than in a hotel bar. In any case, whoever the mystery man really was, Eddie was certain he was human—which meant that he was no match for a cherub, if it came down to fisticuffs. Whoever he was, Eddie wasn't going to let him lay a finger on Cody.

Once Cody was resting comfortably on the couch, Eddie sat in a plush chair across from her. "So let me get this straight," He said. "This guy is your *father*? *Colin Lang*?"

Cody nodded numbly, her face still white. She was staring at the mystery man, who had taken a seat in another chair. He regarded them with a bemused smile on his face.

"You told me you were Saint Culain," Eddie said to the man.

He nodded. "I was. After that, I was Colin Lang. I was a dozen others in between. These days I'm Kevin Baine. I've learned not to get too attached to any one identity."

"How about your *family*?" demanded Cody. "I thought you were dead!"

"I'm sorry about that," said the man. "I have to keep moving. There are...certain factions who would very much like to get their hands on me."

"So what do we call you?" asked Eddie. "Who were you, originally?"

The man sighed. "I'll tell you if you want, but you won't believe me."

"Try me," said Eddie.

"My original name, my birth name," the man said, "was Cain."

"Cain?" Cody asked dubiously. "Like, in the Bible? The son of Adam and Eve? Brother of Abel?"

"That's correct," said the man.

Cody snorted.

"You're right," replied Eddie. "I don't believe you."

The main shrugged. "Call me Culain, then, if you prefer."

"Fine, Culain," Eddie said flatly. "Although I'm not completely buying that either. Now tell me what the hell is going on. What do you have to do with Charlie Nyx and the Anaheim Event and all the rest of it?"

Culain nodded. "It's a long story, and absurdly unlikely, but it's all true, I assure you. You know the account of Cain and Abel from Genesis, of course?"

Eddie replied, "Cain kills Abel in a fit of jealous rage. God curses Cain to wander the Earth, and puts a mark on him so that no one will kill him."

"Hmm, yes," said Culain. "More or less. Except it wasn't a visible mark that kept people from killing me. God changed me. Something about my biology. Made me immortal. Impossible to kill."

"The mark of Cain was immortality?" asked Eddie, doubtfully. "Why would God reward murder with eternal life? That makes no sense."

"Reward!" Culain scoffed. "It was no reward. I was a farmer. It was all I ever wanted to do; all I was ever good at. But God cursed any soil that I worked, so that it bore no fruit. I tried being a potter, but the pots I made were marred by my guilt. I tried weaving clothing, but the yarn snagged and tangled. I found work as an unskilled laborer, but failed even at that. Any enterprise I was involved in would eventually fail. Locusts would eat the crops, or bandits would steal the inventory, or fire would destroy the warehouse. In every case, it didn't take long for the proprietor to determine the source of the trouble: me. If I was lucky, I'd have left town by the time they figured it out. If I was unlucky, they'd beat the hell out of me and then chase me away with pitchforks.

"On the rare occasion that I managed to live in peace with my fellow peasants for a few weeks, *angels* would show up and start harassing me. I didn't know at the time if they were specifically assigned to make me miserable, or if angels just have a special resentment for a human who dares to claim the mantle of immortality—even if it wasn't my choice. Either way, they would ultimately force me to move on.

"They could hurt me, but they couldn't kill me. Nothing could, and trust me, I tried *everything*. Eventually I became a writer, like you, Eddie. I found that writing was the one thing I could do where the mistakes I made were never permanent. If I wrote something and the next day I didn't like it, I would just crumple up the paper and write something else. I got pretty good at it after a few centuries. By that time I had had plenty of time to think about the nature of reality, and immortality, and time… and to research many arcane subjects. I met Pythagoras, Aristotle, Euclid, Augustine, and many others. In what you call the Dark Ages, I spent some time wandering around Ireland, taking on the name Culain. I wrote a number of treatises on the relationship between matter and time. The notions didn't make much of an impression at the time, but Culain attained a bit of notoriety after his 'death,' and was even canonized by the Church. That was my own fault—I tried to stay out of the limelight, but when you survive a fall from the bell tower of a cathedral onto an oxcart full of rotten beets, people tend to talk. I walked away without a scratch, and somebody asked me how I felt. I said, 'Meh,' and kept walking. That's how I became Saint Culain the Indifferent.

"Anyway, not long after that, I had to ditch the Culain identity and move on. I spent several centuries in obscurity. My greatest success as a writer came when I wrote under the name *Shakespeare...*"

"Oh for fuck's sake," Cody spat. "Do we really have to listen to this? Look, I get it, OK? You weren't big on the family thing. I'm over it. You don't have to make up this crazy shit about being Cain and Methuselah and Hemingway."

"Just let him finish," said Eddie.

Cody glared at Eddie. "You're not buying this shit, are you, Eddie?"

"I suspect," said Culain, "that Eddie recognizes the weariness of a fellow immortal."

"Go on," said Eddie impassively.

"I wasn't Shakespeare, exactly," Culain explained. "Shakespeare was a playwright I ran into in London. He needed some help on a play he was working on about King Henry the Sixth..."

"Oh, so you were Shakespeare's ghostwriter," Cody said glibly. "That's *way* more believable."

Eddie interjected, "Many historians believe Shakespeare didn't actually write his plays. Some suspect that Francis Bacon wrote them."

"I suppose you're going to tell us that you're Bacon, too," said Cody.

"It's possible," said Eddie. "We don't know he's not Bacon."

"Well, I did help him with the whole scientific method thing..." started Culain.

"OK, that's it," said Cody, getting to her feet. "I'm outta here. Nice to see you again, Dad. Good to see you're as full of shit as always."

"Cody, wait!" said Eddie.

"It's all right," Culain said. "Cody and I will catch up later."

"Whatever," Cody said. She walked out and slammed the door behind her.

"She always was an impetuous child," Culain mused.

"OK," said Eddie. "Get on with it."

"My tenure as Shakespeare garnered me a little more attention than I wanted," Culain went on, "so I went underground and redoubled my efforts to find a 'cure' for my immortality. At first I had hoped that science might provide the answer, but after a century of experimentation and research, I gave up. The answer always seemed to be just outside my grasp. I then dove headlong into the world of the occult. I met Eastern mystics, attended séances, took part in voodoo rituals, et cetera. I concluded, after some two hundred years, that it was all a lot of bunk. These people were desperate to connect to something beyond the material world, but if there was something out there, it had no interest in connecting with *them*.

"Unbeknownst to me, my dabbling in the occult had piqued the interest of Lucifer himself. One day, as I was about to pack up and leave town once again, Lucifer showed up and offered me a deal. He said that he had discovered the secret to my immortality, and that he could bring my torment to an end: all I needed to do was to write a series of books for him. He gave me a copy of an ancient manuscript that told the story of an orphaned boy who became heroic magician, and instructed me to read it and then write a series of seven books featuring the same character. That was it: write seven books about a teenage warlock and I would become mortal. He gave me a generous advance and even promised to see to it that the angels left me alone so that I could focus on writing. Upon the publication of the each book, I'd get a one-million-dollar advance to write the next one.

"Cody was fifteen years old at this point. I hadn't been around much for her, what with being cursed to wander the Earth and all. Her mother had just died of cancer, so this was a rough time for her. For me, too, of course, but after the first couple of dozen wives, you learn to cope. I promised Cody, though, that things were going to be different soon. The first Charlie Nyx book was due to be published on her sixteenth birthday, and after that, I would finally have some time for her—not to mention a million dollars to buy us a decent house for once.

"I realized after completing the first Charlie Nyx book, though, that something wasn't right. What I had written was more than a book. I knew that nothing good could come from publishing it. I was pretty good at disappearing without a trace at this point, and I decided to take Cody and run away somewhere where Lucifer couldn't find us. But he anticipated my reluctance to follow through on the deal: he kidnapped me and faked my death in a plane crash. He told me that as long as I kept producing Charlie Nyx books, Cody would be taken care of—but that if I ever tried to contact her, she would be killed. Once I delivered the seventh book, I'd be allowed to see her again. And he would live up to his side of the bargain: upon completion of the seventh book, I would become mortal.

"Lucifer let me go, giving me enough money to hole up in a flat in Ireland. After an initial period of defiance, I decided my only option was to buckle down and finish the series. At first I churned out a book a year, but it got more and more difficult with each book—and Lucifer's constant threats didn't make it any easier.

"The Charlie Nyx books, I came to realize, were an abomination. Somehow Lucifer had caused me to tap into something, an arcane power from beyond our own reality, and each successive book was an assault on the very fabric of the Universe. Each time a Charlie Nyx book hit the shelves, the state of the world would deteriorate. Wars, earthquakes, flooding, epidemics, the *Clash of the Titans* remake...things were getting truly out of hand—and I say this as someone who has been on Earth for a *long time*.

"It finally became clear to me how Lucifer was going to deliver my mortality: I was going to die along with everyone else, when the world itself came to an end. This is why you don't bargain with Lucifer, by the way: the devil really is in the details.

"The end came sooner than I expected. After the sixth book, I hit a wall. I just couldn't figure out how to wrap things up. And then the Anaheim Event happened, and I knew the series couldn't possibly be resolved satisfactorily. Real world events had trumped the story of Charlie Nyx. I tried to explain this to Lucifer, but of course he didn't understand. Or maybe he understood but didn't care. All he knew was that there had to be a seventh book—a book that I knew I couldn't possibly deliver, even if I wanted to.

"One night I walked into a dingy pub in Cork, and I saw a man hunched over a stack of papers, writing. Except I could tell that he wasn't a man—I had seen enough angels to be able to recognize one. Curious, I came back the next night, and there he was again. And the night after that, and the night after that. I thought, 'Why is an angel sitting in a pub by himself, night after night, writing? Shouldn't he be out doing the work of Heaven?' I laughed to myself and thought, 'Now that would be a funny story: an angel who has been abandoned in Cork, writing desperate and unread pleas to his superiors to please extract him from this miserable place.'

"And that's when I realized it: the seventh Charlie Nyx book wasn't a Charlie Nyx book at all. Reality had overtaken the story, and now it was time for the story to reassert its supremacy over reality. The seventh book wasn't a Charlie Nyx story; it was a story *about* the Charlie Nyx story!"

Eddie stared blankly at Culain.

"Don't you see, Eddie?" Culain asked excitedly. "There are levels to reality, just like there are levels to the Universe. Above human beings are angels, and above the angels are what you angels call the Eternals. As we near the end of the Universe, all the levels converge. The barriers between the tiers break down and the tiers collapse on each other. That's why so many strange things are happening in the world these days. The earthquakes, the Anaheim Event, the war in the Middle East, the runaway mutant corn in South Africa...the rules are breaking down. The rules of Earth are giving way to the rules of Heaven, and the rules of Heaven are giving way to whatever is above it, and on and on. Everything collapses into a singularity, to borrow a term from physics."

"You've lost me completely," said Eddie. "What does any of this have to do with the Charlie Nyx books?"

"Think of it this way," said Culain. "I am to Charlie Nyx what the angels are to human beings: I'm a mysterious being who exists outside Charlie Nyx's universe, but who somehow controls Charlie's destiny. Mostly my hand is unseen, but occasionally I break into the story to keep the plot moving in the right direction. But

I don't have carte blanche; I can't simply intervene arbitrarily to mold the story to my will. You're familiar with the term *deus ex machina*?"

"God from the machine," Eddie said. "A device that a lazy writers uses to save his ass when he's painted himself into a corner. God basically comes down from heaven and fixes things."

"Exactly!" Culain said. "The problem with deus ex machina is that it destroys the illusion that the characters in the story actually affect their own destiny. If I step in and 'fix' the seventh book so that it goes where I want it to, it stops being a story about Charlie Nyx and becomes a story about me. And that's all well and good, but I don't have the proper perspective to write a story about myself. That's where you come in."

"My head hurts," complained Eddie.

"You see, Eddie?" Culain went on. "The report I commissioned you to write, that's the final book! The story about the story. The levels are collapsing on each other!"

"But then," Eddie said, wheels turning in his head, "doesn't that imply that someone somewhere is writing a story about me writing a story about you writing the Charlie Nyx story?"

"Probably," replied Culain. "And he—or she—is just a character in another Author's story!"

Eddie cradled his head in his hands and moaned. "So when this book is published, it's going to cause the Universe to collapse on itself?"

Culain laughed. "Forget the notion of causality, Eddie. Causality belongs to the world of science, and we're well beyond the bailiwick of science here. What's going to happen is going to happen—or, more accurately, has already happened. Think of yourself as a character in a book that's already been written. You can't *cause* anything."

"Gaaaahhh!" Eddie suddenly screamed, jumping to his feet. "Get out! Get out!"

Culain appeared genuinely surprised. "I'm sorry?" he said.

"I can't think this way!" Eddie exclaimed. "I can't *live* this way! Get OUT!"

Culain got to his feet. "Ah," he said. "Denial. I should have seen that coming. It's part of your character. Good luck, Eddie. I know you'll do the right thing in the end."

"Gaaahhh!" Eddie screamed again.

Culain smiled, and left Eddie alone in his room.

THIRTY-EIGHT

Jacob was escorted by armed guards to the elevator, which brought them back to ground level. The guards then ushered him to a metal door in the base of the Eden Two dome. One of them tapped a code into a keypad at the door and it slid open. They walked into a small, metal-walled room that seemed to be a sort of airlock. An LED display on the wall lit up with a progress indicator, red bars creeping across the screen from the left until they reached the right side. When it was finished, the words BIOSCAN COMPLETE appeared below. The far door slid open and they were hit by a blast of warm, humid air. It had an earthy smell, like the garden department of a home-improvement store.

This is one phenomenally well-stocked garden department, thought Jacob. The contrast with the barren landscape outside the dome was jarring. They hadn't gone more than twenty yards before Jacob completely lost the sense of being inside a structure. The dome's ceiling was seamless and seemed to have been painted a pale azure. It was difficult to tell whether the dome was translucent, letting light pass through from outside, or whether it was artificially illuminated. Very little of the "sky" was even visible, as it was obscured by the mammoth and prolific vegetation. The sides of the dome were covered to a height of over a sixty feet by a fiberglass latticework, to which clung a copious array of vines. A few paces from the base of the dome, massive trees sprang from the jungle floor. The floor of the dome, too, was nearly completely obscured by ivy and exotic flowers and bushes. The entire structure was suffused by a constant buzz of insects and the fluttering of wings, occasionally punctuated by a rustle of branches or a high-pitched call of some strange bird.

A narrow path meandered from the entrance into the thick of the forest. The vegetation blotted out nearly all light, and Jacob wondered that the guards escorting him hadn't thought to bring flashlights. They seemed to have a pretty good idea where they were going, though, and before Jacob had gotten up the courage to complain, he found himself in a small clearing populated by a several bamboo cottages. The guards ushered him to door of one of the cottages.

"This is where you'll be staying," said one of the guards.

"For how long?" asked Jacob.

"For as long as Finch needs you," came the reply. The guards turned and left. Jacob stood for a moment at the door, wondering if he should make a run for it. He was fairly sure he could find his way back to the airlock, but he was less sure that he'd be able to get the doors open. And what would he do if he got outside? The nearest town could be hundreds of miles away.

Jacob opened the door and walked inside. The cottage was simply but comfortably furnished; the generic hangings and décor suggested it was a sort of guesthouse. Sitting on couches in the main room were two men. One of them he recognized as Alistair Breem, his quantum mechanics professor at MIT. Alistair was a tall, wiry man, whose spine was permanently arched in such a way as to give the impression that he was constantly having to stoop to the level of lesser men. He had less hair than Jacob remembered, and what hair he had left was now a dirty gray. Dark rings framed his eyes. The other man was a stranger, tall and lanky, with silver hair.

"Who's the new guy?" said the tall man. "I already called the top bunk. You're going to have to take the sofa."

"Allie?" said Jacob.

"Hello, Jacob. They told me they were bringing in a replacement. I have to admit, I wasn't expecting *you*." Alistair spoke with a crisp, but somewhat indeterminate accent—the result of the Queen's English being gradually worn down by prolonged exposure to Americans, Australians, and Canadians.

"I'm as surprised as anyone," replied Jacob. "How long have you been here?"

"Like, *forever*," said the tall man.

Allie glared at the man. "I've been here for seven years. Mercury got here about twenty minutes ago."

"Mercury?" asked Jacob, turning toward the stranger.

"Hi!" the tall man exclaimed, jumping up from the couch. "Name's Mercury. I'm an angel. "What's your deal?"

Jacob shook Mercury's hand. "Finch seems to think I can get his collider going," he said.

Mercury chuckled. "A lot of men his age have that problem," he said.

"Please," said Jacob wearily. "You're about six hours late with the Viagra jokes."

Mercury sat down, looking a bit put out. He had regained consciousness while being carried over Gamaliel's shoulder down the path to the clearing. Gamaliel had dumped him on the floor of the cottage and left, without explanation. Mercury had spent the next twenty minutes trying to engage Alistair Breem in conversation about something other than quantum physics, which

Mercury understood about as well as Allie understood the infield fly rule.

"So is this chrono-collider device for real?" Jacob asked Allie. "Can it do what Finch says it can do?"

"Reveal the deepest secrets of the Universe?" Allie asked. "I have no idea. What I do know is that Horace Finch is a dangerous socio-path. This was supposed to be a six-week gig for me, consulting on the creation of a physics program at a new multinational African University. Next thing I know, I'm in the middle of the Kenyan wilderness, working on a secret particle collider. When I told him I wanted to leave, he faked my death and told me that if I didn't keep working, he was going to have my wife killed. So here I am."

"That's nothing," said Mercury. "You should hear what happened to *me*. My friend Christine and I went to get the Attaché Case of Pestilence from the Who, but these two cherubim who work for Lucifer showed up and I got struck by lightning!"

Ignoring Mercury's outburst, Jacob turned back to Allie. "So maybe we should just go along with Finch and get his CCD up and running."

Mercury opened his mouth to say something, and Jacob turned to face him. "We get it," Jacob said. "Penis joke. Ha, ha."

This time Mercury looked genuinely hurt.

Jacob went on, without missing a beat, "I mean, what's the worst that could happen? We tear the Universe in half?"

"Hmm," replied Allie.

"That was a joke," said Jacob.

Allie sighed. "I wish I could be as blasé about it. The fact is, there's a reason Finch kept this a secret. Why he funded this whole thing himself and didn't involve any governments or universities."

"Yes," said Jacob. "Because he's a couple of strings short of a unified field theory."

"Maybe," replied Allie. "Or maybe he's just twenty years ahead of his time. I don't know what he told you exactly, but he's planning on doing more than isolating a handful of chrotons. He wants to capture them and control them, like fireflies in a jar. As you know, part of the reason the existence of chrotons—or gravitons, as they are usually called—is so hard to prove is that they aren't detectable by the methods we use to observe other particles. The best that the Large Hadron Collider in Europe can do is to provide very indirect evidence of their existence. And any gravitons they produce only stick around for the slightest fraction of a second, and then they are gone forever. It's hard to conduct experiments on something like that. So Finch's plan is to do one better than the researchers at the LHC: he wants to capture the gravitons and hold onto them. He doesn't want to just *produce* gravitons; he wants to *control* them."

"Why?" asked Jacob. "Is he trying to create artificial gravity? Some kind of tractor beam?"

"No, no," said Allie. "He doesn't care a whit about gravity, remember. These aren't gravitons to him; they're chrotons. He wants to control time itself. Which is to say, he wants to control the Universe."

They were silent for a moment.

Mercury cleared his throat. "Just so we're on the same page here," he said, "When you say 'chrotons,' you're talking about the little crunchy things you put in soup, yes?"

Jacob turned to face Mercury. "Who are you anyway? What is your role in this?"

"I told you," said Mercury. "I'm an angel. My friend Christine and I were assigned to recover the Attaché Cases of the Apocalypse, but my boss double-crossed us, so I had to create a diversion so Christine could get away. And man, what a diversion! You guys ever been struck by lightning? That'll wake you up in the morning."

Jacob and Allie exchanged meaningful glances. Jacob said, "Great. As if we weren't being punished enough, Finch gave us a lunatic for a housemate."

"Hey," objected Mercury. "This is no picnic for me either. My agent told me I was going to be rooming with Natalie Imbruglia and the guy who played Skippy on *Family Ties*."

Jacob shook his head. "I don't know which one of you sounds more nuts."

Mercury rubbed his chin, pointing his finger surreptitiously at Allie.

"It isn't as crazy as it sounds," said Allie. "If the theory is correct, then chrotons are all around us, all the time. But you can't just reach out and grab a chroton, because most of these chrotons are what you could call 'virtual' chrotons. They are, from our point of view, static and therefore invisible. We can't detect these 'virtual' chrotons, but we can detect 'free' chrotons. Now it's difficult to define the exact difference between virtual and free chrotons, but the situation is analogous to that of photons: although photons make up electromagnetic fields, you aren't going to see any light from a static electromagnetic field. You can, however, see *disturbances* of electromagnetic fields."

Mercury's eyes had glazed over completely, and even Jacob was having a hard time keeping up.

"Think of it this way," Allie continued. "You have a pond. The surface of the pond is completely dark except for where ripples on the pond's surface reflect light. The 'free' gravitons are like the ripples and the 'virtual' gravitons are like the invisible surface of the lake. The water is there either way, but it's completely undetectable except for the ripples. From our standpoint as observers of ripples on the pond, the water's existence is completely theoretical, except for the ripples, of which we have some experience—limited and indirect as it is.

"What they are trying to do at the LHC is to throw pebbles in the pond in order to observe the ripples, in an attempt to figure out the nature of the water in the pond. Finch, on the other hand, basically wants to submerge an empty glass in the water, with the opening of the glass level with the surface. He's going to throw rocks in the water in the hopes of splashing some of it into the glass."

"And then what?" asked Jacob.

"Well," said Allie, shrugging apologetically, "that's where the analogy breaks down a bit. You obviously can't literally remove a glass of Universe-stuff from the Universe and hold it in your hand. But clearly this is dangerous stuff. If you could channel a significant number of chrotons, you could conceivably warp space-time itself. It would take an awful lot of them, but once you've got control over time, lots of seemingly impossible things become possible. For example, what if the chrotons warp space-time enough to send the collider a nanosecond back in time, to just before the chrotons were captured? During the next nanosecond, the same chrotons would be captured again, from a previous state in their existence. Then it goes back another nanosecond and catches them again, and again and again. This would become a self-replicating process—call it a space-time virus if you like."

"So time would be frozen in this area?" Jacob asked.

"That's one possibility," replied Allie. "But that would only happen if there were exact parity between the amount of time needed to cause the reaction and the amount of time the collider was sent back each time the reaction occurred. More likely, the effect would be more subtle, such as the reaction occurring a millionth of a second before it should. In other words, the effect would slightly precede the cause."

"That's impossible," said Jacob.

"Not necessarily," said Allie. "Although it's hard to fathom, certainly. Another possibility is that the affected area would be sent infinitely far back in time, essentially blinking out of existence. And when I say 'the affected area,' understand that I'm being deliberately vague. I don't know the spatial range of the phenomena any more than I know the temporal range. In other words, maybe Finch's experiment will just send a few chrotons back in time. On the other hand, maybe the whole Universe will blink out of existence. It's hard to say. The point is that while I don't condone Finch's methods, the basic concepts are sound. There's no solid evidence to indicate he's right about any of this stuff, but there's no evidence to indicate he's wrong either."

Jacob shook his head. "Allie, come on. You know full well that isn't how science works. We don't accept every crackpot theory that comes along until it's disproven. Every hypothesis is tested based on how well it explains known phenomena, and by that standard the Jell-O universe theory is a resounding failure."

"Don't lecture me about the scientific method, Jacob," Allie snapped. "This isn't an abstract scientific problem we're discussing over bad coffee in the faculty lounge. If this machine works, it could literally destroy the Universe. Not just destroy it, *annihilate* it. It could destroy time itself, erasing everything that ever existed or ever will exist. I will grant you that the odds of it working are slim. But what if there's a one percent chance it works? We simply don't know what will happen if Finch succeeds in capturing a chroton."

"I know for certain that we're going to get fed to the lions if we don't get it working," said Jacob. "And since I don't have a clue how to do that, I guess our lives are in your hands."

"I'm sorry, Jacob," said Allie. "I can't risk it. I thought I could work out the unknowns well enough to make the activation of the CCD safe, but I just haven't had time. It will take years to do the necessary background work, but Finch insists on conducting the experiment as soon as possible. I just don't know what's going to happen, and I'm not willing to risk the existence of the Universe to save my own skin."

"So you worked on this thing for seven years and now you've decided, at the last minute, to develop some scruples?" Jacob asked.

"It's not that simple," said Allie. "Like you, I initially thought this whole thing was a joke. It was an interesting theoretical exercise, but I never actually expected it to work. And even now, I'm not exactly sure how he expects to capture the chrotons. That is, the device is constructed to channel them into a receiving chamber, but without something in that chamber capable of absorbing and holding onto the chrotons, they'll just disappear."

"Like a chroton battery!" interjected Mercury.

"Yes, more or less," said Finch. "I assume that Finch had someone else working on the battery, but frankly I don't know of anyone capable of building such a thing. I've done a few preliminary calculations, and the mechanics are so unworkable as to make it a near impossibility."

"Hang on," said Jacob. "You're refusing to activate the CCD because of a theoretical danger of what could happen in the off-chance the device might actually work, *if* Finch has been able to construct a receptacle that would be beyond the understanding of any physicist on Earth?"

"Well," said Allie. "Yes. But understand that it would have been pointless for Finch to build the CCD if it didn't exist."

"In other words," said Jacob, "you've bought into Finch's pseudoscientific nonsense. You've been drinking the Kool-Aid."

"Ooh!" Mercury exclaimed. "This is just like that movie, with Obi-Wan Kenobi."

"*Star Wars?*" Jacob asked, puzzled.

"No, before that."

"There was no movie with Obi-Wan Kenobi before *Star Wars.*"

"You know," said Mercury. "Where Obi-Wan's troops were captured by the Japanese and they had to build that bridge over the River Kwai. What was that called?"

"*The Bridge over the River Kwai?*" offered Jacob.

"Wow, you're like a Jedi," said Mercury. "Creepy. Yeah, it's like *The Bridge over the River Kwai*, where the Japanese make Obi-Wan Kenobi's men build a bridge, and they get so involved in building the bridge that they are disappointed when the Rebel Alliance has to blow it up in the end."

Jacob shook his head. "He's got the details a bit muddled," said Jacob, "but he has a point, Allie. You've been working on this thing for seven years; some part of you has to be hoping that it hasn't all been for nothing. Some part of you hopes that Finch really is onto something, and that the CCD will actually work. But I'm telling you, Allie, as an objective observer, that it's nonsense. There's no chroton battery. There probably aren't even any chrotons. There's no such thing as meta-energy and there's no Jell-O universe. It's all a bunch of bunk. Turn on the man's infernal machine and then maybe he'll let us go home."

"You know he's not going to let us go," said Allie.

"Maybe not," replied Jacob. "But we're definitely going to die if we say no. You can at least buy us some time. Get the machine working, and maybe we can escape while he's preoccupied with his experiment. Between the three of us, we ought to be able to come up with something."

"Don't look at me," said Mercury. "They've got a Balderhaz cube here somewhere, so I can't perform any miracles. Besides, I never even knew you could put croutons in Jell-O."

"We'll figure something out," said Jacob. "Trust me."

Allie sighed heavily. "All right," he said.

"Sweet!" exclaimed Mercury. "This is just like *Star Wars*, where Obi-Wan deactivates the tractor beam! Except that instead, he's going to activate it and maybe kill us!"

THIRTY-NINE
Circa 1,700 B.C.

"No!" Tiamat howled. "They can't do this!"

She had just received an official communiqué from the Seraphic Civilization Shepherding Program overseers informing her that she was being put on probation. She would be allowed to remain in Babylon, but only as an observer. Another seraph would be selected to take her place in the program.

"I've been following all the rules!" she shrieked. "Mostly!"

Mercury cleared his throat. "Maybe they figured out what you're up to," he said, nervously.

"Impossible!" she exclaimed. "Only a handful of seraphim know about the metaverse. There were a few of us who figured it out a couple thousand years ago. Me, Osiris, Quetzalcoatl, and a few others. That's why we've all been working on pyramids. None of us has any reason to tell those paper-pushers in the SCSP."

"What if Osiris or somebody realized you were going to win the pyramid race and decided to fess up rather than let you become Queen of the Universe?"

"You think Osiris would do that?" Tiamat asked. "I always thought he was kind of a sap. Smart guy and all, but not the scheming type."

"You just never know," said Mercury, relieved that Tiamat seemed to be giving the notion some credence. In truth, Mercury didn't think that Osiris would have flipped on her. He was an honorable guy. Not like me, he thought.

The fact was that Mercury had spilled his guts to Uzziel about Tiamat's plans for Universal domination. He felt bad about it, but what could he do? Tiamat was fun to hang out with, but she wasn't the sort you'd want ruling the Universe. Besides, keeping tabs on Tiamat was his job. If he didn't mention the fact that, oh, by the way, she's a few weeks away from becoming Unquestioned Despot of the Universe, he could reasonably be accused of insufficient oversight.

"All I can say is, good luck trying to find someone to replace me!" Tiamat growled. "They're already scraping the bottom of the barrel with this program. I mean, they picked that moron Dagda to run Britain, for crying out loud. At the rate he's going, those people are going to be in the Stone Age forever."

The door to the drawing room opened, and a lanky, good-looking man swaggered into the room. "Hey, babe," he said. "They told me you were in here."

Tiamat's jaw dropped. It was Marduk.

"What have I told you about calling me that?" Mercury replied.

Marduk chuckled politely. "Hey, Mercury. What's up?"

Mercury shrugged. "The usual. Labor disputes, unreliable subcontractors, residents complaining about the chisels going day and night; you know how it is."

Marduk nodded. "Well, things are going to change around here. There's a new sheriff in town."

"You?" Tiamat hissed. "They're putting *you* in charge of Babylon?"

"Yes indeed," said Marduk jubilantly. "Don't worry, I plan on keeping you and Mercury on as consultants."

"Super," said Mercury flatly.

Tiamat sank into her chair, holding her head in her hands. "No," she moaned. "No, no, no."

"Come on," chided Marduk. "It's not that bad. I don't plan on changing much right off the bat. This Hammurabi seems to be working out all right, and we might as well finish off this last ziggurat..."

"Really?" Tiamat asked hopefully. "You're going to let the construction of the ziggurat go on as planned?"

"Well," said Marduk. "Not *exactly* as planned. I have some ideas for making the process more efficient."

Mercury frowned. "More efficient?" he asked doubtfully, forgetting for a moment that the completion of the ziggurat would lead to Tiamat's dominion over the Universe. "The ziggurat is ninety percent done. Wouldn't any changes at this point be, you know, disruptive? Why not stick with what works?"

"Trust me," said Marduk. "We'll finish it twice as fast this way. Check it out." He unrolled a scroll filled with diagrams and notations. "See this here on the left? This is the standard Babylonian system of weights and measures. Six *she* to one *shu-si*. Thirty *shu-si* to one *kush*. Twelve *kush* to one *nindan*. Sixty *nindan* to one *ush*."

"Yes, yes," said Tiamat impatiently. "Every child over six knows this. What's your point?"

"The point is," Marduk said, "that it's all rather arbitrary. Why switch from six units to thirty units to twelve units to sixty units? Where's the logic in that?"

"They're all multiples of six," Mercury said. "Makes the math easy, since Babylon uses a six-based number system."

"Sure," said Marduk. "But imagine how much easier it would be if we used a *ten-based system*."

Tiamat and Mercury sat in befuddled silence.

"Did I just blow your minds?" Marduk asked. "Take a look at this: Ten *grabok-Marduks* in a *brobnig-Marduk*. Ten *brobnig-Marduks* in a *sha-nafurtsen-Marduk*. And ten *sha-nafurtsen Marduks* in a *gamnashtannfurtsenammilok-Marduk*. See how simple that is? I call it the Marduk System."

"Wow," said Mercury. "That is quite possibly the worst idea I've ever heard in my life."

Tiamat groaned and cradled her head in her hands. "Where do you come up with this idiocy?" she asked.

"I wish I could take all the credit," said Marduk, "but let's just say I had a little inspiration from *above*." He winked meaningfully at Tiamat. "All right, Mercury," he exclaimed. "Let's head out to the ziggurat and tell the men the good news!"

The men, it turned out, were delighted to hear about the new measurement system. Marduk interpreted their response as enthusiasm about being able to finish the ziggurat more quickly, but Mercury knew better. The workers were looking for any excuse not to finish the ziggurat, and Marduk had handed them a solid gold excuse on a silver platter. None of them recognized the mysterious stranger, of course, having been born long after Marduk's disappearance, but rumors spread quickly that this was indeed their long-awaited savior. And if their savior expected them to fuck up the ziggurat, who were they to question him?

Mercury returned to find Tiamat in tears. "Centuries of work down the drain," she moaned. "The final ziggurat will never be completed. I'm telling you, Mercury, the deck was stacked against me. First the labor disputes and the invasions, and then the flood, and now this!" She shook her fist at the sky. "Someone up there has it in for me!"

A sickening feeling came over Mercury. What had Marduk said? That his system had been an "inspiration from above?" Tiamat tended to be paranoid, but that didn't mean she was wrong. Maybe someone *up there* was screwing up her attempts to open a portal to the metaverse. He pulled Michael's card from his pocket. He shuddered as he reread the message.

The rain comes from above.

Was that what Michael had meant? Had the Eternals sent the rain to disrupt Tiamat's ziggurat-building? Having failed to stop her, had they then manipulated Marduk into promulgating his idiotic System? His mind reeled with the possibilities. How many other little ways might the Eternals have subtly discouraged the completion of the ziggurats? Spreading dissention among the builders? Provoking neighboring provinces into attacking Babylon?

His thoughts were interrupted by a loud banging on the door to the drawing room.

"Enter!" shouted Tiamat angrily.

A servant opened the door. "Ma'am," he said with a bow. "My apologies, but I have some urgent news."

"Out with it, then," said Tiamat.

"Ma'am," said the servant. "The Elamites have attacked southern Babylon. It sounds like we're going to need all the workers from the ziggurat to help hold them off."

Tiamat sighed heavily, letting her head drop to her hands once again. Her shoulders began to shake, and Mercury at first thought she was sobbing. But when she looked up, he saw that she was laughing. "Tell Marduk," she said. "It's his problem now. I quit."

"You can't just quit!" Mercury exclaimed in disbelief.

"I can quit ziggurats anytime I want," declared Tiamat, and stalked out of the room.

Around the corner, a mysterious figure quietly slinked away, smiling to himself. Tiamat might have given up on unlocking the mysteries of the Universe, but others within Babylon had been watching her efforts with great interest, and they weren't about to concede failure simply because Tiamat had fallen out of favor. It was bound to happen, the way she conspicuously flouted the will of Heaven. What was required here was a subtler touch. It might take hundreds or even thousands of years, the man knew, but eventually the Order of the Pillars of Babylon would succeed where even the gods themselves had failed.

FORTY

Mercury, Jacob, and Finch sat in the CCD control room, watching Alistair Breem type some final instructions into the CCD computer. Armed men stood guarding the exits. Allie pressed the Enter key, slid his chair away from the console, and held up his hands in a gesture of either resignation or supplication.

"It is finished," he said.

A monitor at the front of the room now displayed the message:

CAUTION: CCD ONLINE

Finch leaped from his chair. "At last!" he chirped. "Now I, Horace Finch, shall tear the veil behind which lies the most closely guarded secrets of the Universe!"

"Don't get ahead of yourself, Finch," said Jacob. "Your machine is useless without a receptacle for the chrotons."

Finch smiled wickedly. "Oh, didn't I tell you? I happened to find such a thing, just a few days ago. It must have slipped my mind." He walked to a wall safe, tapped a combination into a keypad, and pulled open a thick steel door. Reaching into the safe, he pulled out a square metal box about half the size of a shoebox.

Finch proclaimed, "Babylonian prophecies foretell that the key to the secrets of the Universe will be found hidden beneath a sacred shrine guarded by an ancient race of people since the beginning of time. Behold!" He opened the box to reveal, resting on a cushion of velvet, what appeared to be an apple made of crimson colored glass. "This is a device from beyond our own reality, constructed specifically to harness the power of chrotons," he crowed. "My moment of triumph is at hand!"

Allie glared at Jacob.

Jacob paled.

"Uh oh," said Mercury.

"*Your* triumph!" said a voice behind them. They turned to see three figures enter the room from the southern hallway. It was Uzziel, flanked on either side by Izbazel and Gamaliel. "No, Horace. This is the moment of *my* triumph!"

"Uzziel, you jackass," said Mercury. "I knew you had something to do with this."

"I wouldn't miss this for the world," said Uzziel. "The Apocalypse Bureau has been watching the Order of the Pillars of Babylon for thousands of years. I knew that the OPB's plan to tear open the veil concealing the higher reality was nearing fruition, but they were missing a key element: a receptacle for the chrotons. The Babylonian prophecy states that the key to the portal is hidden under a mountain between two streams, and the OPB had of course assumed that the two streams were the Tigris and Euphrates. But even after searching for centuries, they had turned up nothing. It was I who realized that the two streams were not rivers but *energy streams*. There are lots of mountains on Earth between two energy streams, but I figured it was most likely someplace known to the Babylonians—which left the Middle East, Eastern Europe, and Northern Africa. The likeliest candidate became

Mbukuoto, the holy site of the Tawani people. The prophecy fore-
tells that the key will be guarded by an ancient people, and that it
will fall into the hands of a 'silver-haired stranger,' who will hold
the fate of the world in his hands. Clearly the prophecy referred
to Horace Finch. All I had to do was guide Finch to the Tawani."

"Clearly," said Mercury. "Isn't this scheme a little out of your
jurisdiction, Uzziel? You know, while you hang out here on Earth,
reports are going unfiled and files are going unreported."

"Silence, Mercury!" Uzziel growled. "I did my job without
complaint for seven thousand years. I followed every rule, every
bylaw, every regulation. I attended all the meetings, filled out
all the paperwork, reported to all the committees. But when the
Apocalypse fell through, I realized I had been a fool. In the end,
I had no more control over Armageddon than anyone else. My
whole existence had been a joke, a fraud. Well, I'm done following orders. I want to see the man behind the curtain. I want to see
who's really in charge of the Universe. And if I have to break a few
rules—or risk the annihilation of our reality—then so be it."

Mercury shrugged. "Well, as long as you've thought it
through."

Uzziel went on, "I knew you'd have interfered if I had given
you a chance, Mercury. But I couldn't have you and Christine
detained without raising suspicion. That's why I assigned you
to get the Attaché Cases of the Apocalypse. As soon as you left
my office, I had Izbazel and Gamaliel released from holding and
assigned them to track you down. Everything is going according
to my plan!"

"*Your* plan!" hissed a voice from the side of the room. The
assembled group turned their respective heads to see a severe-
looking but not unattractive middle-aged woman enter the room,
flanked by two cherub guards.

"Tiamat!" gasped Uzziel. "What are *you* doing here?"

"Oh, Uzziel," Tiamat said smugly. "As endearing as it is that you believe that you've played a key role in bringing about the culmination of OPB's plan, I'm afraid I must steal the spotlight. After all, it was I who started the Babylonians on the path to seeking a higher reality. There would be no OPB if it weren't for me. If anyone can claim this as a moment of triumph, it is I!"

"Ah, Tiamat," said a voice from the opposite end of the room "Always eager to take more than your share of the credit. You abandoned the Babylonians nearly four thousand years ago, and now that their efforts seem to be about to bear fruit, you rush in to take credit. Classy."

A tall, blond figure entered the room, flanked by two demons.

"Lucifer!" exclaimed Tiamat. "Come to sabotage my plans, as you always do?"

"On the contrary," replied Lucifer. "I am here to see that *my* plan is brought to its proper conclusion. Your piddling efforts to break through Mundane reality are of no interest to me. You see, a while back, I had a bit of a disagreement with the authorities in Heaven. I had hopes that we'd be able to work things out satisfactorily, but I implemented a failsafe plan, just in case. I stole an anti-bomb and hid it where no one would ever find it. For seven thousand years, that glass apple remained unmolested inside a remote mountaintop in Africa. If my surprise attack failed, I still had an ace up my sleeve: an anti-bomb powerful enough to destroy the entire world!"

For a moment the room was silent, as everyone tried to make sense of what had just happened. After a few seconds, Mercury spoke.

"I'm afraid I must disappoint you all," he announced. "Truly I tell you," he said, "the moment of triumph is *mine!*"

All eyes turned toward him.

"And then I pull off a mask and it turns out I'm really Hitler," said Mercury. "What do you think? Too much?"

Uzziel nodded at Gamaliel, who punched Mercury in the stomach. Mercury doubled over and fell to the floor.

Horace Finch spoke up. "Look," he said. "I don't know who most of you are or how you got in here, but if you don't mind, I was about to flip this switch and uncover the deepest secrets of the Universe. Does anyone have a problem with that?"

Jacob stood up. "I do," he said, trying to keep his voice from quavering. "Listen, Mr. Finch. I'm a scientist. My job is to analyze disparate data and make sense out of it. I understand the desire to break things down and then try to put them together again, in order to better understand them. But there are some things that can't be put back together, and I'm pretty sure the Universe is one of those things. If that means we're doomed to never fully understand the Universe, then so be it. Maybe there are some mysteries that were never meant to be solved."

Finch nodded at one of his guards, who punched Jacob in the stomach. Jacob doubled over and joined Mercury on the floor.

"Anyone else?" said Finch.

Lucifer shrugged. "Regardless of whether your little science experiment works, the anti-bomb will soon implode, destroying the Earth. All you're going to do is speed things up a bit. Heaven loses. I win. Do it."

No one else spoke up.

"OK, then let's do this," said Finch. He removed the glass apple from its padded box and held it aloft in his hand. The apple began to sparkle in the dim light of the control room. "Interesting," said Finch, regarding the transfigured anti-bomb.

"What does sparkling mean?" Jacob whispered to Mercury, who was lying next to him on the floor. "Sparkling can't be good."

"Sparkling is never good," said Mercury. "It means that the anti-bomb is about to blow. Or suck, as it were. We have maybe an hour left, tops."

"Wait a minute," said Jacob. "The apple is an anti-bomb? You mean that's…?"

"Yeah," Mercury replied. "That's what imploded Anaheim Stadium. Except this one is about ten thousand times as powerful. When that thing goes off, it's good-bye, Earth."

"My God," gasped Jacob. "But maybe the CCD will neutralize it."

"Maybe," said Mercury. "Or maybe it will increase its potency by a factor of a billion. Care to place a bet?"

Finch pressed a button on the CCD control panel. A metal arm with circular receptacle about the size of a cup holder slid out from the panel and Finch placed the anti-bomb into it. He pressed the button again, and the arm slid into the CCD.

Finch turned to Alistair Breem, who had been sitting in silence at the control panel. "Would you care to do the honors, Allie?" he asked.

"Go to hell, Finch," said Allie.

"Fine, then," replied Finch. "I'll do it." He reached for the switch and everyone in the room held their breath.

"Not so fast, Horace Finch," said a small but authoritative voice from the north end of the room.

Everyone turned to see a diminutive, hooded figure enter the room. To the figure's right was Christine Temetri, and flanking them were a dozen cherubim wielding fiery swords. The figure removed her hood, revealing locks of curly black hair.

"Michelle!" gasped Mercury, struggling to his feet. "And Christine! And...I'm sorry, I don't know the rest of your names, but I'm totally happy to see you all!"

"Whoever you are, you're too late!" hissed Finch. He flipped the switch.

The display now read:

CAUTION! CCD IS ACTIVE

A low-pitched, almost subaudible hum filled the room. Lights on the control panel blinked crazily as dozens of prepro-grammed processes woke from their slumber. Below the surface of the panel, millions of electrons shuffled from place to place, like commuters in a vast city of copper and silicon. If these indi-vidual particles had any idea that all their efforts were part of an incomprehensively complex machine whose goal was to direct a train car filled with their quantum cousins to a subatomic con-centration camp, they might have hesitated a bit, but insulated by ignorance and propelled by urges beyond their understanding, they all did their parts to bring the monster to life.

"No!" Christine screamed.

Before anyone else even knew what was happening, Jacob leaped onto the control console and launched himself at the ceil-ing, his arms stretched as high as they would go. His goal, the rest of the congregants belatedly realized, was a clear plastic tube about four inches in diameter that ran the length of the ceiling. It looked like the vacuum tubes that used to be used for transport-ing messages between floors in office buildings.

Jacob wrapped his fingers around the tube and hung there, willing himself to weigh more than his one hundred and forty pounds. As if in answer to his prayers, Horace Finch grabbed him by the ankles, trying to break his grasp on the tube.

There was a CRACK! and the tube came apart at a joint a few inches from Jacob's fingers. The section of the tube he was hanging from bent downward and the glass apple, now sparkling brightly, rolled from the opening toward the floor. Jacob fell on top of Horace Finch, knocking him out cold.

The display now flashed:

ERROR! CCD OFFLINE

Mercury dove across the room, his left hand outstretched, landing on his back and sliding nearly a foot across the floor. The apple landed without a sound in his hand.

For several moments, no one dared breathe.

At last, Mercury spoke. "I wasn't sure the infield fly rule applied in this case," he said, "so I thought I'd better catch it."

"Nicely done, Mercury," said Michelle. "I will open a temporary portal and have the anti-bomb transported somewhere safe. Then I will be taking Lucifer, Tiamat, and Uzziel into custody. These wicked schemes stop right now."

Lucifer stepped forward. "Please do," he said. "If you try to transport the anti-bomb through a portal at this point, you'll set it off. I'm afraid these pointless heroics have only delayed Earth's doom by a few minutes. There is no stopping the anti-bomb from imploding now."

"He's right," said Uzziel. "The anti-bomb is too unstable to be transported. There's nothing we can do but wait for it to go off. The end of the world is at hand!"

"My work is done here," said Lucifer. "I'll be heading back to the Infernal Plane if no one has any objections."

"I've really got to be going as well," said Tiamat. "As much as I'd love to stick around and be ripped apart by a massive rift in this plane with the rest of you, I've got work to do."

"No one is going anywhere," declared Michelle. "If anyone sets a foot outside this room, I'll call down a Class Five pillar of fire and take out this whole place."

"Wouldn't that set off the anti-bomb?" Christine asked. "And, um, kill us all?"

"It seems you mortals are going to die either way," said Michelle. "And I can't let Lucifer and Tiamat escape. They must pay for what they've done. A pillar of fire will transport them to Heaven, where they can be dealt with."

"You wouldn't dare," said Lucifer. "You'd be killing all of these innocent people."

"You've forced my hand, Lucifer," Michelle replied. "I won't let you escape again, whatever the cost."

Mercury stepped forward. "OK, let's not forget who's holding the sparkly apple here," he said, the anti-bomb sparkling brightly in his hand. "Now, hear me out. While it's true that we can't stop the anti-bomb from imploding, that doesn't mean we have to let it implode *here*."

"Where do you recommend?" asked Michelle. "This is perhaps the most remote location on Earth."

"I was thinking someplace not on Earth," replied Mercury. "I could fly the anti-bomb into space and let it implode there."

Uzziel shook his head. "That's not how an anti-bomb works," he said. "It's not like a conventional bomb that can safely detonate in a vacuum. The anti-bomb creates a vortex that reaches out to suck in any available matter. It keeps expanding until it finds enough matter to equalize the pressure between this plane and the plane it's opening a rift into."

Jacob interjected, "You're contradicting yourself. If the anti-bomb goes off in a vacuum, creating a rift onto an empty plane, then the pressure is already equalized. You've got a vacuum on both sides, so there would be no implosion."

Uzziel replied impatiently, "When I say 'pressure,' I'm not talking about air pressure. This isn't conventional physics. Each plane is made up of its aggregate total of matter and energy. The total is different for each plane, and when you open a rift between two planes, matter rushes out of the higher density plane into the lower density plane. That's why opening portals between planes is so expensive: it takes a tremendous amount of energy to create what is essentially an airlock between the two planes. Except that it's not an airlock; it's a matterlock."

"Ah," said Mercury wistfully. "Where is the folksy wisdom of Matterlock when we need it most?"

Uzziel, who was accustomed to Mercury's non sequiturs, went on, undeterred, "On the higher density side, the anti-bomb vortex expands until it has consumed a sufficient amount of mass. The older the anti-bomb, the more mass it takes. With an apple of this vintage, it's going to take somewhere around a hundred trillion kilograms of mass to satisfy it. Even if you transported it ten thousand miles into space, it would still suck in a hundred trillion kilograms of Earth's atmosphere, setting off thousands of massive hurricanes across the globe. The death toll would be in the hundreds of millions, if not billions. And that's *if* you could get it ten thousand miles into deep space, which is impossible, even for an angel. There's no time."

"What if I aim for the moon?" Mercury asked. "If I can get close enough to the moon, then the anti-bomb vortex will wreck the moon instead of Earth, right?"

"There's no time, you fool!" Lucifer snapped. "This discussion is futile. Michelle, if you're going to call down a Class Five, go ahead and do it. Otherwise, I'm leaving."

"He's right, Mercury," said Uzziel. "We've got maybe half an hour until the anti-bomb goes off. Even flying at top speed, you don't have a chance to get anywhere near the moon."

"I've got to try," said Mercury. "Matterlock would have wanted me to."

"Mercury, you're not listening," said Christine. "It can't be done. We just need to accept the fact that the end of the Earth is at hand."

"Well, what's the point of *that*?" Mercury asked.

"Actually," Tiamat said, "he just might be able to do it."

All eyes turned toward Tiamat.

"We've got twelve angels here," she said, "not counting Mercury. If he were to fly straight toward the moon, and we were all to push him, he might be able to get close enough to the moon to save the Earth."

"What do you mean, 'push'?" said Christine.

Tiamat explained, "Flight is just a matter of using the interplanar energy to overcome gravity. Mercury pushes against the ground, and we push against him."

Christine now understood how Gamaliel had been able to catch Mercury outside the WHO building: Izbazel had been *pushing* him. With the combined power of two angels, Gamaliel had been able to fly twice as fast as Mercury.

"We're right between two energy streams," Tiamat was saying, "so there's plenty of power. In essence, we transfer our power to him. If each angel pushes as hard as we can, we may be able to get him to the moon before the anti-bomb goes off." She paused and then said, "Let me stress that he would need the help of *every angel here.*"

"What's your game, Tiamat?" Lucifer asked.

"We help Mercury get to the moon," Tiamat said. "In exchange, Michelle drops all charges against us. We get to leave, scot-free."

"Forget it," Michelle said, shaking her head vigorously. "I'm not letting you slip between my fingers again."

"Then the Earth dies," said Tiamat. "And good luck explaining *that* to the Senate. See if you hold onto your job after that one."

"Please," said Christine to Michelle. "It's the only way. You'll have another chance to catch Tiamat and Lucifer. You can't let seven billion people die because of a grudge between angels."

"Let me know what you come up with," said Mercury. "I'll catch you all later." He made his way to the elevator that led to the floor of the dome. The angels looked expectantly to Michelle for a cue.

"Fine," she said at last. "But I don't have the authority to absolve you of your crimes. All I can do is give you a head start. If Mercury succeeds, I'll let you open portals and get out of here. Even you, Uzziel, if you can find someplace willing to take you. But if Mercury fails, I'm calling down a Class Five and taking you all in. Take it or leave it."

Lucifer made no effort to hide his disgust. "I've been waiting seven thousand years for this moment," he growled. "Why should I give up now?"

"Self-preservation," said Tiamat. "Yes, you'll have the satisfaction of destroying the world, but do you really want to spend the next ten thousand years in Heavenly custody? They will make you pay for every one of those seven billion deaths. Be reasonable, Luce. There will be other opportunities to destroy the world."

Lucifer gritted his teeth, narrowing his eyes at Mercury. This was the second effort of his to destroy Earth in the past two months that had been foiled by this uppity cherub and his little human sidekick. First they had absconded with his Antichrist, ruining his attempt at a surprise attack via the linoleum portal, and now they were going to steal his failsafe, his doomsday device, the anti-bomb that had been ripening silently inside a mountain for seven thousand years. How did this keep happening? Somehow fate itself was interfering with his attempts to wipe out the Earth.

Lucifer scolded himself for pursuing this line of thought. Lucifer was the original empiricist; he believed in reason and cold, hard facts. That was why he had rebelled against Heaven in the first place: he was sick of being told to just do what he was told and trust that there was some sort of "higher order" that was going to make sure everything turned out OK. *Fate* and *destiny* were the last refuge of the weak and incompetent.

But there did seem to be something to the whole Charlie Nyx thing. With the publication of each successive book in the series, the situation on Earth got exponentially worse. He had always known there was something powerful about that ancient tale of the teenage warlock, but had never put much stock in the prophecy that the books were somehow going to bring about the Apocalypse. He had always thought of the Charlie Nyx books as just another way to spread Satanism and chaos, but the connection between the publication of the books and the progression toward the Apocalypse was becoming difficult to deny. Was the ancient prophecy right after all? If it were, then it was no wonder Lucifer kept failing: the world couldn't end until the seventh Charlie Nyx book had been published.

The rational side of his mind continued to rail against this notion. His whole purpose in trying to destroy the world was to prove that there was no meaning, no higher power, no Divine Plan. There were only accidents, entropy, and destruction. And if the world was going to have to end, *he* was going to have to end it. He couldn't rely on humanity's half-assed efforts to wipe itself out, or on self-interested schemers like Tiamat, or on Fate or Destiny. The Apocalypse wasn't something that just *happened*; it had to be brought about, and Lucifer knew that he was the only one in the Universe who was up to the task. The anti-bomb was his ace in the hole. If he gave up this opportunity, he'd never get another chance. On the other hand, if the occurrence of the Apocalypse really *was* dependent on the publication of the final Charlie Nyx book, then his attempt to use the anti-bomb to destroy the world was premature and doomed to fail. Not only that, but as Tiamat said, he'd most likely spend the next ten thousand years in prison. That might be tolerable if he succeeded, but if he failed, he would have to spend a hundred centuries regretting the premature implosion. No one would be around to ensure that Culain delivered the final book, and the human race would simply limp along miserably for countless millennia, with no one to put them out of their misery.

In the end, Lucifer did something that he hadn't done for seven thousand years: he ignored his rational side and made a leap of faith. There was simply no point in resisting Destiny. He clenched his fists and let loose a howl of rage. "Let's get this over with then," he spat, and followed Mercury to the elevator.

"First floor," Mercury announced. "Hardware, lingerie, and the freaking *moon!*"

The lot of them joined Mercury and Lucifer, packing the elevator to capacity. The elevator took them to the floor of the dome and they made their way outside, where a full moon hung in the night sky. Uzziel placed his Balderhaz Cube into its shielded box, so that it wouldn't interfere with the angels' ability to channel energy. The angels gathered in a circle around Mercury, while Christine, Jacob, and Allie stood back from the group. They had left Horace Finch and his guards in the control room.

"Any last words, Merc?" said Michelle.

Mercury held the glowing red apple aloft and said, "I would like to take this moment to officially forgive the other reindeer for not letting me join in any of their reindeer games."

With that, he leaped into the air, a red beacon twinkling in the night sky. Michelle stepped forward, raising her hands heavenward to channel her supply of interplanar energy toward Mercury. One by one, the other angels joined in, adding their power to the stream.

By the time Lucifer had begrudgingly joined in, Mercury was traveling so fast that he had to channel all of his own strength into shielding the anti-bomb from the heat caused by the compression of the air ahead of him. A few minutes later, though, he was free of the atmosphere, soaring far above the Earth. The full moon grew larger and larger, until he could make out hundreds of individual craters in the gray orb—and still he continued to accelerate. The apple now positively glowed in his hand.

After a few more minutes, the moon loomed larger than the Earth. The farther he traveled, the faster it grew. The twelve angels on the ground continued to push, and with the lack of atmosphere and diminished gravity of space, there was nothing to limit his speed. Fear gripped him as he realized that he could easily be traveling over a hundred thousand miles per hour—and as he entered the gravitational pull of the moon, he accelerated even faster. The apple shone so brightly now that he had to shield his eyes from it, and it actually seemed to be vibrating in his hand. The apple got hotter and hotter, and soon it was burning his hand. He held it for as long as he could, and then pulled back and hurled it with all his might into the center of the silvery disc.

FORTY-ONE

"We've lost him," said Tiamat.

"What do you mean, you've lost him?" Christine demanded. "Did he make it?"

As they watched, there was a pulse of light in the center of the moon, and then it went dark. Where the light had been, a black spot appeared and continued to grow. Massive chunks of the moon were breaking off and being sucked into the void.

"He did it!" Christine said. "Right?"

The rest of the group cast nervous glances at each other. Suddenly the earth began to shake.

"What's that?" Christine asked. "An earthquake?"

"A third of the moon just got sucked into another universe," said Jacob. "It's affecting the moon's pull on the Earth. There are going to be some earthquakes. And tsunamis. And volcanic eruptions. And probably some hurricanes, too. Things are going to get ugly."

"The important thing is that we lived up to our side of the bargain," said Lucifer. "Now if you'll pardon me, I've got some pressing matters to attend to." He could only hope that he was right about the Charlie Nyx books. His number one priority was now to make sure that the seventh book was published as soon as possible.

A portal appeared on the ground near Lucifer's feet. He and his minions stepped onto it and disappeared.

"I've got to be going as well," said Tiamat. Another portal appeared at her feet.

"Wait!" cried Uzziel. "Take me with you!"

"Bah," said Tiamat. "I have no use for a paper pusher," she said. "Izbazel and Gamaliel may come with me, however, if they reaffirm their allegiance."

"OK, whatever!" said Izbazel. "We pledge our allegiance. Just get us out of here!" Gamaliel nodded, and they joined Tiamat.

Tiamat took a step toward the portal.

"Wait!" Uzziel cried again. "I have information!"

Tiamat's brow furrowed. "What kind of information?"

"If you agree to let me come with you, I'll tell you who betrayed you in Babylon. I'll tell you who leaked your plan to open a portal to the metaverse."

Tiamat shook her head. "That matter is settled. My intelligence indicated it was Osiris. He has been dealt with."

"Osiris!" Uzziel exclaimed. "Where did you get that idea?"

"It seemed obvious," said Tiamat. "He was jealous because he couldn't get his portal working, and Mercury assured me that…" Her voice trailed off.

Uzziel smiled.

"He wouldn't," Tiamat said coldly. "He was my lieutenant, my right-hand man. I trusted him."

"I've got proof," said Uzziel. "Take me with you, and I'll show you."

"Fine," said Tiamat. "But you'd better not be lying. And if you're telling the truth, Mercury would be wise to never show his face on any known plane again."

Tiamat and her entourage stepped onto the portal, and Uzz-iel, Izbazel, and Gamaliel followed.

"I must leave as well," said Michelle. "I need to mobilize my troops to try to stem the chaos on Earth. Thank you for your assistance, Christine."

"Wait," said Christine. "What about Mercury? Where is he? Is he all right?"

Michelle sighed. "The short answer," she said, "is that I don't know. An anti-bomb opens a rift between two planes. Any matter that gets sucked into the rift will reappear in the corresponding location on the target plane. The problem is that with anti-bombs, there's no controlling which plane that is, and the farther you get away from Earth, the more remote the target plane is likely to be. Mercury is an angel, so his physical form will reincorporate wherever he ends up, but that could be on some completely uncharted plane."

"Uncharted?" Christine asked, a queasy feeling in her gut. "But you can get him back, right?"

Michelle sighed again. "Possibly," she said. "He may be able to tap into Angel Band from whatever plane he's on. But on some remote planes the signal is very weak. If he can't reach anyone on a known plane, then we can't open a portal to him."

"Meaning what?" Christine demanded. "He's alone on some deserted plane? Stuck there by himself, forever?"

"It's a possibility," Michelle admitted.

"So he saves the world, and this is the thanks he gets? Exiled to some godforsaken plane for all eternity?"

"We'll do what we can to find him," Michelle said. "I promise. But now, I really must go. Duty calls."

"Fine," said Christine. "Go."

Michelle and her angels left as well. The three humans were left alone on the Kenyan plain, a cold wind howling in their ears.

"We haven't officially met," she said to the two men. "I'm Christine Temetri. I'm an Apocalypse magnet."

"Hi, Christine," said Jacob. "I'm Jacob Slater. This is Alistair Breem."

"Allie, please," said Allie, shaking Christine's hand.

"Nice to meet you," Christine said. "What do you say we steal a car and get the hell out of here before Horace Finch wakes up?"

FORTY-TWO

Mercury regained consciousness reclined on a molded plastic bench. The sky was completely dark and devoid of any stars. The air was crisp and cold. Beneath his feet was concrete, but he couldn't make out any buildings in the darkness. Before him were several figures in tattered clothing, huddled over a steel drum in which a fire flickered brightly.

He stood up and approached the figures. "Uh, hello," he said, uncertainly.

"Hey, look who's awake!" one of them exclaimed, a filthy, toothless old man who seemed to be wearing at least four overcoats. There were seven figures altogether, and Mercury judged that four of them were men and three of them women, although it was difficult to be sure, given the dim light and the fact that each of them was wearing an entire wardrobe of mismatched clothing.

"You want some beans?" asked one of the ostensible women.

Mercury shook his head. "I'm good," he said. "Where am I?"

The group burst into laughter. "Where am I?" one of the men echoed jovially. "Oh, that's a good one. Haven't heard that one in…" His voice trailed off. "Anyway, it's been a while. Come closer to the fire. Don't be a stranger."

As Mercury approached the drum, the group's members shuffled aside, making room for him.

"It's cold here," said Mercury.

"Ha!" said the toothless man who had spoken first. "This is the warmest it's been for a long time. My name's Ernie. This is Thelma, Edith, Ronald, Neal, Agnes, and Lester."

"Nice to meet you all," said Mercury. "I'm Mercury. So seriously, where am I? Who are you people?"

Suddenly the fire flared brightly, flooding them with a wave of warmth. The assembled group moaned appreciatively.

"That was a Charlie Nyx burning," said Ernie, and the others nodded in agreement. "Gotta love those. Stir it up a bit with your stick and see if you can get another one, Ronald."

Ronald grumbled something and poked a long wooden stick into the drum.

Mercury leaned over the drum to get a look at the source of the fire.

"Wait, don't!" Ernie yelled, pulling Mercury away from the drum.

Mercury staggered backward, falling onto the cold concrete. His eyes had been blinded by the glare, but his mind was assailed by a thousand images—and not just images, but slices of time, complete with sounds, smells, and tastes: ancient peoples tearing down temples, barbarians sacking Rome, Inquisitors burning heretical texts, Reformers throwing rocks through stained-glass windows, Fundamentalists chanting over piles of flaming Charlie Nyx books.

"What is this place?" Mercury gasped. "What are you burning?"

"*We're* not burning anything," said Ernie. "We didn't start the fire. It was always burning, since the world's been turning."

"We just poke at it once in a while," said Thelma. "Sometimes it gets really cold here."

Now black smoke was pouring from the drum, and the odor of burning hair filled the air.

"Ugh," said Ernie. "Damn Tawani, burning goats again." He leaned over the drum. "Enough with the goats already!"

"Hey, what's that?" asked Lester, pointing at something in the drum. "Are they building ziggurats again?"

"You want me to knock it over?" asked Ronald.

"Hang on," said Ernie. "That's just a hotel in Las Vegas. No danger there."

"Sorry," said Lester. "I guess I'm a little overly cautious since that thing with the Babylonians."

"Yeah, that was a close one," said Ronald. "We almost ended up putting out the fire completely that time."

There were nods and murmurs around the group.

Suddenly the fire popped and showered them with sparks.

"Uh-oh," said Agnes.

"Yeah," said Ronald.

"What?" asked Mercury. "What is it?"

"Well," said Ernie. "The good news is that it's going to get a lot warmer for a little while."

"And the bad news?" asked Mercury.

"Then it's going to get very, very cold."

FORTY-THREE

Eddie spent the night in his hotel room, trying to put Culain's fatalistic nonsense out of his head. By the time the sun rose, he felt somewhat better, and he decided to drive to the Beacon Building and level with Wanda Kwan about the missing Charlie Nyx book. Rehearsing his speech on the drive over, he was so preoccupied that he barely noticed the series of earthquakes that were rocking Los Angeles. L.A. did seem a little crazier than usual; he had to put the top up on the BMW and turn up the radio to drown out the sounds of pedestrians who were panicking about whatever it was that pedestrians panicked about.

The *Beacon's* valet wasn't at his post, so Eddie parked the car himself in a spot that seemed to promise that he would be transported to his destination from the parking lot in a sort of wheeled chair. This hope also proved disappointing, and after several minutes of waiting in vain for the wheeled chair to appear, he decided to simply walk to the elevator. Adding to the inconvenience was the fact that he had to dodge several pedestrians who were fleeing the building in terror. Say what you will about Cork, thought Eddie; at least it wasn't packed with panicked pedestrians. L.A. was becoming downright unsafe. He found himself hoping that Cody was OK, which was silly: one thing Cody was good at was taking care of herself.

Eddie managed to make his way to Wanda Kwan's office, finding her sitting at her desk, a worried expression on her face.

"Eddie!" she exclaimed. "What are you doing here?"

"Hello, Wanda," Eddie said, in practiced tones. "I've come to talk to you about the final Charlie Nyx book. You see, Wanda..."

"Eddie, this is no time to be talking about Charlie Nyx books!" Wanda said.

"It isn't?" Eddie asked.

"Haven't you seen the news, Eddie? There are earthquakes and tidal waves and hurricanes all over the world! A third of the moon has fallen out of the sky!"

Eddie frowned. "Really?" he asked. "So you don't want the final Charlie Nyx book anymore?"

"Of course not, Eddie. This isn't the time for silly children's fantasies. The world may be ending!"

Eddie rubbed his chin, deep in thought. "So no more Charlie Nyx books? Ever?"

"Eddie," Wanda said. "I understand that you writers can be a bit self-absorbed, but look around you. The world isn't the same place as it was yesterday. The Middle East has erupted in war. Massive earthquakes have rocked Rio Di Janeiro, Beijing, San Francisco, and Mumbai. Japan's been hit by a tsunami. Paris is in flames. The military has been called out to handle riots in London, Warsaw, New York, and Chicago. It's the end of the world, Eddie. This isn't the time for a book about a teenage warlock fighting monsters underneath Los Angeles!"

Eddie sank into the chair across from Wanda. The seriousness of the situation was finally beginning to sink in. While he had been scurrying around, trying to find the manuscript that was going to jumpstart his writing career, literally earth-shaking events had been occurring. Wanda was right: if this wasn't the end of the world, it was a damn good trial run. There was a time and a place for books about teenage warlocks, and this wasn't it.

Eddie met Wanda's worried gaze. He took a deep breath, trying to calm his nerves. "OK," he said. "How about a story about a rogue angel at the brink of the Apocalypse?"

Wanda's eyes met his. "I'm listening," she said.

"It's a riveting story," Eddie said. "Based on actual events. The only concern I have is with the ending."

"What's wrong with the ending?" Wanda asked.

"Well, the book is about the Apocalypse, but the Apocalypse doesn't actually occur. On some level, people might be disappointed."

"But you could have it happen in the sequel, right?"

"I suppose," said Eddie. "I wasn't really planning on another book."

"Oh, we have to do another book. Actually, a trilogy would be even better."

"Hmmm," replied Eddie. "You don't think that the readers will feel like I'm stringing them along?"

Wanda laughed. "Oh, Eddie," she said. "It's so sweet of you to be concerned. Now about this book..."

"Yes?" asked Eddie.

"How many explosions does it have?"

FORTY-FOUR

Horace Finch sat alone in the control room of the CCD, holding an icepack on his head. Somehow things had gone horribly wrong. Was it all a dream, or had a group of bickering angels really stolen the magic glass apple and ruined his experiment? The broken plastic tube hanging from the ceiling attested to the veracity of his memory, but still he found it hard to believe.

The Order of the Pillars of Babylon had believed in him, had given him their backing and entrusted him with sacred teachings that had been passed down for thousands of years. He, Horace Finch, was supposed to have been the gatekeeper standing between the end of human history and the beginning of a glorious new age in which the genius of humanity was constrained by neither space nor time. But he had failed.

He wanted to curse the angels and demons who had meddled with his destiny, but he knew that was a cop-out. When one aspired to tear down the veil that concealed the ultimate reality, one had to be prepared to deal with angels, demons, and whoever else showed up to the party. It was all part of the deal. The Babylonians had known that. The OPB had taught him that the gods themselves were not to be trusted, and they were right.

But it was not, in the end, the gods who had stolen his destiny from him: it was that annoying little cipher, Jacob Slater. "Jacob Slater," he hissed to himself, the words becoming a curse as they left his lips. "Jacob Slater, you will *pay.*"

While he fantasized about the myriad horrific tortures to which he would subject Jacob, his finger absently pressed a button on the console and a robotic arm slid out. At the end of the arm was an empty container where the glass apple should be.

"Empty," he hissed. There had been one magical glass apple on the planet, and it had been wasted—tossed at the moon like just another fifty-cent golf ball.

Wait a minute, he thought, looking in the receptacle. What's this?

The cup wasn't quite empty after all. Something very small glittered in the bottom. He reached in and gingerly pulled it out. Holding it between his fingertips, he appraised the item in the dim light. It was the most beautiful thing Horace Finch had ever seen.

There was no doubt about it: the thing was made of the same substance as the apple itself. In the anti-bomb's death throes, it had shed a small piece of itself—a teardrop of rosy glass.

Horace Finch tossed his head back and laughed. Perhaps his plans hadn't been foiled after all; just delayed. For in his hand he held the key to the secrets underlying all of reality: a glass apple seed.

ABOUT THE AUTHOR

Robert Kroese's sense of irony was honed growing up in Grand Rapids, Michigan— home of the Amway Corporation and the Gerald R. Ford Museum, as well as the first city in the United States to fluoridate its water supply. In second grade he wrote his first novel, the saga of Captain Bill and his spaceship *Thee Eagle*. This turned out to be the high point of his academic career. After barely graduating from Calvin College in 1992 with a philosophy degree, he was fired from a variety of jobs before moving to California where he stumbled into software development. As this job required neither punctuality nor a sense of direction, he excelled at it.

In 2006 he started his blog, www.mattresspolice.com, as an outlet for his absurdist wit. Around the same time, he was appointed to be a deacon in his church, and this juxtaposition of roles prompted him to create the character Mercury, the star of *Mercury Falls*. Kroese (pronounced KROO-zee) currently lives in Ripon, California, with his wife and two children.